# MURDER

# IN

# PROVIDENCE

**The Second Hawkridge Book**

British Library Cataloguing In Publication Data
A Record of this Publication is available from the British Library

ISBN 1846852161
978-1-84685-216-9

First Published June 2006 by
Exposure Publishing, an imprint of Diggory Press,
Three Rivers, Minions, Liskeard, Cornwall, PL14 5LE, UK
WWW.DIGGORYPRESS.COM

**BY THE SAME AUTHOR**

The End of an Era

*In the Hawkridge Series*

Murder in the Park
Murder in Providence
It couldn't happen in Dorset
The Qatar Affair
Diamonds in Dorset
Bedsits in Bath
Problems at Portland
Nuclear. No! How?
Submarines and Swindlers
Requiem for a Sapper
Politics and Property
The Body in the Churchyard
Chain of Circumstances
Murder in the Theatre
The Irish Affair
The Spetisbury Mystery
Death isn't Particular
Family Affairs
Nemesis
Satan's Disciples

# ABOUT THE AUTHOR

Jack Daniel lives in Bath, England with his wife, Elizabeth and two small long haired dachshunds.   He has two sons.

He is a naval constructor, now retired.

He saw sea service with the British Navy in World War 11 and was assigned to the US Manhattan Project for the Bikini atomic tests.

He subsequently designed several classes of warships for the Royal Navy, notably frigates and nuclear attack and ballistic missile submarines, reflecting his lifetime association with submarines.

He was Head of the Royal Corps of Naval Constructors when he resigned and joined the Board of British Shipbuilders.

His memoirs, the End of an Era, were published in 2003.

Murder in Providence is the second of twenty books featuring the Hawkridge family and their friends in pursuit of the ungodly.

*For Liz and the two boys*

*Who make everything enjoyable*

# Chapter One

DOCTOR Elizabeth Hawkridge dozed fitfully in an armchair in the annex to the Accident and Emergency unit in Southmead Hospital in Bristol. She didn't really belong there; she was from the Bristol Royal Infirmary but had agreed to do a week in the A & E for experience and to help out colleagues in the hard pressed unit. She had helped the staff deal with the crop of injuries from bar fights and drunkenness, which usually climaxed around eleven o'clock in the early days of the week and things had quietened down. It was nearly one a.m. and she listened with half an ear to the talk show broadcast from one of the local radio stations. She always listened to this station because it was one of her brother Timmy's stations and she knew a little of the background of Chuck Williams, the show's anchor man.

She listened idly. Chuck Williams greeted Phil who evidently was a regular,

*"Hello Phil, good to talk with you once more, where have you been this time?"*

*"Hello Chuck, it's good to be back. Had to take a load to Holland and the crossing was rough both ways, boy was I glad to see Harwich."*

*"Why don't you go through the Channel Tunnel or at least by one of the short sea crossings?"*

*"My boss has a contract with the people from Harwich and us poor sods have to lump it, it's not so bad in the summer but at times like this I'd rather not go."*

*"What are you planning to do now, Phil?"*

*"Well, I'm going to have a meal and then get to bed."*

*"No, what I meant is, where is your next trip?"*

*"The boss has been looking for trips to Eastern Europe and perhaps I'll get one of those, I wouldn't mind seeing Hungary, they say it's beautiful. And the girls aren't bad."*

*"Talking of girls does a truck driver have a wife in every car-port?"*

*"I don't know about that, I've got one upstairs who'll give me hell if I don't stop talking, so long Chuck, talk to you next trip."*

*"So long Phil, take care of yourself."*

The people who phoned in to air their views between midnight and two a.m. were not infrequently people who had just finished a late shift and were relaxing before going to bed. The remainder was the usual mix, insomniacs, lonely souls, inadequate souls and oddballs of various sorts, usually with grudges or axes to grind. They were an odd section of the population. During the present week Liz had heard what she was sure was the same person phone in with the same question about when were they going to do something about the drains in the city center. She still had no idea what the problem was.

*"Hello Rosemary, what can I do for you? We haven't spoken before have we?"*

*"No, and you've got to do somethin' about it."*

*"Do something about what Rosemary?"*

*"'Baht these council geezers who shut up the houses where I used to kip down, boarded 'em up, winders an' all. A body 'as ter kip down in the open if there's no room at the Salvation."*

*"I know that it's rude of a man to ask a lady her age but, if you don't mind me asking, Rosemary, how old are you?"*

*"I shall be seventy seven next birfday."*

*"And when's that, Rosemary?"*

*"January. Just after Christmas. I'm one of the unlucky ones, born too close to Christmas and always got one toy for both Christmas and me birfday. Me Mum said I was born unlucky, never 'ad a chance."*

*"Where are you going to sleep tonight, Rosemary?"*

*"I got a nice place down a basement spotted and I'm off there now, G'night."*

Liz wondered what would be the response if she were to phone in and protest that the dedicated staff of the A & E unit, who were already overworked in coping with the growing workload from motor and other accidents, domestic violence, accidents in the home or at the workplace, street violence, drug overdoses and suchlike, were now being overwhelmed by people who present themselves at the unit demanding treatment for cuts, bruises and pains because they considered it a more convenient and quicker way of getting medical care than attending their general practitioners surgery. They had realized that the medical staff dare not refuse to see them because they might actually be an emergency. She imagined the headlines, 'Dying woman turned away by Bristol Hospital.'

Liz marveled at Chuck William's temperament, no matter how rough, awkward or downright rude the caller was, he or she was treated with courtesy and consideration. Chuck was a master of the 'soft answer turneth away wrath,' school.

She had met him and his wife Betty quite recently; when Timmy and Helene had been down to visit Timmy's stations in the West Country and had learnt something of his background. Chuck Williams had built up a reputation in London as an outspoken commentator on affairs and critic of authority and petty officialdom. He had been lured to Bristol ostensibly by a higher salary but he had told her that actually he had wanted to leave London because he was sick and tired of the same people ringing in, night after night, with the same unwholesome questions. And towards the end there had been threats to 'do him' because of his campaign for the re-instatement of effective policing in what had become police no-go areas. The thugs had known when he was on the air and had been able to slash his car tyres at their leisure. It was not difficult to work out that he would leave the studio some minutes after the end of his broadcast and he had been jostled and punched by men in the dark. But of course he had jumped from the frying pan into the fire, for in Bristol, in places like Saint Paul's and Saint George, he found the same situation.

She supposed that Chuck's slot was important. It occupied a period when a lot of people were still awake and receptive. After two a.m. this changed, all the Hawkridge stations took the canned music and hourly news programme from Hawkridge Media Central in London until six a.m. when they again went their separate ways, but taking the Central news on the hour every hour. Her brother's policy was to provide the same programme formula in all of his stations in the UK, Canada and the USA, a mixture of light music, the better known classics, news and comment on current affairs and local gossip, with, of course, sponsor's advertisements. He had little trouble in getting his station managers to keep to this policy for they, too, like the advertisers, could see that there are millions of potential customers out there who don't want to listen to the meaningless gibberish of the top of the pops all day.

The reception at which she had met Chuck was at the station headquarters on Bedminster Down on the southwestern side of Bristol. The building had been built by one of the electricity generating boards as its headquarters. She had thought what a wonderful position it occupied with green fields and open countryside extending into the distance on three sides and the A38 on the other. She wondered if someone in the heady days of nationalization had allowed it to be built on green-belt land. It suited Hawkridge Media admirably with its transmitter nearby. The office space was generous and Timmy more than covered the expense of running the station with the rents he collected from the small companies who rented office space. He had found that people liked the movement and the sense of participation that surrounds a media presence. In America he liked to put a station in an hotel to the benefit of both the hotel owner and the station. Of course Timmy had been helped in doing this in America by the fact that the only daughter of the owner of the Maier hotel chain was married to his elder brother, David, a major in the British Army.

Liz was brought back out of her reverie,

*"and he keeps touching me as he walks past, and that."*

*"Are you saying, Joan," said Chuck, "that the man you work for in that shop is molesting you, deliberately touching your body or is it just that there's not much space behind the counter?"*

*"Oh he does it in the stock room as well, specially, 'cos customers can't see in."*

*"You know that what he's doing is not only nasty but it's against the law, have you told him to stop and that if he doesn't stop you'll go to the police?"*

*"Oh I can't do that 'cos I need the money to bring up my baby."*

*"Look Joan, on your day off you go down to the Citizens Advice Bureau. There are some nice ladies there and you can tell one of them exactly what this man does and then you do what she says. They can help you get another job and help you with the baby too. Goodnight love, don't you worry, you do as I say. Goodnight."*

Liz could picture the scene in the small studio. Chuck Williams at his console with turntables and CD players to hand and opposite, his producer, the person who actually took all the incoming calls and decided which ones to put directly through to Chuck and which ones she should tell that she would ring back 'in a few minutes' for use when calls became scarce. It was the producer whose responsibility it was to monitor the content of the calls and delete any obscenity or material that might form the basis of a libel case, made possible by the short inbuilt delay between what was being recorded from the microphones and what was actually going out on the air. Chuck's usual producer was Sally Evans. Sally was in her early thirties, an attractive blonde who always seemed to be on duty at the station. Liz wondered if she was on duty tonight.

Chuck was saying,

*"I can't hear you very well, can you please speak louder."*

*"I not speak English good an' I frightened to speak loud in case man come."*

*"What's your name, please?"*

*"I called June here in Blistol but real name Ah Ming."*

*"Why are you calling, Ah Ming?"*

*"I blought to England for work but bad men make me sleep lots men, do bad things to me and other girls."*

*"Where do you live in Bristol, Ah Ming?"*

*"In house like plison near many traffic road all day and night."*

*"Can you give me the address?"*

*"Don't know address, oh, no, no, don't, let go, help, help...."*

*"Ah Ming, are you there?"*

There was the noise of a phone being slammed down.

"I'm sorry listeners but someone seems to have interrupted our caller. You may rest assured that this station will do all that is within its power to help that young lady who seems to have come from abroad."

Liz's pager buzzed and she went to deal with an incoming patient. She spent the remainder of the night alternately dozing in the annex or answering calls to examine and perhaps treat an incoming patient, knowing that she would be expected to do a days work at the BRI before returning here tomorrow night. But only for a week, thank goodness and then she would be able to go home to her parents in Dorset on Saturday and sleep a whole night through. Like all newly qualified doctors she worked over seventy hours each week and accepted it as the price to pay for becoming what she had wanted to be ever since she could remember, a doctor.

The following evening she was once more at Southmead Hospital and the pattern of accident and emergency patients was as before. Between calls she dozed and listened to the Chuck Williams show on Hawkridge Radio.

Alfred was explaining about his knee. *"They don't seem to 'ave any ideal wot's wrong wiv' it at the 'ospital. I bin in four times an' they say they can't find nothink wrong wiv it an' say it's all me imagination. It's me right one, see, the one I used to score goals wiv when I played for the Rovers, see."*

Liz expected that Chuck had also got the real reason for the call. He had.

*"Oh, so you played for the Rovers did you Alfred, when was that?"*

*"In nineteen fifty six, when they was in the second division an' we 'ad a good run in the cup, too, see."*

*"What position did you play, Alfred?"*

*"I was left half for the first team but I played everywhere except goalie in the reserves. Often fort I would be a better goalie than some of 'em. Proper rubbish some of 'em was."*

*"What are you doing now, Alfred?"*

*"Well, I done nothin' much since me wife died two year ago, just bits an' pieces for folk, like mowing their grass an' cleaning winders but I ain't much good at that now 'cos I can't climb ladders, it's me knee, see."*

*"Why don't you go round to the hospital tonight, or rather this morning, and see what they say about your knee?"* said Chuck.

Liz could have killed him.

*"Can't get there at this time of night an' anyway I went last Fursday an' they told me to push off, sayin' there was nothin' wrong wiv me knee. They was a bit fed up 'cos I been there on the Toosday and Wensday as well."*

*"Well you take care of yourself and that knee, Good bye Alfred."*

The next caller was George.

*"Where are you calling from, George?"*

*"Fishponds. I'm calling about the previous caller, Alfred. I think that must have been Alf Titman who played for the Rovers about then."*

*"Are you a Rovers supporter, George?"*

*"Have been all my life. My Dad used to take me to Eastville when I was a kid and I remember Alf from those days 'cept that I think he played right half and not left half."*

*"Do you still go to see them?"*

*"No, I stopped when they left Eastville Stadium. I don't know the ins and outs of it but it seemed a stupid thing to do, and then wander around Bristol looking for somewhere to play. They played on Bath City's ground for a bit, can you imagine what that did for their supporters?"*

*"Well they've settled at the Memorial Ground now and it's not too far from Fishponds."*

*"The old Rovers magic has worn a bit thin these days, Chuck. Tell me, do you ever wonder why it is that Bristol can't support a Premier League side, surely the area is large enough and rich enough?"*

*"Can't say that I've given it much thought, I'm a rugger man myself, but we've got the other league club, Bristol City who are doing pretty well, haven't we?"* said Chuck.

*"If you like that sort of thing, I suppose so but I'll always be a Rovers man myself."*

*"Then why don't you go and support them? Goodnight George."*

Liz found the mysteries of the local soccer clubs somewhat less than arresting and in her mind was reviewing the night's events so far. Had she diagnosed that man correctly and was this the right treatment until a bed could be found for this woman? Then there was the Asian woman who had been brought in earlier accompanied by a man. The paramedics had given Liz a hint that they didn't believe what they'd been told and she was sure the woman's injuries weren't the result of falling down the stairs like her husband said. The woman was obviously scared stiff of the man. Now if this was Dorset she'd have had a quiet word with her family doctor, Dr Browne, who happened to be the police surgeon and someone would have asked the husband some awkward questions. Here in Bristol, she had learnt, one got no thanks for causing trouble in the ethnic communities. She reflected that it was a sad reflection on British society generally and that a doctor's lot is not necessarily always a happy one.

*"And who have we next?  Alice, and where are you calling from, Alice?"*

*"I'm calling from St Georges and I think it's time someone did something about the druggies who leave all their dirty things around here.  Where are the police, we never see a policeman on foot and you can't do much sitting in a car which is all they seem to do these days?"*

*"You say that there are lots of people using drugs out your way?"*

*"Yeh, you see people quite openly selling little bits of what looks like paper to youngsters, they're a danger to our children and the police do nothing about it. Nor does the Council."*

*"What do you think Bristol Council should do to improve the situation, then, Alice?"*

Liz was not destined to hear what Alice had in mind, for she was called to the Emergency unit as an ambulance arrived with its lights flashing.

The patient was a young girl of oriental appearance who had been rescued from drowning in the Floating Harbour.  She seemed to have swallowed a deal of water, which the paramedics had pumped out of her and was suffering from exposure.  As she was undressed it became clear that she had also been badly beaten.  Liz learned the whole story as she supervised the team's efforts to save the girls life.

It seemed that a young police constable on foot patrol near the Lloyds Bank Building had seen a car stop and two or three men drag a bundle from the car and carry it to the waters edge. He had run towards the spot and shouted, at which the men had pushed the bundle into the water and rushed to their car and away.  The constable had not got the number of the car but had run to the dock edge where he could see in the inky darkness that the bundle appeared to be a human being. He had radioed for help before diving into the water and pulling the bundle to some adjacent dock steps from whence he and the bundle were rescued by the ambulance crew and fellow police officers. But for the policeman's prompt action and bravery, the girl, for such she was found to be by her rescuers, would surely have died. As it was her chances of recovery appeared slim as the medical team laboured throughout the night. By dawn they had stabilized her condition and she recovered consciousness for a short while. In a short moment of lucidity she whispered to Liz that bad men who make her sleep with other men, had beaten her because she spoke on the telephone and thrown her into water.

Liz recalled the small voice she had heard on the Chuck Williams show the night before, "What is your name?" she asked.

"Ah Ming," replied the girl.

"How did you come to England?"

"In a big boat full of cars. We hide in car till dark then bad man came and took us to house. Say sleep with men to get money or we bring police, you not got papers and no right be in England and police send you back."

She slipped into unconsciousness as she was moved into Intensive Care.


In making out her report on the patient, Liz reported the brief moment of lucidity and the girls name Ah Ming and separately added a brief note on the previous night's telephone call to Chuck Williams. Liz suggested that in view of the girls injuries and attempted drowning, she could be in some danger, since, should she recover, she could be in a position to identify her attackers and therefore should receive police protection. As far as Liz could tell the police showed little interest other than to say that '*they had more important crimes to deal with than illegal immigrants. If they get murdered that's one less on the social security.*' But the police told the resident hospital security officer to ensure that the girl should be detained if she attempted to leave. Since the girl was at deaths door the security man considered this to be a pretty silly instruction and returned to his perusal of the Evening Post.

## Chapter Two

WHEN she reported for duty the following evening, Liz went into Intensive Care and asked the charge nurse how Ah Ming was progressing.

"She is gaining strength but isn't out of danger yet, she had a brief moment of consciousness this afternoon, just after her cousin left."

"What cousin?" asked Liz.

"A young coloured man came in just after lunch and created a scene because we wouldn't let him see his cousin who fell into the harbour the night before. The more he argued the more he put our backs up and we sent for the security man and he made the man leave."

"The girl is an illegal immigrant," said Liz with some heat, "the chances of her having a cousin here are infinitesimal, he was probably sent to finish the job by the pimps who tried to kill her last night. Do you have any CCTV cameras working in the daytime?"

"Yes, doctor, there is one at each end of the corridor and one in each ward, they're on all the time, day and night. The night shift nurses find them useful for keeping an eye on things and matron sometimes runs the tapes to check up on us nurses."

"Do you know who changes the tapes and when?"

"The security man would know, you should ask him," said the nurse.

"Thanks sister. Look I know I'm not a member of this hospital's staff but please tell everyone that the Asian girl is not, repeat not, to be allowed visitors, only real hospital staff and real policemen. Someone tried to murder her last night and it looks as if they might have tried again this afternoon. Her life's in your hands in more ways than one. I'll have another go at the police, this time, I hope, with the security tapes."

Liz sought out the night security man. He liked attractive young women and Liz was certainly attractive, so he gave her his attention. He said,

"There's nothing in the log about a man causing a disturbance in Intensive Care this afternoon."

"Well, there certainly was before your colleague got there, it'll show up on the CCTV tapes, when are those changed?" asked Liz.

"I change them at midnight, put new tapes in and put today's tapes in the cupboard where they remain for forty eight hours in case they're needed, you've no ideal what they show sometimes, nurses and patients getting up to all sort of things."

"Please listen carefully," said Liz. "Someone tried to murder one of the patients last night and I believe that they sent someone to finish the job this afternoon but the nurses wouldn't let him in. It's possible that the police might be able to identify this afternoon's man from the CCTV tapes so their safety is important and you'll realize that you must be alert because they might try again tonight."

"If she's that important you'd think the police would guard her. On the TV there's always a copper sitting on a chair outside the room the patient's in and the crooks or goodies, depending on whether the patient is a crook or a goodie, try to lure him away from his post so that they can get in."

"I'm going to have another go at the police and if I can, I'll come over from the A & E at midnight to watch you deal with the tapes."

A worried Liz went to the annex. What should she do, she didn't know anyone in the Bristol police – the Avon and Somerset Constabulary, to give it its proper title – what should she do? She would do what she had always done since she was a very little girl, she would ask her brother Timmy, although what he would do in London – if he weren't abroad – at seven thirty in the evening, she couldn't imagine.   But she'd ring Tim. If he wasn't there Helene might be and she was as inventive as Timmy.

She dialed Timmy's number on her mobile and after what seemed an interminable time, Timmy answered.

"Oh Timmy I'm so glad you're in, it's Liz."

"Yes, I recognized your voice, are you coming home this weekend? We'll be there."

"Yes Timmy, is Helene there?"

"Yes, do you want to talk to her?"

"No, well, yes as well, if you know what I mean. Timmy I need help and it can't wait."

"What's up, kitten?"

"I'm helping out at Southmead casualty unit where a girl was brought in last night nearly dead.  I think that she is a recent illegal immigrant who has been forced into prostitution. She phoned Chuck Williams and tried to get away and was beaten and thrown into the harbour. A policeman rescued her and she's in this hospital. The police don't seem to care what happens to her and this afternoon a coloured man, posing as her cousin, tried to get at her but was prevented by the nurses. I'm going to try to impound the CCTV tapes from Intensive Care where he might show up but I'm afraid that whoever tried to murder her last night and this afternoon will try to get at her tonight. There should be a police guard on her room. How can I get that?"

"You certainly pick them, Liz. Look, on the strength of what you say, I'll ring Chuck Williams and get him to use his police contacts to get a man posted to guard the girl. I'll authorize Chuck to say that Hawkridge Media will pay for the officer for as long as you, Liz, think protection is necessary. Chuck will also say that if anything does happen to the girl now that the police have been warned, Hawkridge Media will give nationwide, no, worldwide publicity to the police failure. How about that?"

"You are an Angel, Timmy, is Helene there?"

"She's right here asking to talk with you, I'll put her on while I phone Chuck on another line. I suggest that you ring Chuck in, say, an hour's time unless he rings you. I'll give him your number. Don't worry, Liz, and keep up the good work, see you at the week end, Bye."

"Hello Liz, I could hear all that you said," said Helene, "do you have any idea how long the unfortunate girl has been in England?"

"No, but she said that she came in a big ship and came ashore in the back of a car and a bad man came and made her sleep with men because she had no papers. Helene I'm telling you the story backwards. It started with Chuck Williams' phone-in show two nights ago. She phoned in and said, in broken English, that she was made to sleep with bad men in a house like a prison near a road busy with cars all the time, or words like that. Chuck will have the tape. The call was not completed she was pulled away from the phone. Next she is beaten and thrown into the harbour, you heard the rest, didn't you?"

"Yes, poor little soul, she probably thought that she was coming to a better life in England," said Helene. "What a good thing you heard the broadcast and then recognized the girl. Tell me, don't they have big boats that bring cars into Bristol or ship cars out of Bristol or perhaps both? If what the girl says is true, and why shouldn't it be, all sorts of people and things could be arriving in the boots of new cars. Keeping watch on the port might be a starting point, mightn't it? Please take care Liz, they sound like nasty people. We'll see you at the week end."

Liz's phone rang an hour later.

"Is this Doctor Elizabeth Hawkridge? This is Chuck Williams. Your brother spoke with me earlier and I've been on to the police. The man I spoke with is a good man who would move mountains for us if that was possible but even he can't beat the system, the time is too short to switch men to Southmead, they really are stretched, you know. My friend, Detective Chief Inspector Roger Hardwick, who's on the Headquarters staff, was aghast to learn that there is no police guard on this unfortunate girl. Someone has slipped up badly but that doesn't help us. In the circumstances I've hired two Securifirm guards to sit outside the ward tonight and Roger is squaring it with the hospital authorities."

"I'm most grateful to you Mr Williams, now I'll call you Chuck if I may for that's what I know you as from your broadcasts and I'm Liz. Did Timmy explain that this all started with your programme two nights ago?"

"No, how was that?"

"I'm helping out at Southmead Hospital A & E for a week – I belong to the BRI – and I listen to you between casualty calls. Well, the girl in intensive care is the girl who telephoned-in two nights ago and didn't finish her call, she said that her name was Ah Ming and she was being made to sleep with bad men, I hope that you remember and that you still have the tape of that night's calls."

"Now I remember and yes we still have the tapes."

"I don't want to interfere with your freedom of the air sort of thing, but I think that in the interests of the girl's safety, you will have to think fairly deeply about whether you mention any of this on the air for the next few days," said Liz.

"I can see that it could be tricky, but it's a pity to let a scoop pass by."

"I'm sure that there'll be others," said Liz.

Liz went into the Intensive Care ward and spoke to the ward sister,

"Sister, you know me, I'm helping out in the Casualty unit for a few nights. I'm worried about the safety of that girl who was brought in last night after someone tried to drown her. Someone posing as her cousin tried to get at her this afternoon and I fear that they may try again tonight and they could hurt hospital staff in the process. The police have slipped up and can't provide a guard tonight so my brother has hired two Securifirm men to do the job. They should be here soon and I know you'll tell them where to sit, and look after them and see that they stay awake all night!"

"I was surprised that there was no police guard, doctor," said the Sister. "There usually is in cases like this. Nowadays we try to keep the unit doors locked at night but until about eleven o'clock there is a fair bit of coming and going with people visiting and afterwards with staff clearing up and so on and it's difficult."

Liz went to the night security guard.

"Because the police aren't able to provide a guard to that girl who someone tried to murder, two Securifirm men have been hired to do the job. They'll be here soon and are to go to Intensive Care. The ward sister knows all about it."

"There was no need for them to hire people. I won't let anyone get in."

"I know," said Liz diplomatically, "but you have so many other wards to watch over and I expect you could do with a little help."

"Well, there is that I suppose, the powers that be don't seem to care how much work they expect a body to do these days, cutting costs and waiting lists is all they've got time for."

At that moment a Securifirm van drove up to the barrier and the guard bustled out to check their identity and lead them to Intensive Care.

Feeling that she had done everything that she could, Liz returned to the A&E and checked on the early evening patients. When she could, she returned to the annex and rang Chuck Williams on the number he had given her. His wife answered the phone and Liz explained who she was. She was asked to wait a minute and then she heard the now familiar voice,

"Hello Doctor, more problems?"

"No, just to let you know that the Securifirm men have arrived and by now should be sitting outside Ah Ming's door. Thanks for your help."

"I feel that this thing could be bigger than we might imagine and I'd like to keep in touch if I may, there could be a big story here."

"I promise to tell you everything that I learn, but I am only going to be at Southmead for another few days and could well lose touch. Anyway, thanks again."

Liz was kept busy as evening became night and the number of people brought in rose towards the nightly climax. Sometime after eleven o'clock there was a great noise of sirens and flashing blue lights as two police patrol cars raced into the hospital and stopped outside Intensive Care. Several minutes later, two men came running along the covered way from that unit, forced their way through the people in the Casualty unit, knocking people and equipment over and ran away into the night. Two policemen came after them but stopped beside Liz to phone for reinforcements and the helicopter. She heard the officer report that 'at least we got one of them.'

Liz made her way to the Intensive Care Unit and to the ward sister who was talking to a police sergeant,

"Here she is," said the sister, "this is the doctor who hired the guards and a jolly good job she did." She turned to Liz,

"They came, just as you said they would, three of them, a white man and two blacks. They pulled things over their faces the moment they came in and the white man got hold of me and sent the other two along the corridor towards the girl's room. Of course they didn't know about the guards and all hell broke out with them fighting and shouting. The guards seized one of them and the man let me go and he and the other man ran off. It was terrible."

Somewhat aggressively, the police sergeant said, "Who are you?"

"My name is Doctor Elizabeth Hawkridge."

"How did you know there'd be an attempt on the immigrant girl's life?"

"I didn't, but since someone tried to murder the girl last night and tried to get at her in this hospital this afternoon, I reasoned that there was a fair chance that they would try again, probably tonight, so my brother hired Securifirm to provide some guards. He did it through Chuck Williams of Hawkridge Radio. A Detective Chief Inspector Roger Hardwick from the Avon and Somerset police headquarters knows all about it."

"Well doctor, it seems that we owe you a vote of thanks," said the Sergeant with whom the names Hawkridge and Hardwick had suddenly struck a chord.

Liz had a word with the Securifirm guards and congratulated them on their capture. Yes, they would be there for the rest of the night as ordered.

She put her head in the door of Ah Ming's room and found her fast asleep. She checked her pulse and found it much stronger than the feeble flutter of the night before.

Back in the A&E annex she telephoned Timmy. Helene answered the phone.

"Helene, it's me again. I was right. What a good idea to put two Securifirm guards outside that poor girl's door. Three masked men came into the Intensive Care unit tonight and tried to get to the girl. They didn't know about the guards and there was a fight which resulted in two men running away and one being caught."

"Slow down Liz, you say they tried again and were foiled by the guards?"

"Yes, the police have got him and they're looking for the other two."

"You say Securifirm guards, not police?"

"Yes, Chuck Williams spoke to his police contacts who were as surprised as we were that there was no police guard on the girl but were unable to do anything at such short notice, so Chuck hired Securifirm who could provide men at that late hour."

"Well done Chuck and well done private enterprise," said Helene.

"I was going to ask Timmy whether Chuck should mention the girl and her attackers on his programme and the part the station had played in protecting the girl. I know that Chuck would like to but I suppose it could put him in danger, these crooks seem to be beastly. I haven't spoken with Chuck since the attack and I expect that he doesn't know. But I should tell him, shouldn't I?"

Liz could hear Helene talking with Timmy.

Presently Timmy's voice came on the line " Hello, kitten, you must tell Chuck about tonight's attack but please tell him that I would advise him not to mention the part that he and the station played in protecting the girl. He would be exposing himself to danger. If he decides to ignore my advice, so be it. Well done Liz. Goodnight from us both."

Next, Liz phoned Chuck at the radio station. She got his producer Sally Evans.

"Sally, you probably don't remember me. I'm Liz Hawkridge, Timmy's sister. Chuck has been helping me."

"Yes, I know, Liz, he told me when he arrived a moment ago, he's about somewhere."

"I really have to hurry as I'm supposed to be in Casualty. I wanted to tell him that the enemy made another attempt to get at Ah Ming tonight and was driven off by the Securifirm guards who arrested one of them and handed him over to the police. I told Timmy and he said that because the enemy seems to be really nasty he would advise Chuck not to mention the part that he played in providing the guards. It's up to Chuck but that's Timmy's advice. He asked me to pass the message."

"OK Liz, I'll pass it on verbatim," said Sally.

In between her calls to deal with patients, Liz dozed in the Annex and listened to the radio. She heard the beginning of the Chuck Williams show and the first few callers, she marveled at the average caller's belief that theirs was a complaint hitherto unknown to medical science and opinion that all medical specialists were myoptic idiots.

With half an ear she heard,

*"... it all started when my landlord sold the house to this new man."*

*"What started, Hilda?"* asked Chuck.

*"Why, all this bother about paying more rent or moving out."*

*"Tell me Hilda, how long have you lived in your house?"*

*"Ever since my Mah died, must be over thirty years."*

*"And is your rent controlled?"* asked Chuck.

*"I don't know about that, my hubby did all that but now he's passed on."*

*"Let me put it this way then, how often does it get increased?"*

*"'Bout every two years they put it up a bit but the Council helps so I don't fret."*

23

*"What's bothering you, if your rent's controlled and the Council gives you Housing Benefit you are sitting pretty, surely Hilda?"*

*"You'd fink so but this new landlord says he wants me out or else. My neighbours on both sides 'ave gone they couldn't stand him always at the door, like."*

*"You should complain to the Council and the Rent Service officer."*

*"I bin to the Council office in South Bristol but the man said its nothink to do wiv 'em."*

*"Look, you stay on the phone and talk to my producer, Sally and you give Sally your address, love. Don't worry we'll try to sort something out."*

*"You are tuned to Hawkridge Radio Bristol and this is the Chuck Williams Show, where listeners air their views. Before I take any more of your calls I want to say this to all my listeners and especially the old and frail. If you are having problems with your landlord go to the Citizens Advice Bureau and tell them. The law is very strict about landlords and tenants and the rents that may be charged, especially if you've been there a long time. But always be sure to pay the rent that's in the rent book and make certain that the payment is recorded in the book at the time you pay."*

*"Now I've got something else to say. Some of you will remember two nights ago a frightened foreign girl phoned in and asked for help, saying her name in England was June but her real name was Ah Ming, She said that bad men were making her sleep with men for money and she didn't finish the call because someone pulled her away from the phone. Well, the next night she was badly beaten and thrown into the harbour. Luckily a brave young policeman saw something fall into the water and dived in and kept her afloat until help came. The men who threw her in, escaped.*

*She was taken to Southmead Hospital where doctors worked throughout the night to save her life and I am pleased to say, it looks as if they might have succeeded. But that's not the end of the poor girl's troubles because there have already been two attempts by outsiders to get at her while she lies nearly dead in hospital. I'm pleased to tell you that during the second attempt not two hours ago, a man was arrested. You may be able to help. Did you see a car somewhere between St Paul's and Southmead sometime after ten o'clock this evening with a white man and two black men in it? Or one going the other way in a hurry, with a white man and one black man just after eleven?"*

Chuck went on,

*"It's clear that there is something evil in Saint Paul's and we, the good citizens of Bristol have got to do something about it, we can't simply leave it to the police. Someone must have noticed strange men going into a house or houses and coming out again after a half hour or so, or that lights are on at all hours or even noticed signs that there are girls being kept in a house. It's your duty to report what you see. If you're reluctant to speak to the police, simply phone this station, we'll give out an 0800 phone number and we won't ask for your name or address. Just call us and tell us what you have seen. Don't worry about wasting our time. Someone will be here to take your call, twenty four hours a day."*

Liz thought blimey, Chuck, you've really put Hawkridge Radio on the spot. I wonder what Timmy will say. Knowing her brother, he'd probably say 'Well done.' Anyway, it would keep; she'd mention it when she saw them at the weekend.

The next afternoon, on duty at the BRI, she was asked to go to Reception where she had a visitor. Mystified she went down and found a tall, slender, good looking, man with light coloured hair and blue eyes in the small waiting room.

"I'm Doctor Elizabeth Hawkridge. I gather you want to see me?"

"Yes, my name is Roger Hardwick, Detective Chief Inspector Roger Hardwick to be precise. I'm the Chief Constable's staff officer. You've never seen me before but I've seen you, you came up to Trinity one day with your parents while Timothy and I were there."

"Oh," said Liz, "that was ages ago."

"But that's not why I'm here. Well it is really, because I want to talk with you, sort of off the record. I was the one, or perhaps one of several, police officers that Chuck Williams called last night to try to get a guard put on that unfortunate girl. I'm sorry that all I could do was to make it possible for the Securifirm chaps to be accepted by Southmead. What a blessing that you did what you did, you undoubtedly saved her life, if this was ancient China she'd be bound to you for the rest of her days."

"How can I help you, I can only spare a few minutes….."

"It's about Chuck Williams' broadcast. I didn't hear it but I'm told that he is setting up a phone-in arrangement to encourage people to report suspicious things."

"I was on duty all night at Southmead and I heard it. My only questions are whether my brother will like the cost of about three extra staff to take the calls, few though they will probably be, and what does the station do with the information when they've got it?"

"That's really why I'm here, to try and start a dialogue on where do we go from here."

"I'm terrified that Timmy will see this as another crusade, you probably don't know it but Timmy and his wife Helene were instrumental, recently, in breaking up a car smuggling racket, a drug smuggling racket, solving a murder and played a vital role in destroying a counterfeiting operation that was flooding Europe with twenty dollar bills, all while he was courting Helene."

"Well I sort of heard rumours, good old Tim. Look, how do we go about keeping us in touch with the Chuck Williams initiative? He's doing what Crimewatch tries to do except he's not the police, and to some of the people who we want to help us, that's important."

"I don't know, I'm going home this weekend and Timmy and Helene will be there. I'll talk to them and phone you early next week if you give me your number."

"Please tell him that the Chief Constable has no intention of rushing in and fouling up his station's initiative and that I'll be your only link with the police force. No one but the Chief and I will know of the arrangement."

"Alright, Roger, I'll tell him, and now I must rush, Goodbye. By the way did you simply park outside? How nice it must be to have a police car and be able to stop where mere mortals dare not go."

The next night, her last at Southmead, Liz covertly checked that there was a policeman on guard outside Ah Ming's door.

# Chapter Three

TIMOTHY Hawkridge's secretary, Penny looked up as Helene walked in with her coat over her arm and sat down.

"He's got no-one with him, you can go in," said Penny

"No, I'll wait, let's not hurry him, any time we gain now we'd probably lose getting out of London."

"I had lunch with old Sin, you know, Cynthia Smith, Peter Davenport's secretary, the other day," said Penny. "She nearly swallowed her false teeth when I told her that you and Timmy had married and that Sid and I had been the witnesses. She said that probably accounted for Peter being so bad tempered."

"Oh, Peter's all right, he was probably annoyed that I'd resigned from his bank, but we'll make it up to him and anyway he can't afford to lose an account like Timmy's."

"Old Sin was more surprised at the speed of the thing. You don't know it but at the bank the younger managers called you the Ice-Maiden because you didn't respond to their advances. Then you come here and, bingo, you fall in love and marry the boss."

"Penny dear, I surprised myself," said Helene. "Ever since I was about fifteen I have been dodging men who wanted to take me to bed, in the Finishing School in Lausanne, at the LSE and since. Then I meet Timmy and I'm practically asking him, asking him would you believe, to take me to bed."

Timmy buzzed Penny and asked if Helene was about and Helene went in.

She could never enter this room without remembering the first time she'd met Timmy. He had asked his bank if they had anyone who could speak Arabic to help him in some negotiations about setting up a commercial radio station in the Gulf. She had spent the first seven years of her life in Jordan and was a banker and so she had been a natural selection. She'd walked in the door and held out her hand and said 'Hello, I'm Helene Taylor. I'm told that you want a finance person who can speak Arabic.' Timmy had stood there practically open mouthed and her heart turned over. His side of the story is that Penny told him that his visitor from the bank had arrived and he had said 'Show him in' and the most breathtakingly beautiful girl he had ever seen walked in. It was the same now, she was lovely and now she was his wife.

"Hello Angel." He kissed her, "have you been waiting long? You should have come in, have you had a successful day? You can tell me all about it on the way down."

He helped Helene on with her coat, put his on, locked the safe, put what Helene called his weekend homework in his briefcase and they both went out, saying goodbye to Penny on the way.

They followed their usual route to the hotel restaurant in Walton on Thames where they had a light dinner and thence, after avoiding the M25, by the M3, M27 and the A31 through the New Forest to Tolbrite and Timmy's parents at the Manor House.

They were greeted by Timmy's mother, Margaret, Lady Hawkridge, and the butler Sergeant Holmes, who had been General Hawkridge's batman and driver. The sergeant had followed him into retirement and his wife was now the Manor House housekeeper.

"Helene darling and Timmy, so glad you've arrived safely, I can't help worrying with all the traffic these days. I know by now that you've already eaten so run along and put your things in your room and come down for a drink with Daddy. Oh and by the way, David and Sally-Ann and the children and, of course, Liz, are coming down so we shall all be here this week end."

The General greeted them warmly. Every time he saw his new daughter-in-law he was struck by her beauty, she was gorgeous, there was no other word for it, and she was clever as well, what a rare combination. Margaret watched as Helene kissed him quite naturally on both cheeks and thought what a lucky chance had brought her into their lives- the fact that a school friend of her sons who's father was the Emir of Qatar, wanted a commercial radio station.

Saturday morning followed the now usual pattern, Timmy worked at his papers and Helene and Lady Hawkridge – Margaret - went out and about the Manor park and the home farm, the village or visited one or other of the five farms that made up the estate. The walk to the village meant passing the church and usually the vicar's wife, Mary Ford, was there to have a word as they passed. The other landmarks in the village were the Tolbrite Arms, the Old Forge Garage, the Cosy Tea Room and an antiques shop. This morning, as they passed the garage Helene was sure that she heard a faint wolf whistle and knew that ex Royal Marine Commando, young Will, Old Will's son, was behaving true to form. Village boy young Will had played with the Hawkridge boys and Liz when they came home from school for the holidays and there was a real bond of affection that had lasted through the years. Helene knew that she and Timmy would find their footsteps leading to the garage sometime that afternoon, probably with David's children and the dogs, to exchange news with young Will. This morning, Will had clearly recognized two pairs of trim ankles and that one pair was the squire's wife, hence the faintness of the whistle. Dear Will, he didn't realize that the squire's wife knew more about him than he thought and she had understood the faintness of the whistle and grinned at Helene. Young Will claimed that he lurked underneath the cars he was repairing waiting for trim ankles to appear, when he would emerge and engage the possessor of said trim ankles in cheeky chatter. He had to be a little careful because the garage was immediately opposite the Tolbrite Arms and he and the barmaid, the landlord's daughter, Gloria, were an item.

The way that the family walked to and from the village was usually across the park rather than the longer way down the front drive and along the Winterborne road. Without comment Margaret and Helene took the long way home and had barely turned in past the Lodge and said good morning to the general's gamekeeper, Charlie Towers, when a car overtook them. They heard the cry "Daddy stop, Daddy stop, there's Granny and Helene." The car stopped and two little figures and two little dogs emerged. They exchanged a few hello's with David and Sally-Ann who drove on while the children ranged themselves on either side of the two adults and, with the dogs running here and there, made their chattering way to the house and big hugs from Granddad and questions about Auntie Lilibets pending arrival.

Margaret Hawkridge had something to think about. She had noticed the same smart car parked beside the lodge as had been there on several weekends and she had noticed how much smarter and vivacious Maisie, the gamekeeper's daughter was these days, much different from the little mouse of a girl she had been when she had first come to the Manor House as a maid. She had grown into a thoroughly nice, attractive girl and it had only been a question of time before Mr Right came along. It seemed that he might have arrived. The problem would be her father, Charlie Towers, who, according to her informants on such matters, the Sergeant and his wife, lived only for his daughter and his young pheasants. What on earth would happen when Maisie got married?

That morning, Saturday, Liz went straight to her flat, changed and drove to Tolbrite. As she turned in at the lodge she saw two little figures and two small dogs lurking behind some shrubs and sure enough as she drove slowly ahead the children ran beside her crying "Aunty Lilibet, Auntie Lilibet, Stop, Stop for us." She stopped the car and the two children and their dogs clambered in for the less than half mile or so remaining up to the Manor House.

She was welcomed by her mother and Sergeant Holmes.

"Hello, darling, Timmy's been telling us how you saved a poor girl's life," said her mother.

"Well, not exactly, Mummy, but what we did certainly confounded the ungodly."

Over lunch she told the entire story leading up to Chuck William's promise of an 0800 telephone line and Roger Hardwick's call on her.

"Do you remember a Roger Hardwick at Trinity, Timmy?"

"There was an earnest chap who was rather clever and a good athlete as well. I think he was called Hardwick. His people were in property in the Home Counties if I remember correctly and if it's the right man," said Timmy. "I'll look out some old photographs and a yearbook or two."

"What are you going to do about Chuck's 0800 phone-in?"

"I can't see what else I can do but honour his promise. I expect that the station manager, Joy Philips, has already faxed me for approval to hire the extra staff, hinting at Liz as the reason she expects approval, which means that Chuck has been doing his stuff."

"OK," said Helene, "you approve the proposal. Now what do you do, we've got to set down some guidelines for the people who are going to man the phones, how they speak to callers, how they record the conversations and above all, what they do with the tapes afterwards. How do you think the taped data should be analysed and by whom?"

"Good points, Angel," said Timmy. "I don't know yet who'll do the analysis, for the first two or three weeks it could be us, sitting around this table, just to get a feel for things. The first step will be to assign the calls to four or five major subject heads, like drugs and drug dealers, bad landlords, bad tenants, prostitution, robbery, cars, and medical to name a few. Most will simply be moans that we should ignore but there's a chance that people will be more willing to talk to us than to the police."

"Although your man Chuck has given a promise of anonymity, it would be useful to know the caller's telephone number," said David. "Say that one of your callers is found dead the next day, you wouldn't know but it might be foul play. Can't your whiz kids fix it so that the numbers are recorded say on a separate tape that even your call station people don't know about?"

"That would be useful. I'll speak to Bill Lawrence about it on Monday," said Timmy, "and think about it some more this afternoon. What are we doing this afternoon, Helene?"

"We're going for a walk with you and Aunty Helene and have tea in the Cosy Tea Room, aren't we Aunty Helene?" said David, aged six,

"And we're taking Maxi and Oliver, they'll be ever so good in the tea place," said Anne, aged four.

"Well, that's it then, we're going for a walk across the park to the village."

"And over the bridge across the river past the bathing place to Long Wood," said David.

Helene said that she had a problem with so many Davids,

"Daddy calls me David three, he's David two and Granddad General is David one and he's a Baron something, aren't you granddad? Retired General Sir David Hawkridge GCB, DSO, MC Bart., smilingly confirmed that this was so.

Liz came as well. They all put on Wellington boots from the cloakroom and off they went across the bridge to the Long Wood, skirted the wood then back along the far bank of the river, across the bridge and then eastwards along the south bank and towards the village; holding adult hands, rushing off, throwing sticks for the dogs and chattering the whole while.

They made their way to the garage and young Will emerged from beneath a car and said, "Spotted you coming."

"What the trim ankle test, Will? Did we both pass?" asked Helene.

"Yes," grinned Will, "and your Mum passed this morning too." Looking at Liz, "It's nice to see you Liz, how is the doctoring going, cut up anyone I'd know?"

"I'm a doctor, not a commando," smiled Liz. "It's good to see you too, Will. We've just been walking in the Long Wood like we four did when we were children, those were happy times when the sun always shone and days seemed to last forever."

Timmy watched Will. Will made no secret of his admiration of the blonde beauty of Helene and now she was side by side with the beautiful brunette he had known from childhood. They made a stunning pair. Who would have thought that old Liz would grow up to be such a beauty.

"'Ave you got any new adventures planned, Tim, it's getting a bit dull around here since that business you took me to in France. I saw that the drug man Thomas got eight years and his sidekick Tiny got twelve for manslaughter. Serve them right," said Will.

"Not at present, Will. Although Liz has been dealing with some thugs in Bristol this week, we'll keep you posted."

The girls and children wandered on towards the tea room and Timmy said,

"Seriously, Will, things are going alright with you, aren't they? If you need any help you let me know. I mean it."

"OK Tim, we're just about keeping our head above water. I'll let you know if the good ship Conway is about to sink. I'll try to keep it going till the old man dies."

"Do you still look after Jane's car and does she still go off to Bournemouth six nights a week?"

"Yes, she's still the Exotic Dancer – Jane, stripping for her living at the Half Moon Club. She's still the same nice person, funny isn't it?"

"And Gloria?" asked Timmy.

"She's still the same, and trying to steer me to the altar."

"I can strongly recommend marriage. See you tonight."

Timmy rejoined the party in the tearoom. Liz had just ended the 'Have you washed your hands' routine with her ex-village schoolmistress, Miss Daisy, who ran the tearoom with her younger sister, Miss Mary. This had been Miss Daisy's standard greeting for the past twenty-odd years and Helene knew how much this grated on Liz.

They would have just cups of tea for the adults and lemonade for the children, over whom the sisters made a fuss, and three cream cakes one of which was cut in halves for the little dogs which lay quietly beneath the children's chairs. Helene was not unaware that, in addition to the cake that they shared, most of little Anne's cake also disappeared under the table. She resolved to remind the children that the reason that she didn't get the dogs a cake each wasn't meanness, it was just that cakes aren't very good for little dogs health. She could imagine the barrage of questions that would spark.

They made their way back across the park, walking, running throwing sticks and holding hands while some important childish thought was imparted. Anne was most pleased at how good the 'boys' had been and how they should have an extra dog biscuit tonight. Liz, who had had little sleep for some days, had retired early from the more vigorous bits of the walking-home games and by the time they reached the Manor House Helene felt exhausted. Not for the first time, Helene's heart went out to Sally-Ann who had these small dynamos full time. But they were lovely children.

While they were dressing for dinner Timmy told Helene what young Will had said after she had moved away. She said,

"I'm glad that Jane's alright and still enjoys what she's doing."

"I should have asked him what happened to Pierre and the counterfeiters," added Timmy, "but I suppose that he'd have mentioned it had he known. Never fear, we are bound to hear in due course."

He held her close until she said "Stop it, Timmy, I must put my dress on or we'll be late for dinner and spoil Sally-Ann's record of always being the last one down. She told me that they tried to get David to be the last one to say goodnight children and close the door but the kids wouldn't have it, it has to be Mummy with endless kisses and goodnights and so she's always the last one down."

Timmy had found some photographs taken during his university days and with a glass of sherry in their hands he and Liz pored over them looking for anyone who looked familiar. She found someone who looked like Detective Chief Inspector Roger Hardwick and Timmy said that he thought that was a chap called Higginbotham from Crewe but he could be wrong.

Sundays at Manor House were a slightly later breakfast, a walk across the park to the village church at which the General, as squire, read the lesson, and then a walk back for drinks and lunch. If it rained they took their cars. Liz asked to be excused and stayed in bed. As they left the church both Margaret and Helene spotted a slight figure sitting in one of the pews near the door and of one accord went and sat on either side of her.

"Hello Jane," said Helene, "how lovely to see you, I hope that all goes well and that the troubles are now firmly behind you."

"Hello, yes, thanks to all of you up at the Manor I can look the world in the face again."

"Are you still working at the same place?"

"Yes, and I'll let you into a secret, Bruce and I are going to be married in a few months time when memories of recent events in both families have dimmed."

"That's wonderful, June, we're so pleased for you," said Margaret. "May I give you a word of advice?"

"Of course."

"Never, no matter how much you love you future husband, never, ever, tell him the truth about that dreadful night. Remember, you came home at 3 a.m. and went to bed. Let sleeping ghosts lie."

"I will, and thank you both. I'll never forget what I owe to you."

They left to rejoin the family party.

After lunch Timmy called a meeting of the Manor House Trust. Timmy had admired the way his parents had tackled the ever-mounting costs of running the estate and knew that this was becoming a great worry to them. He'd decided that he should do something about it without it seeming to be outright charity. Helene agreed and they had set up the Trust to meet the expenses of running the estate, guaranteeing to put in sufficient money each year to keep the Manor House and park, church, farms and the village in good repair and support other  worthy causes, like university fees and so on.

The General chaired the meeting, which all family members over eighteen could attend and Helene was its executive officer. The whole idea was new but since there was a backlog of essential things to do, and this included seeing that those who worked for the estate were properly rewarded, they had little difficulty in deciding the first years programme. The question was, as Helene put it, who was to oversee the work on a day to day or perhaps weekly, basis; to be the Manor House Trust Clerk of Works and general handyman? The General and his wife thought that they could start the thing off, like getting young Will to do the church heating system, but agreed that there would be a need for someone later, an honest, versatile person. This was the second meeting. Margaret had enjoyed the first meeting because they had agreed to give every employee and the vicar a long overdue ten percent increase in pay. She looked at Tim, the son who had made all this possible, sitting quietly in the background, dear Tim, and now he had a wife. How time flew.

David two, Major David Hawkridge was on regimental duty that night and so with many hugs and kisses and a few tears, David, his American wife, Sally-Ann, the children and dogs departed in late afternoon. The others left for London and for Bristol after an early evening meal.

# Chapter Four

AS EXPECTED, a fax from Joy Philips was in the pile of papers that Penny brought in on Monday morning. Timmy put it to one side and prepared for his regular Monday morning management meeting and individual discussions with his senior managers that followed. Helene joined him for a sandwich lunch. He had chosen his corner office in Canary Wharf with views down the river and to the South and had furnished it sensibly with a desk, some chairs and a settee along the two sides of the room under the windows. Whenever she looked out there was always something happening and more often than not they would finish their lunch standing side-by-side watching the never-ending pageant on London's river. He showed her the fax from Joy.

"Joy seems a bit put out at Chuck committing the station to this 0800 phone-in business without consulting her or us. There's an element of clearing her yardarm in it but she does have a point. Somehow we've got to appear to re-establish her authority while not turning Chuck off. Could you go down there, Angel and tell her what a grand job she's doing and put the 0800 monitoring arrangements in place while making Joy think it was all her idea? You could take the Bentley but you'd be wiser to go by train. If she's free you could rope Liz in as well."

"If you want me to I could go tomorrow but I think that it might take two visits, tomorrow to set up the system and put in hand the recruitment of the people and a visit later in the week or early next week to interview the candidates that the agencies produce and give the final go-ahead. If there's time Liz could take us both out to meet the Detective Chief Inspector," said Helene.

"Honestly, darling I don't know how I ran this company before you came, no, I mean it, put that paperweight down and tell me that you love me."

"Timmy darling, that's not office talk, but I do. And while we're on the subject I'm pleased that you're letting me make a few changes at home to make the décor lighter."

"Angel I wasn't on that subject."

36

"No darling but I was. I'll go and tell Joy that I'll be with her tomorrow and would appreciate Chuck being there too. I'll also let Liz know that I'll be down."

She went to Bristol on an early train and took a taxi to the radio station offices at Bedminster Down, arriving at about half past ten. She thought again what a remarkably good choice the site had been, set in its own grounds beside the A38 on the southwestern edge of the city and within a mile or two of Bristol International Airport. Joy Philips said that she had asked Chuck to be there at eleven and sure enough, he arrived on the dot.

Helene thanked Joy for her fax and said that Timmy has asked her to come down and help set up the arrangements for the 24 hour telephone watch.

Chuck interrupted to say,

"It would only be twenty two extra hours since Sally and I will take the calls between midnight and two a.m."  Helene said,

"While that is undoubtedly true it is not very helpful since presumably someone would have to do it before you and Sally arrive and after you've left."

Chuck said "Sorry."

"For your ears only, at the highest level, the police think that the phone-in could be helpful and would like to keep in touch with the enquiry.  They recognize that the official way they have to proceed, asking every informant or witness for their name and address, puts people off and welcome an initiative that might encourage some of the shy or frightened people to speak up. How do you react to that, Chuck?"

"Not very well at first glance, we'll find that they'll go marching off and arresting someone and then want to use our tapes as evidence and no-one will ever trust us or Hawkridge Media again."

"I agree with Chuck, lets keep the police at a very long arms length," said Joy.

"OK, suppose we limit our co-operation to a willingness to provide them with a summary of something that looks important, like quote, we have had a number of reports that there seem to be a lot of foreign people arriving and then leaving a house near so and so public house in Bedminster, unquote or quote, we have had a number of reports that the man in the end house of such and such street is dealing in stolen cars, unquote."

"I wouldn't object to that," said Chuck and Joy nodded her agreement.

Helene said "We'll need watch-keepers each day for seven days a week and we should plan on keeping the operation going for a month and then review progress; if calls are still coming in we might extend it for a further two weeks and so on. All calls would be recorded and the tapes would be evaluated by the three of us and perhaps Timmy's sister, Liz."

"How will we go about getting the watch-keepers, should I get on to the employment exchange or whatever it's called this week?" said Joy. "We have to be so careful since this government made even casual workers pensionable."

"I thought about that in the train," said Helene, "we won't employ anyone, we'll use undergraduates. I'll call on the Head of the Social Sciences Faculty in the University and suggest to the Professor of Sociology that his or her undergraduates man the phone as part of their work experience. We won't pay them but we'll give them £5 an hour to cover their expenses. That will avoid the station having employees and the youngster's having grant problems. The job shouldn't be exacting, I doubt whether there will ever be more than five calls in a day and so they can study at our expense. If they're the type of young people I think they are, we'll be able to rely on them arranging their timetables to suit. One thing that we must do is pay, sorry, give their expenses to each participant when he or she finishes each shift, we don't want any arguments afterwards. This means that they'll sign in and sign out. Furthermore they won't be allowed to chop and change shifts in the middle of the night."

"What happens if the University won't play?" asked Joy.

"Then we go to Bristol's other University, the University of the West of England," said Chuck, warming to the idea.

"Now for the real work, we must provide the watch-keepers with a set of questions that they should ask each caller and I suppose a warning of questions they must not ask, like 'what's your name' or 'what's your address,'" said Helene. "This is very much in your court Chuck. Will you have the first shot? We can use Chuck's free-phone number. Do you have a small office for the watch-keepers to which the 0800 calls can be directed during the other twenty two hours?"

"Yes," said Joy, "and I'll put in a kettle and the things for making coffee."

"Good, then lets plan on starting next Monday, better to get things going for five days before the young people have to organize themselves around a weekend," said Helene. "I'll ring the Dean and see if Joy and I can see him immediately after lunch while you prepare the set of nice encouraging questions to give to the watch-keepers, Chuck. I'll be coming back here before catching my train but I don't want to take up more of your time than I have to, so perhaps you'd fax the questions to London when you've talked with Joy."

"Sure," said Chuck.

"Next, publicity, I'd stake my life that the majority of those who would like to phone us will be well over the age of retirement and not many of those will be regular listeners to Chuck's programme," said Helene, "so we have to advertise our phone-in invitation in the daytime hours. Off the top of my head I'd say six times a day for this week and perhaps four times a day thereafter, I'll accept your judgement. The advertisment should be on the lines of what Chuck said the other night, that the preservation of law and order is the duty of all the good citizens of Bristol and not just the hard pressed police and that it will be absolutely confidential, no names and no addresses."

Meeting the professor turned out to be more difficult than Helene had planned and it wasn't until after four o'clock that they were ushered into his study. Helene explained their mission, giving the background about the attempts on Ah Ming's life and the radio station's proposal to enlist the eyes and ears of the citizens of Bristol in an endeavour to reduce crime. She explained that she had first thought of going to the Students Union in Clifton to offer young people from all faculties the chance to earn some pocket money but would much prefer that the arrangement might present a semblance of work experience.

"The Dean told me that you would be approaching me and asked that I do my best to help. I'm sure that my predecessors would have had nothing to do with such a proposal," said the professor, "but, frankly, they lived in a different world. My students are themselves the victims of street crime, unscrupulous landlords and so on and I think that sufficient of them will be intrigued by what you are planning to do."

"We don't want to disrupt their course work and attendance at lectures," said Helene, "is it possible for them individually to work their day around an eight hour or four hour shift at Bedminster Down?"

"You don't know my students, they'd plan their way round an earthquake if it suited them."

"Would you mind if we used your department to recruit the students," said Helene. "We'd send you an explanation of what we're doing and why, the duties required of a watch-keeper, and perhaps the questions that should be put to the callers-if any- and the questions that must not be put, and, of course, the undertaking to pay expenses of £5 an hour, guaranteed for a month. This would be putting all the facts on the table with a vengeance. If you think it necessary, Joy could come in and talk to them, sign them up, and organize the roster for the first few days, but remember that she's also got a radio station to run."

"The more I think about this scheme the more I like it," said Professor Young. "I can see the outline of an interesting social paper in it."

"We would simply ask the students to reply to the callers and ask questions from a list that we will provide," said Helene. "The only judgement item for the students might be to assign the caller's question to one of five or six categories like, sex, cars, street violence, housing, drugs and crime generally. The calls will be recorded and other people will analyse their substance and draw what conclusions are possible."

"That's fine," said the professor. "If you'd send me a statement on the lines you've suggested I'll talk it through with my second year students and let you know the outcome. Then we'll get down to a duty roster for the first week from next Monday onwards."

"Thank you," said Helene. "One final question, we'll be advertising the project and its 0800 number in our daytime programmes throughout the week, would you mind if we mentioned your faculty's assistance when we've ironed out the details?"

"No, please do so it will increase the students interest."

Chuck had gone when they returned to the radio station but he had left his list of questions. Helene tried to ring Liz and found that she had been on duty all day. She spoke with Joy, "I'm leaving now. I'll take a copy of these questions and the other papers and work on them in the train. In the morning I'll e-mail the statement that I want you to send or give to Professor Young and then you can deal with him on the lines that we discussed. I think that's about all and now, bless you, you can start your real days work."

The train drew into Paddington and there, beside his precious Bentley, was her husband, in amiable conversation with a policeman.

"Oh it is lovely to see you, Timmy, and thanks for coming to meet me, you are such a dear."

"What shall we do, Angel, go straight home or go down to Walton on Thames for dinner and then home?"

"I finished my work in the train, what about you? If you haven't got any homework let's go slowly down to Walton and a leisurely dinner and then home to bed, darling. I'll fill you in on today's events as we go."

And thus it was.

The next day she e-mailed the data to Joy together with a suggestion that Hawkridge Radio Bristol should put a sizeable advert in the local paper on the lines of Chuck's statement.

Timmy asked Bill Lawrence, his technical and research manager to see him. He explained what was being set up in Bristol and asked him to ensure that there were an adequate number of voice-actuated recorders there. He asked if it was possible to automatically record the number from which an incoming call was made as an aid to checking the locality from whence the call originated. Bill said that he thought that it might be done with the ordinary phones but that some mobile phone calls might be a problem. Timmy asked that whatever was possible should be recorded.

They spent the weekend at the Manor House as was becoming usual but on Sunday evening Timmy returned to London alone. With each mile he hated it more.

It had seemed a good idea that Helene should be in Bristol for the first day of the 0800 phone-in, so she went to Bristol with Liz. With each mile she hated it more.

Each realized that since the visit to her mother at the Chateau Bouchier this would be the first night they would be apart. He had suggested that he should cancel his Monday meetings and come as well and had been firmly reminded by his young wife that he had a business to run. Helene now regretted her firmness but at least she would sleep at Liz's and not in an hotel and anyway Liz wasn't on duty until after lunch and was coming with her to the radio station, which solved a minor transport problem. The next day would soon pass if she kept busy.

Timmy's Monday morning management meeting went well. He received reports from his divisional managers and it seemed that they were on course to exceed their profit forecasts. Bill Lawrence reported that the required equipment was installed and would shortly be working in Bristol. He relayed a report from Joy Philips that the undergraduate situation was more than satisfactory; Professor Young had done his stuff.

He worked doubly hard for the rest of the day but it was clear to Penny that part of his mind was elsewhere when he reminded her for the fifth time that she must tell him the time of arrival of Helene's train at Paddington.

Helene and Liz arrived at the radio station about 0830. The first undergraduate was sitting in the room set aside for monitoring the calls with the list of questions in front of her and various sociology textbooks and notebooks to one side. They had a choice of a speaker or headphones to receive incoming calls and this young woman had her headphones firmly on. She had seen the pictures on the TV and disc jockeys always had earphones on. She told them that since the station had been advertising the confidential phone-in, the number of callers on the Chuck Williams Show had increased. They were impressed that this young woman understood the reason the questions were phrased the way they were and the importance of maintaining the trust of any caller and gently drawing out what the person wished to say. The students had arranged four-hour shifts until midnight when the next person would do eight hours until 0800, when the cycle would be repeated. Girls would do the daylight hours and boys the hours of darkness. How sensible, they thought.

They spent the morning speaking with Joy and the staff and tried not to impede busy people. By the time the first shift ended and the first young lady had been relieved by an equally serious fellow student, there had been three calls, one to complain about the Council's failure to clear away a pile of old mattresses, refrigerators and the like that had been dumped near her home, one to complain about a neighbour's loud radio playing all night and the third a man making sexual proposals to the student. For some reason Helene hadn't considered this and was embarrassed. The student said think nothing of it, if I'm to do social work I've got to get used to that sort of thing. Liz asked her under which headings she had assigned the calls and saw that there were two neat entries under housing and one in red ink under sex.

Liz had to go at lunchtime and Helene decided that she might as well go too. The Bristol people had the situation well under control. She made a mental note to thank Professor Young. Liz took her to Temple Meads Station and Joy dutifully reported to Penny that the boss's wife would be on the 1300 train.

Timmy was at Paddington to meet the train and they both went back to the office. Penny watched them come in and thought them the two happiest souls she had seen that day. Come to think about it, that week.

On the following Monday, Joy Philips reported that the score for the past week had been sixty calls, which the students had categorized as 8 sex, 12 cars, 6 street violence, 18 housing, 10 drugs and 6 crime general. In addition, out of the more than a hundred calls that Chuck took in the week on the Chuck Williams Show, forty-two calls could be taken as complaints. These had been added to the recording of the confidential calls to provide a total sound record for the week. Chuck's complaint calls were 7 sex, 9 cars, 5 street violence, 9 housing, 9 drugs and 3 general crime. Where should she send the tape?

Helene told her to make two further copies and send one to her in London and the other to Professor Young. The plan was that they should analyse what was said and see if there was a discernable trend or concentration, like half the callers about sex mentioned the same local public house or a third of the complainants about housing had

43

the same landlord.    She added that she would prepare a note about this trend analysis and send copies to the radio station and the professor. She urged Joy to use Chuck as much as possible because he should have developed a feel for such things. Because they were all busy people she would suggest that they should exchange brief notes on the trend analysis and get together towards the end of the four-week period to make a more detailed review and decide on future action.  She made a note to write to the professor about paying him a fee.

She decided that she would visit Bristol once more at the end of the second week and this time she would take Timmy if he could get away.  She conspired with Penny to keep his diary clear on that Friday and arranged to see Professor Young in the late morning and Liz for lunch.  They'd go on to Tolbrite afterwards and back to London on the Sunday evening.

# Chapter Five

FRIDAY came and they made their way to the M4, quite painlessly since they were going against the main traffic flow. Helene snuggled down in the passenger seat and recalled the time, just a few months ago, when Timmy had first taken her, his 'financial adviser who could speak Arabic,' down to his parents house. The big car silently ate up the miles to the M4 / M5 interchange where they turned south and crossed the River Avon over the bridge that seemed to be constantly under repair and turned sharply inland to reach Bedminster Down, their route barely touching the city.

They discussed station affairs with Joy and her staff and assured them that any extra costs arising from the phone-in exercise would be met from headquarters. They put their heads in to the monitoring room where a mirror image of the girl who had initiated the watch-keeping was sitting studying a text-book, and wearing headphones. They gestured hello and goodbye and withdrew. Joy said that the whole exercise was going well and the people who were so quick to ring in and criticize the undergraduate population should be made to eat their words. This transposition from the days of the printed word interested Timmy. The pattern of calls was much the same as before with perhaps a bias towards housing and the complaints were becoming more specific. The usual report and copies of the tape would be made on Monday.

They took a taxi into the city and the University. Helene introduced Timmy to the professor and said, "We've all been impressed with the behaviour of the under-graduates, they're doing a splendid job which must really be awfully boring, sitting for hours and then responding to a call from someone they don't know who most times makes little sense to them."

"You are discussing the sociologist lot," laughed the professor. "They are a remarkably mature set of young people, aren't they?"

"Yes," said Helene, "have you had an opportunity to listen to the tapes yet?"

"Yes and a pattern is beginning to emerge, it's early days yet, but what you are turning up might, just might, be of great help to the police and, perhaps, the benefits people."

"I thought that might be the case," said Timmy, "and that's probably a racial minefield."

"That's something that we're only too conscious of in my profession," said the professor, "so much so that there's bound to be the inevitable back-lash against what is seen by many of the poorer white section of the community as positive discrimination, untrue as that might be."

"I suggest that we get together at the middle of the fourth week," said Helene, "and see what tentative conclusions might be drawn from the first three weeks and decide whether or not to extend the enquiry to six weeks; if you and the young people are agreeable, of course. This would give them time to plan their duty roster for the extra two weeks. If staffing were difficult we could eliminate the midnight to 8 a.m. session, because the first two hours are already covered by the Chuck Williams Show and after that the sort of person who wants to complain is usually asleep in bed."

They agreed to meet at the radio station at 11 a. m. the following Wednesday when the discussion could continue over lunch.

They walked down the road to the Bristol Royal Infirmary where they asked that Doctor Elizabeth Hawkridge should be paged. In a few minutes Liz came running, she was ready and waiting for them. They climbed into her car and she drove up the M32 motorway explaining that lack of parking made lunching in the city center difficult and they were going to an hotel on the northern ring road. She explained that it wasn't a totally random choice because she intended to pop into Southmead hospital on the way back and see how the Asiatic girl Ah Ming was progressing and, bye the way, she had asked that policeman who said he was at Oxford with Timmy, to join them.

Detective Chief Inspector Roger Hardwick was waiting for them in the foyer. His face lit up as he rose and greeted Liz then quickly turned to the other two. He and Timmy instantly recognized each other as Liz introduced Helene. The girls attracted a great deal of attention from fellow patrons who could be seen wondering which TV show or film they had seen them in. They decided to go straight in to lunch and there was a hush as the girls passed through the main body of the restaurant to a table for four in the window.

"I didn't see your shiny blue and yellow car in the car park and thought you weren't here," said Liz.

"We daren't use our official cars for social occasions, if I'd come in my shiny blue and yellow cruiser you can bet that Tim's 0800 line would be jammed with complaints by concerned citizens."

They ordered their meal and Timmy asked Helene to chose the wine. She found a red from her mother's vineyards, but not a particularly good year, she explained. Roger was going back to his police duties and drank water.

Conversation was largely about the radio station's phone-in enquiry and the results to date. Helene did most of the explaining.

"The results to date are much what you would expect. Although it wasn't necessary, we asked the undergraduates to put the calls in one of six categories, sex, cars, street violence, housing, drugs and crime in general. We also put the calls that Chuck Williams gets each night into the same categories and the results after two weeks were sex 34, cars 40, street violence 26, housing 66, drugs 40 and general crime, 20, a total of two hundred and twenty six. There was an increase of twenty percent in calls in the second week compared with the first but I would expect the number of callers to fall off in the third and fourth weeks."

"You mean that the people who want to complain will have got it off their chest, so to speak," said Roger.

"Yes. Of course we don't know how many of the complaints recorded are repeats by the same person with a grudge and I haven't included the threatening calls."

"You've recorded them, I hope," said Roger, "because our voice analysis people can work wonders identifying people and uttering threats is an offence. That could be useful."

Liz said, "I gave Roger a brief summary of your summer adventures with a murder, car thieves, drug smugglers and counterfeiters."

Timmy looked at Helene and they both grinned.

"I can certainly recommend criminology for romance," said Timmy.

"That's my brother who used to think that kissing was soppy and who's only use for girls was wicket keeping and fielding while he and our brother, David, took it in turns to bat and bowl. I've never liked cricket since," said Liz.

"Returning to the phone-in," said Helene, "we're having a review of the first two or three weeks results next Wednesday at 11 a.m. at Bedminster Down, you're welcome to come. I expect that the discussion will go on while we have lunch and enable busy people like yourself and Professor Young to get away immediately afterwards."

"I'd be pleased to come. I accept that I'll be at a disadvantage in not having heard the raw data from the tapes but I'd like to hear the other people's digest of what the tapes contain. Have you discovered anything useful from the first two weeks?"

"The most positive thing is that two people phoned to say that a lock-up at a Fishponds Industrial Unit is being used to store stolen cars. Next, there seem to be a number of complaints about one particular property company and third, agreement that drugs are on sale in at least two public houses with the landlord's knowledge," said Helene.

"That should be enough to be getting along with," said Liz.

"Unfortunately suspicion isn't enough to secure a conviction these days."

After a pleasant lunch Liz walked with Roger to his car and then came back for those she called the 'young lovers.'

"You'd think that he'd have a British car, wouldn't you, being a policeman?" said Liz. "I'm going to drop in and see Ah Ming, I've visited her a few times she must feel very much alone. Perhaps you'd come in Helene and make another visitor for the poor girl. She's made a remarkable recovery and I expect that the police and immigration people have a problem in what to do with her."

"I'd love to see her, remember she's the reason why we're having the phone-in," said Helene. She turned to Timmy, "You'd better not come in, my pet she probably goes in fear of the male sex."

"Good," said Timmy. "Come to think of it that was probably God's intention when he created woman, to go in fear of man."
"Ouch, that hurt."

Liz showed her pass and talked Helene into the hospital wing where Ah Ming was seated beside her bed in a room still guarded by a woman police constable.

"Hello, Ah Ming, remember me, Doctor Hawkridge. I've brought my sister Helene to see you. How are you today?"

"ello Doctor Liz, doctor say I am better. I walk round wing."

"Have you remembered where the other girls are?"

"No, no wemember, I not able tell," she said something in another language.

Helene could hardly believe it. The girl was muttering in a dialect of Arabic that she had last heard one small girl use twenty years ago in her school in Jordan.

She spoke to Ah Ming in Arabic and the girls eyes lit up and she clutched Helene's hand.

"Oh, help me please in the name of Allah."

Gradually Helene coaxed the story out of her.   She had been sold by her parents when she was ten years old and brought to Qatar. She had been taken to a house on the outskirts of Doha and made to work in the house and garden. The man of the house and his sons had made her sleep with them and beaten her if she tried to refuse. When she was about fifteen, the man got new small girls and sold her to a man who took her to a town in Saudi Arabia where her life was as wretched as it had been in Doha.   She was there for two years and had a baby who died and she was sold to a man in Jeddah. This man made her sleep with many men but she didn't have more babies. A rich white man had come who said I take this one to England. A big ship full of motor-cars had come to Jeddah to bring some cars and she was smuggled on board at night and put in a compartment with about twenty other girls. The ship's crew made all the girls sleep with them.   When they reached England the crew put them each in the boot of a red car and they were driven ashore. It was very hot in the boot and she was very frightened.   Next night the rich white man had come and taken her and the other girls to a place called Saint Paul's where she was given a room and made to sleep with many men each day.

Helene had translated for Liz as the girl spoke.

"How did you escape?" asked Liz.

"Man who sleep me left door open and I go out and ran. Inside the door was some money, which I used for telephone but big man had seen me along street and caught me while I was telephone. He took me back and beat me and I cried all night and next day.   Man say I no good and next night he beat me and put me in bag and threw me in water."

Liz and Helene told her that she was not to worry and they would see that she didn't have to go back to that bad man. They said they would visit her next Wednesday.

They rejoined Timmy and told him the story. "What on earth do we do now?" said Liz.

"I don't know about us, but Ah Ming's got two problems, the bad white man and the British Immigration Service," said Timmy.

"But we can't just abandon her," said Liz.

"Let's think aloud," said Timmy, "what would happen to her if she were to be deported, where would she be sent? If she was allowed to stay in this country on parole, would you personally be prepared to assume responsibility for her if it could be arranged?"

Helene said "Hold on, that last question's unfair, Liz is simply the doctor who helped save her life. If anyone's responsible we all are."

"OK Angel, remember we're just thinking aloud. The hospital will discharge her soon and doubtless she'll be required at the trial of the man who was arrested at Southmead, especially if the police succeed in linking him with her attempted drowning. Where does she go meanwhile, what about taking her down to Tolbrite?"

"That's what we should have discussed with Roger," said Liz.

"Do you often discuss things with Roger, then, kitten?" said Timmy.

"Quite often, brother dear, you'd be surprised at what we young doctors get up to."

"I don't know much about the British police but it seems to me that he's young to be a Chief Inspector," said Helene.

"Yes, I said that to him," said Liz, "and he laughed and said that it was because the people who make the police promotions discovered that he could do joined-up writing as well as read."

"At the rate he's going he'll be a Commissioner or something by the time he's forty," said Timmy, "and probably entitled to use his shiny blue and yellow car for social visits."

"Well, at least he seems decent," said Liz.

"Bless you, kitten, he seems a nice chap and, after all, he did go to your brother's college, didn't he?"

Liz drove them back to the radio station by what she said was the scenic route, which incidentally was the most direct, across Durdham

Down, down Bridge Valley Road, along the Portway and beneath Brunel's famous Suspension Bridge, across the mouth of the Floating Harbour, past the Bristol City football-ground in Ashton Park and then up on to Bedminster Down. When they passed under the bridge Liz explained that Roger lived in a rather nice house on the other side in Leigh Woods. Helene thought this to be one of the most attractive parts of any place she had seen in Britain.

Liz left with promises to see them in Dorset the following day.

They had a final talk with Joy Philips. She surprised them by saying,

"I'm becoming a little concerned about Chuck. As station manager I seldom see Chuck. I rely on his producer Sally Evans for his day-to-day management and would see him about once a fortnight if there were something to discuss at my progress meeting. I hear his broadcasts, of course, and I've noticed that he's become more strained and touchy in the past months. His decision to ignore your advice, Timmy, and announce the 0800 phone-in was, in my opinion, unforgivable."

"Yes, I realized that from your fax. I'd noticed that our audience figures for his show have been falling and he may have seen the Ah Ming story as a life belt, if that's not a too-close-to-the-wind analogy," said Timmy.

"Before this happened I was waiting an opportunity to suggest to you that we pulled his show and gave him a day-time slot, say in the morning for the housewives and retired folk," said Joy.

"Is there any reason you can suggest for the change in Chuck?" asked Helene.

"Well, it could be that the threats have become more frequent and nasty, they've even got to me," said Joy.

"Are they worse than the usual rubbish calls?"

"Oh yes, you listen to the tapes, the man or men who have been threatening us have been recorded in the past fortnight. The undergraduates drew attention to them."

"Does Sally Evans share your opinion about Chuck?" asked Helene.

"Yes and no," said Joy. "She is concerned at the audience ratings and thinks we should do something but she has a loyalty to Chuck. She can't see him in a daytime slot like I can. I think he could be great."

"I'm glad you raised this, Joy, we can't do anything until we've finished the month's phone-in and then we'll see how we stand," said Timmy. "Helene will listen to the tapes this weekend."

"My lord and master has spoken," smiled Helene. "Goodbye Joy, I'll see you next Wednesday and I'll bring Timmy too if I can fix his diary. Get someone in to do the lunch for four visitors plus yourself and Chuck and whoever else from your staff you think should be there, won't you?"

They went out to the Bentley and Helene elected to drive. Timmy thought this an admirable arrangement and proof positive that he loved the girl. Before he met Helene the very thought of anyone driving his car made him go grey and here he was opening the drivers door, catching a glimpse of perfect long legs as she swung in, helping her fasten her seatbelt and loving every moment of it as she made her way smoothly through the southern suburbs to the A37 for Shepton Mallet, then across to Shaftesbury, Blandford and eventually, Tolbrite.

# Chapter Six

"HOW lovely", said Margaret. "You're early. Off you go and change and then you can tell us all that has been happening. Liz told me last night that you'd be with her today and she was hoping that you'd go with her to see that poor girl, so you must have lots to tell us."

Over dinner Timmy and Helene recounted the day's events, not least the fact that Helene could speak the 'poor girl's' dialect. They spoke of meeting Roger Hardwick at lunch and the significance of the look that Helene and his mother exchanged was not lost on Timmy. They said that they would have to spend a lot of the weekend listening to the tapes of the callers to the Bristol station.

Timmy had the work that he'd brought with him to do on the Saturday morning, plus a bunch of e-mails that Penny had sent on the Friday while Helene settled down to listen to the tapes. She soon realized that it was an enormous task, far bigger than she'd envisaged, a hundred and two messages from the first week and a further hundred and twenty four from the second. And, in two days time a further hundred or so from the third week would arrive and a week after that a further hundred or so. She confessed to Timmy later that it was at that moment that she decided that four weeks would be enough. She decided that she wanted six tape recorders, one of which would be reserved for each of the six categories of complaint. She would then play the first weeks tape and re-record each complaint on the appropriate recorder and repeat the process for the second weeks tape. She would finish up with six subject tapes each of which would present a more meaningful story than sitting there playing the master tape with her mind jumping from sex to cars to street violence to housing to drugs and to crime general.

Having decided that she needed six tape recorders and tapes she went to interrupt Timmy.

"Timmy, this job is enormous."

"I know, Angel, I did a quick sum and decided that it would take nearly eight hours just to listen to the two tapes. I didn't like to dampen your enthusiasm and I thought that it'd keep you out of mischief."

"You rotter, and who was it taught me all about mischief?"

He stood up, turned, put his arms round her and lifted her off her feet, saying,

"You didn't require much teaching, sweetheart."

"Put me down Timmy, what I suggest is that we get six tape recorders, one for each category, and re-record the messages so that each presents a more coherent story and our minds don't have to keep jumping from category to category."

"You mean that when you start on sex you want to keep on thinking about sex. What a good idea, I'm a good mind to pick you up again." He put his arms round her waist.

"Please be serious, darling, what shall we do about the tapes?"

"Well, first, what you suggest is good, we'll do it. The work of copying the tapes could be done by anyone who can tell the difference between a sex matter and a car matter and so on. There's some urgency, because we want the six separate tapes by, say Tuesday morning so that we can listen to them and draw some conclusions before we, or you, go to the meeting in Bristol on Wednesday next. OK so far?"

"Yes," said Helene. "Mr Swift or Bill Lawrence?"

"You've got it in one, Angel. Bill will have the equipment and he can probably assign a couple of chaps to the job. We'll take the tapes into the office and get Bill to do it. I'll ring him now and warn him. It conjures up a lovely image of Bill Lawrence standing in front of an orchestra of tape recorders and pointing to the appropriate one as the messages come from the master tape. I rather think that we'll have to settle for reviewing only the first two weeks tapes on Wednesday, there won't be time to get the third weeks tape transcribed."

"Thanks darling, I'll just have a little listen to a few of the calls to get the flavour."

Liz arrived just before dinner and was hugged by her mother and told to hurry down and tell her all the news. When she came down,

"Timmy and Helene have told us all about your lunch and the poor Arab girl, so exciting," said her mother, "and about meeting your policeman."

"He isn't my policeman Mummy. He's just the contact about Ah Ming."

54

"Oh, that's a pity, dear. Timmy thought that it might be a good idea to invite him down one weekend soon to discuss this broadcasting thing that you're doing in Bristol."

"Well Mummy if Timmy thinks that it'd be a good idea...."

"I see dear, anyway they said that he's a nice man and he was at Trinity with Timmy, wasn't he?"

The conversation ranged widely over dinner, from what a good job young Will had made of the church heating system to the recent illness of the vicar's wife. "Such a cold house, the vicarage, perhaps young Will could do something about it," ventured Margaret.

"Excellent idea," said the General. "He seems to be a capable chap; they get good training in the services these days. Turn their hands to anything."

"I'll ask Mrs Ford whether he can come and have a look, then."

"A thing we want to ask you Mummy," said Liz "is, if the police would allow it, could the Asian girl Ah Ming come here to finish her recovery. She could help Mrs Holmes and sleep in one of the old servants bedrooms, Helene and I would get it ready," with an appealing look at Helene.

"Oh yes, that would be a Christian act, for I don't know where she'd go otherwise," said Helene. "She's been treated horribly ever since she was sold into slavery as a child and deserves some kindness in her life. She told us the whole horrible story."

"It's funny you should raise the subject but I can see us losing the services of Maisie one day in the not too distant future," said Margaret. "The young man with the Volvo saloon seems to be a frequent visitor and haven't you noticed the care she now takes with her make-up and clothes, she's a different girl these days."

"If she goes it'll kill poor Towers," said the General.

"Well, perhaps they'll work something out," said Margaret. "The lodge has three bedrooms and is big enough for three grown ups, but we could still have the need for another pair of hands."

"So if I could fix things with the police, father being a magistrate etc etc, could I offer to provide a safe home and employment for Ah Ming? Remember that she may have to give evidence one day at the trial of the man who tried to get into her room and this could attract the attention of some shady characters," said Liz.

"I doubt if he could be charged with anything more serious than trespass," said Timmy. "His lawyer could claim that he fought the security men because he thought that he was the one being attacked because he's black, Of course, if the police charge anyone with her attempted murder by drowning, it would be different."

"What do you say, mother?" said Liz

"I don't know what to say, we mustn't bring a sickly person in who will need looking after, everyone has enough to do as it is."

"I'll take that as a qualified Yes," said Liz.


Helene and Timmy spent the Sunday afternoon listening to the tapes, she took the first week and he took the second. Margaret had arranged an early dinner and Liz departed immediately thereafter. Timmy and Helene were not long afterwards and they compared their impressions of the calls on the two tapes during the journey back to Chelsea.

Bill Lawrence had been warned and took the tapes on Monday, seeming amused at having to decide which category and hence which button to press to assign the calls to the appropriate subject tape. At lunchtime he reported that it was going well but he and his chaps no longer found it amusing. The original tapes and the six subject tapes were finished by six p.m. and Helene spent that evening and the whole of Tuesday listening and making notes. By lunchtime Helene had decided that the tapes were potential dynamite and that Timmy should be at the morrow's meeting in Bristol and she and Penny rearranged his diary to make this possible.

They went by train to Bristol and were getting an update on the arrangements from Joy Philips in the Radio station by ten thirty. Professor Young and Detective Chief Inspector Hardwick arrived at about ten fifty and Chuck Williams on the stroke of eleven. They went into the conference room and Timmy said,

"Before we start I have to remind you that some of the calls received and recorded make accusations against named individuals. Collectively we have no means of verifying the accuracy of such claims. My lawyers tell me that we are entitled to listen to the tapes but we must not, under any circumstances, divulge to others what is alleged thereon about people or companies."

"I assume that by us you mean employees of Hawkridge Media," said Joy. "What about the professor and the chief inspector, can they listen?"

"Yes, of course. The professor and his undergraduates were, and are, acting for us and the police are sitting-in because of the allegations of crime made by some of the callers."

"All of us here today and those associated with the phone-in can listen and draw conclusions but we must not divulge specific calls. Sounds reasonable to me," said Helene.

"You mean I can't re-broadcast any of the calls?" said Chuck.

"Of course not Chuck, you yourself gave the promise of anonymity," said Joy.

"I don't see why I shouldn't use the actual calls, after all if I hadn't started the thing you wouldn't have any material at all," insisted Chuck.

"Look Chuck, be reasonable, the last thing any of the callers would expect would be to hear their confidences being broadcast over the air. You yourself gave our promise of confidentiality. In any case we have to watch our step and I'd remind you of what Timmy's lawyers have said."

"We all know how timid lawyers are. If editors took note of what the paper's lawyers said we'd have no daily newspapers. We've got to use our own judgment and I say broadcast the lot."

"You can't really mean that," said a startled Joy.

"Sure I do. You're the station manager. Do you want to miss what is probably the best scoop of the year?"

Timmy and the others had listened to this with mounting astonishment. Timmy said,

"Look Chuck, you evidently still haven't grasped how serious this is. Let me put it this way, if I hear that you've referred directly to what any of the callers said, you'll never work in broadcasting anywhere in the UK again. Do I make myself clear?"

"Keep your shirt on. You might own the station but I'll say what I like on my show. I don't need you to tell me what I can and can't say. I'll decide what should or shouldn't be said on the Chuck Williams Show, not you."

"I'm sorry to do this Chuck but I can't take any chance of being landed with a multi-million pound slander suit as well as losing the Hawkridge reputation for honesty. We all recall that it was because you chose to ignore my instruction that you shouldn't mention the Ah Ming thing that night that we are embarked on the present exercise. I'll concede that the process is turning up potentially useful information for the forces of decency and law and order but it is information that must be used with great care. Today all those present have heard your evident wish, indeed your insistence, to use the contents of the tapes on your programme. Do I have your solemn undertaking that you will not broadcast or quote from any of the material that the callers have provided?"

"No you most certainly do not, I decide what's broadcast on my show, you seem to forget that it's people like me who keep your station going."

"Very well," said Timmy. "I've forbidden all reference to the tapes but you seem set on going your own way and in the circumstances I have no alternative but to remove any possibility that you might do so. The only safeguard possible is to take the Chuck Williams Show off the air and cancel your contract."

He turned to the station manager,

"Joy, the Chuck Williams Show is terminated from this moment. You will give Chuck a statement of all the monies due to him and see that he removes all his belongings and himself from this station by 12 noon today. I'm genuinely sorry Chuck but I can't take the risk that you evidently pose. You've become a loose cannon, and as such there is no longer a place for you in Hawkridge Media. Will you please leave now?"

In a shocked silence Chuck and Joy stood up and left the room with Chuck muttering something about Timmy had not heard the last of this.

"I do apologise for that happening in your presence. I'd have avoided it if at all possible but I am not prepared to face an expensive and time-consuming lawsuit because of Chuck's ego. Now let's hear Helene's report."

A somewhat subdued Helene began,

"In the time available we've only been able to deal with the first two weeks tapes. The only way we could see of making sense out of the two hundred and twenty six phone calls received in those first two weeks was to sort them out and re-record in six subject categories on separate tapes. This means that you don't have to keep switching your mind from cars to sex to housing and so on as the tape is played. We found that the assignment to subject that the undergraduates made was surprisingly good and we don't question their breakdown in numbers. I'll start first with the thirty-four calls about sex. These break down into three main sorts, general street prostitution, suspected brothels and gay bars and the like. The important disclosure is the addresses of two brothels that have young girls in them."

"I'll go next to General crime if I may, you'll see the reason. When Chuck made his broadcast appeal on the night that someone tried to get at Ah Ming in Southmead Hospital, he asked if anyone had seen a white man and two blacks in a car between St Pauls and Southmead between ten and eleven that night or a white man and one black going the other way shortly after eleven. Well, the first call on that tape gives three names, one of whom is the man the security guards captured."

"That's quite remarkable," said Roger Hardwick.

"There's more to come," said Timmy. "There was one caller with a cultured voice who said that one of the most senior men in the Civil Engineers Department is in the pay of one of the Council's biggest contractors."

"Next, calls about cars," said Helene. "There were forty calls which could be broken down into four sorts. General moans from the housing estates about teenage tear-aways, road racing and burnt out cars, car theft and what are the police doing about it? Car sales places that wind back the mileage recorders and dealers in stolen cars. Two winders back and two places to which stolen cars are taken for alteration are identified."

"Drugs also attracted forty calls. These were much more general and ranged from complaints about the implements of drug taking being left about as a danger to children, to naming three public houses where drugs seem to be available across the counter and finally the name of a prominent citizen who was said to finance the drug barons."

"Calls about street violence were what you would expect but did indicate where most of the muggers come from and again St Paul's tops the list. Names and addresses of some thugs are given."

"Last but by no means least, we come to housing. There were sixty-six calls about housing which fell into four areas; why should refugees and illegal immigrants receive better treatment than young people whose parents fought for the country and pay penal taxes. The second area was the failure of the Council and Housing Associations to maintain property, a whole string of detailed complaints. Third was a list of people that informants said were receiving benefit but working as well but the fourth was worth the whole exercise, chapter and verse on landlords and property developers who harass elderly tenants so they can put up the rents or re-develop sites for large profit. Descriptions of the methods used for intimidation are given. Three of the callers gave their names and addresses and invited further discussion, all relate to the Old Market area."

"That's a quite remarkable tour d' force," said Professor Young, after a pause. "How you folk who are running a big business could find time to make that analysis, I can't imagine, but well done. I've only sampled the tape in places but where I have my impressions are exactly the same as yours."

"I've not had access to the tapes," said Roger, "but they seem to contain some powerful information on lawbreakers and lawbreaking. We can take action on several of them without breaking your assurance of anonymity, by which I mean its things we could have found out for ourselves, the people who ring cars and the dealers who turn back the clock, for example. We can maintain a watch near the pubs and find out where the brothels are and we can do the same thing at the drug dealing pubs. And best of all, in the immediate future we can arrest the two men named for the attack at Southmead hospital. We might then frighten one of them into admitting that he was one of the three who threw Ah Ming into the harbour. The remaining items require a lot of work, we can't accuse Mr X of financing a drug cartel or Mr Y of accepting bribes for civil engineering contracts and the benefits people would be the agency to investigate some of the other items. Would it be possible for me to have a copy of the master tape and copies of the six subject tapes? You have my word that they won't leave my possession."

"Of course," said Timmy. "How do I make certain that they actually come to you in these days when every parcel is opened in some secure place lest it be a bomb? Would you come here, or have someone come here on Friday and collect them from the station manager, who I see has just come back into the room after performing a most unpleasant duty? I'm sorry Joy."

"I'll call here and collect them," said Roger.

Joy resumed her place at the table and nodded

"I'm sorry about that Joy," said Timmy, again.

"Oh, it had to be done and I'm just grateful that you were here to do it. As I said to you the other day, I was going to pull him off the night show and find something else that he might do. Your way is better and perhaps kinder in the long run although he won't see it that way. Timmy, lunch is ready next door."

"We've nearly completed today's business," said Helene, "and we must remember that we'll have two more weeks worth of tapes to review. The decision that we should make today is whether to continue the exercise for a further period. Since it depends on the undergraduates' cooperation could I ask for your view, professor?"

"I'm sure that you'd get volunteers for a further two weeks but frankly I feel that you've done enough, more than enough, in fact. You've given the police valuable information and you've given me enough material for a number of research items and I'm grateful. I suggest that you draw stumps, don't you agree Chief Inspector?"

Roger nodded.

"OK, then we will stop. Will you tell the young people, professor or should we put up a notice in their listening room?" said Timmy.

"I'll tell them and thank them on your behalf. They've done well."

After lunch they sought a private word with Roger and told him about the visit Helene had made with Liz to Southmead Hospital and the remarkable fact that Helene could speak the dialect of Arabic that seemed to be Ah Ming's mother tongue. Helene outlined the girl's life story and suggested that they should think about what is going on at the Bristol docks. She understood that car shipments through Royal Portbury Dock were fairly frequent but perhaps not all the carriers called at Jeddah. If it was up to her and Timmy they would find out when the next car ferry that had stopped at an Arabian port was due, and mount a covert surveillance operation on the dock. She understood that cars are unloaded by a team of drivers who drive the cars from inside the ship to parking lines ashore, hundreds from each voyage, and the cars are then moved in slow time to dealer's showrooms across Britain. Clearly the men who come for the girls couldn't open the boot of every car in the parking lines and neither could the girls make a noise so there must be a system. Ah Ming had mentioned red cars, so it would be as well to keep an eye on where the red cars were positioned. She and Timmy had no idea whether the cars were parked randomly or whether they were grouped by colour.

Timmy remarked that there must be a link between this girl smuggling operation, the brothels, the attempt to drown Ah Ming and the subsequent attempts to get at her. There was an outside chance that the same men were involved and that drugs were also being imported.

Roger said that he'd look into it, but the police resources really were stretched and it was difficult to allocate men on the basis of supposition. Give him hard evidence and he would move heaven and earth. Timmy pointed out that the police had one man in custody and the names of his two accomplices, surely that was sufficient justification?

In due course they took leave of Joy Philips and returned to London.

The following morning the Western Daily Press contained a short piece in which Chuck Williams (46) said that he had left Hawkridge Radio Bristol because the proprietor insisted on trying to censor what he could say over the air, particularly suppressing evidence of lawbreaking gathered as the result of a phone-in that he, Chuck Williams, had introduced. He had information on brothels, drugs and housing scams and the people who were making a fortune from them, which he intended publishing soon, naming names. Joy Philips, (38) the station manager confirmed that Mr Williams' contract with the radio station had been terminated.

# Chapter Seven

CHUCK Williams lived with his wife in the village of Long Ashton to the west of Bristol and on the old coaching route to Weston-Super-Mare and the South-west. It got its name in part from being the longest ribbon village in England, strung out for several miles along the Weston road. It had developed by throwing lateral roads up the fairly steep hill to the west and the Williams' lived towards the top of one of these roads called Providence.

That evening Betty Williams went out to see friends as she always did on a Thursday. When she returned she found her husband's body slumped just outside the front door of their house, he had been shot in the head. She ran inside, the front door was not locked, and phoned the police. It took some time to get the police to understand what she was saying and it was a further fifteen minutes before a police car arrived. The constable explained subsequently that the dispatcher hadn't realized that it was the road that the Williams lived in that was called Providence, she had thought that the distraught wife was saying that it was an act of providence.

The following morning the Western Daily Press contained a much longer piece reporting that Chuck Williams (46) had been found dead at about ten p.m. the previous evening outside his home at Providence, Long Ashton. He had a gunshot wound in the head. His wife Betty (35) had discovered the body when she returned to the house from visiting friends in Bristol.

Joy Philip picked up the item on the teleprinter and telephoned Timmy, Penny put her through,

"Timmy, this is Joy, some dreadful news, somebody murdered Chuck Williams last night. His wife came home and found him lying outside the front door. He'd been shot in the head. Do you think it had anything to do with us?"

"What do you mean Joy?"

"Well, you know, those phone calls we were talking about on Wednesday, or the ones I didn't want to bother you with."

"Were they that bad?"

"I didn't tell you but one of the reasons that I was going to pull Chuck's show was the increase in threatening phone calls we've been getting recently," said Joy.

"Why on earth didn't you mention them when we had Liz's tame policeman with us?"

"I didn't want to be a nuisance, what with all the bother Chuck caused."

"Did Chuck know about the threatening calls and did they mention his show?"

"Yes to both," said Joy "I'm sorry Timmy. Should I tell the police if they ask me?"

"Yes, we must have no secrets from the police as far as Chuck is concerned."

"Alright."

"Don't worry Joy, Now, listen, it's our policy to record all telephone conversations, I hope that you've still got a record of the threatening phone calls?"

"Yes, I kept them separate."

"Do they sound the same? I mean does it seem that the same person is making the calls?"

"Perhaps," then, "I can't be certain."

"The best thing for you to do is send them up here to headquarters for Bill Lawrence and his boffins to listen to. They'll analyse the sound spectrum and virtually fingerprint the caller's voice. They've already done it for the more important voices on the six tapes we discussed on Wednesday."

"What use can you make of that, Timmy?"

"Oh, I'll think of something. Imagine that one of your reporters calls on the Bristol Council Civil Engineers Department to discuss the possibility of making a short radio programme about something that they're doing. Your man would naturally record what the man or men say and when we get the recording we analyse the voices and find that one of them is the soft spoken cultured voice that said that one of the most senior men in that department is in the pay of one of the Council's contractors or potential contractors."

"Wouldn't that break the promise we gave of anonymity?" asked Joy.

"Not as long as we use the knowledge as a means of discovering who the crook is without disclosing our source and anyway, someone's been killed, which lets us bend the rules a little."

"Do you want me to send someone into the Civil Engineers Department?" asked Joy.

"Yes, your reporter could ask about that big development by Temple Meads Station that has done so much to improve the area, you know the sort of questions, what it cost over-all? Was it completed to time? How many men employed? What office space created? Rents and which members of the Civil Engineers staff supervised it? That sort of thing."

"Alright Timmy, it's always reassuring to talk with you. I'll send you the last set of tapes on Monday."

"Goodbye Joy and don't worry."

He told Helene about Joy's call that lunchtime. She thought that the timing of the murder was like something out of grand opera.

Helene said that she had consulted Lloyds List and it seemed that a car transport vessel called the Octavia Maru had called at Jeddah and was due at the Royal Portbury Dock the following Tuesday when the tide would be suitable. She asked,

"Shall we bring it to the attention of the police? Perhaps they already know."

"We haven't a clue what Roger's doing, if anything," said Timmy. "What about getting Mr Swift to keep an eye on things?"

"You're incorrigible, my pet, the last time you asked Mr Swift to keep an eye on things, as you so quaintly put it, you ended up being a murder suspect – briefly I admit – but that policeman from Hell said it, didn't he?"

"But look what it got me, the nicest girl in the world disguised as a banker who could speak Arabic."

"In point of fact, I was already there when it happened. It's simply that I want you to quit while you're still ahead."

"If we're being pedantic, Angel, I would remind you that I was a murder suspect for some time after we brought Mr Swift on board."

"What exactly is that intended to prove?"

"I haven't the foggiest idea. You started this bit of the conversation."

Later that afternoon he spoke with Mr Swift, the proprietor of Confidential Enquiries Limited.

"Mr Swift, this is Tim Hawkridge, remember me?"

"Mr Hawkridge, how could I ever forget you? You asked me to do a business surveillance operation and we finished up with smugglers, counterfeiters, stolen cars and a murder, I didn't leave anything out, did I?"

"You could have mentioned Jane, the striptease artiste otherwise I think that's the lot."

"My operatives still talk about it. It was the high point of their careers to date. What can we do for you this time?"

"It's a long story and I would prefer to brief you on Monday, say immediately after lunch but it will entail keeping observation at night on a lot of cars that will have just been unloaded from a Japanese ship at Royal Portbury Dock on Tuesday next."

"How long will my people be required?"

"If the ship docks on Tuesday as planned, they should be through by the following morning."

"All night observation, you say?"

"Yes and it's an exposed site and perhaps the police will also be keeping observation."

"Oh Lord, now he tells me; alright Mr Hawkridge, I'll be over on Monday, goodbye."

They left for the weekend at six. Helene settled comfortably in the passenger seat of the Bentley. They had stopped for dinner at the usual place and were on the M3.

"I've been thinking about Chuck's murder," said Helene.

"Tell me," said Timmy.

"I have every intention of doing just that, Timmy dear. His murder can be the result of something to do with his private life or his work with the radio station. We know little about his private life except that he is, was, married to Betty, who teaches at Colston School, no children. Turning to his work with the radio station, it's difficult to imagine how his answers to the questions phoned in could be sufficiently dangerous to someone to justify murder. I suppose that Joy has the records of his recent programmes and we could listen to those but somehow I don't think that the answer lies there. That brings us to the recent phone-in exercise and I can recite the calls off the top of my head. People who could take offence include;

The men who run the import of girls,

The men who run the brothels. That word makes me shudder, Timmy.

The men who steal or alter cars

The man who allegedly is in the pay of a contractor,

The men who terrorise people to leave their houses,

The men who bully tenants into paying high rents,

The publicans who sell drugs,

The prominent citizen who, someone says, finances the drug operations.

But, and this is a big but, with the exception of the men who run the brothels, who are probably the same men who got the girls out of the cars at Portbury and tried to get into Southmead Hospital, these people don't know that we have information about them, via the phone-in tapes or otherwise, unless someone on what I will call our side, has warned them. This brings me to who is on our side?"

She recited

"There's us and Joy and Sally.

The undergraduates who each know the calls they took.

The professor and the chief inspector.

Now consider the weapon and the speed with which the deed was done.

The reaction to Chuck's threat to tell all could not  have been quicker."

Few people have a hand gun and bullets."

Timmy didn't comment and she went on,

"What do we know of what happened that evening? I don't think you've heard this. The radio news gave an interview with Betty Williams. She said that just before she went out, at about six thirty, Chuck took a call on his mobile phone that delighted him. It was from BBC Television to say that they wanted to interview him and would half past eight be all right because they wanted to put it out on the ten o'clock news? Chuck was delighted. BBC Television Bristol, have said that they made no such call. So that was probably the murderer. Simple, wasn't it, come to the door to be interviewed and Bang, you're dead."

She continued. "The question that arises is, did the murderer know that Betty would be out? Think about it, the television people are coming to interview the husband, so naturally, in the normal course of events the wife hovers about near her husband. Unless the murderer knew that she'd be out, he must have been prepared to kill her too.  This gives me a woman's intuition sort of feeling that Chuck's murder was nothing to do with the tapes."

"I tend to agree, Angel. We have to know a lot more about their private lives, but you've missed out a member of what you term 'our side' haven't you?"

"Who's that?"

"Why, Chuck, the murdered man," said Timmy. He reached across and touched her to emphasise what he was saying. "Something has bothered me from the outset but I couldn't put my finger on it, your recital has done the trick. What was bothering me was the statement that Chuck made to the Western Daily Press immediately after he'd been sacked, that *'He had information on brothels, drugs and housing scams and the people who were making a fortune from them which he intended to publish soon, naming names'."*

"Why does that bother you, or am I being dense?"

"We both were, my love, Chuck wasn't supposed to hear what was on the tapes until the meeting on Wednesday at which you reviewed the content of the tapes. I fired him and he left the room before you started."

"Oh yes. That can only mean that he had a sneaky preview. I wonder how he managed to do that?"

"He probably arrived at the studio early and went into the undergraduates listening room and listened to what had come in that day," said Timmy. "He could have been in trouble if a call had come in while he had the tape run back, but our machines have very high speed fast forward and rewind capability and the undergraduate would only need to stall the caller for a minute or so."

"How can we find out if he did something like that?"

"On Monday I'll ask Professor Young if he would be so good as to ask the young people whether anyone claimed access to the tape material while they were on watch."

"You think that Chuck could have approached someone mentioned on the tapes, don't you?" said Helene.

"It's a possibility, you must agree."

They arrived at the Manor House and when they joined Margaret and the General, the latter said,

"The paper said that a man who works for you in Bristol had been shot. Do you know anything about it?"

"Actually, we do Father, you see I fired him the previous day."

68

"Shot on successive days, that's the English sense of humour I suppose?" said Helene.

"We're not going to have some damn fool policeman saying you're their number one suspect like they did last time, I hope?"

"No, and this time I've got a cast iron alibi, at the time in question I was with my wife. You see, Angel, there are some good things about marriage. What a wonderful thing it is, it provides alibis as well."

"What time is the next sailing from Poole to France where men know the true value of romance?" smiled Helene.

"Seriously, though it's not going to be bothersome, like having a body dumped in the park was?" said the General.

"Fortunately the policeman, Roger Hardwick, was there when Chuck went crazy and I fired him."

Liz arrived late on the Saturday afternoon and had to be told the latest developments. She wondered whether her mother had given any more thought to having Ah Ming at the Manor House. It was agreed that Liz would bring the girl down on her day off and see how things went. Margaret stressed that it would depend very much on what the Housekeeper, Mrs Holmes, felt.

On the Monday Timmy held his management meeting and saw his departmental managers to clear up outstanding issues before asking Penny to get him Professor Young in Bristol University. She buzzed to say the Prof was on line two,

"Good morning Professor, I hope that I haven't dragged you away from something important?"

"Good morning Mr Hawkridge, no you haven't, as a matter of fact I was having a seminar with the second year students on the subject of exercises like the one you sponsored to produce the tapes. I had to warn them that such exercises don't usually end in murder. That was a nasty climax wasn't it?"

"That's why I'm ringing. A curious anomaly is bothering Helene and me. When Chuck sounded off to the Western Daily Press reporter after his sacking, he said words to the effect that he had the dirt on brothel keepers, drug barons and housing scams that have made certain people rich and he intended to name names. What needs to be cleared up is how and when did he have access to the tapes? He left before my wife gave her summary. He wasn't supposed to hear what was on them but I admit we didn't say as much to anyone. My suspicion is that he went into the student's listening room while they were there and wound back the tapes and listened. Could you ask the young people if this happened while they were on duty? This casts no reflection on the students, for as far as they were concerned Chuck was the instigator of the exercise."

"I fully understand. Give me your number and I'll ring you back."

Professor Young rang back a short time later.

"Your supposition is correct. Several of the students say that he and his girl friend came in at about eleven p.m. and spent best part of the hour to midnight running the tape backwards and forwards. Some of the youngsters were annoyed at his behaviour and one says that he missed recording a call because of it. Fortunately the call wasn't important. One student said that Chuck heard one message and seemed cock a hoop and turned to his girlfriend and said something like '*Sweetheart, this could be the key that let's us start our life together*' or words to that effect. Is that helpful?"

"That's marvelous, please thank them for the sterling work they did."

Timmy told Helene all about it at lunchtime.

"Who do you think his girl friend is?" said Helene and added "or was?"

"I haven't a clue but I expect that his producer, Sally Evans, would have an idea, I'll ask Joy."

He telephoned Joy Philips.

"Joy, this is Timmy. We've been making some enquiries as to how Chuck got to know the contents of the tapes and it appears that he was in the habit of going into the students listening room and running the tapes back and forth to listen to the messages."

"Well I'm blessed," said Joy.

"What I wanted to ask you is who went with him because the students are insistent that his girl friend was always with him. Do you think that Sally would know?"

"Sally's in a dreadful state, crying all the time, I've had to send her home. I rather think that poor Sally must be the girlfriend. I know that her marriage is a disaster and she had or still has a minor drug problem. She always wanted to produce Chuck and be around him, poor girl."

"Be kind to her, Joy, and when she's got over it a bit we'll have a talk with her."

Timmy remarked to Helene that it looked as if Chuck may have tried to blackmail somebody.

"Clearly he must have done it by phone and it would be helpful if we could see his phone bill."

"Or, perhaps, Sally's or even the radio station's," said Helene.

Mr Swift arrived promptly at two p.m.

Timmy told him the entire story, starting with Ah Ming's call to the Chuck Williams Show right up to his recent talk with Joy Philips. He also said that, during their visit to Qatar, he and Helene had met the uncle of Sheikh Abul, the Emir's son, and, in conversation, Helene had heard the uncle accused of importing young girls for his pleasure. The accuser had asked, in passing, what happened to the girls afterwards? Perhaps what happened to Ah Ming provided a hint.

"Things seem to happen around you, don't they, Mr Hawkridge?" said Mr Swift

"I don't see how anyone could blame me for anything that has happened as a consequence of one of my late night disc jockeys having a rush of blood to the head, but you're right, Helene said as much this morning."

"Now about this car transporter and Royal Portbury Dock, I've sent two of my people down to do a reccy and see how we might keep observation on the big car park in the hours of darkness. We rather thought of a couple of pretend British Telecom vans which I can hire from one of the companies that supply props for television shows which would explain my chaps up the poles fitting image intensified TV cameras. The thing that bothers me, site unseen, is how the crooks get the girls out. Unless everyone is bribed or scared stiff, which I think is hardly credible, they must have a plausible reason to take a medium sized van out of the car park during the night or at dawn. Or is it possible that they go by boat?"

"I really don't know, all we have is what a very frightened girl said. We've no proof that she really came in on a ship or, if she did, whether there will be girls on board this time. If there are, the most important thing is to find out where they are taken to."

"What about the police, Mr Hawkridge, how much of this do they know?"

"They know all of it, except what we've found out today about Chuck getting access to the tapes."

"And what are they doing?"

"Lord alone knows, Mr Swift I've tried to convince the man who was at Oxford with me who, I think, would like to know my sister Elizabeth better than he does at present, if you know what I mean, and I expect that he's doing his best but every time we see him he tells us how stretched the police resources are and complains that when they catch crooks some stupid magistrate lets them off."

"If you think about it, the cost of setting up and operating the trade would be considerable and hardly justified by supplying a dozen or so girls to Bristol and Bath. It's likely that this girl smuggling thing provides girls for other towns large enough to provide a sufficient market for that sort of thing," said Mr Swift. "We could be fishing in deeper waters than we think."

"That had crossed my mind, I don't want to become a one-man crusade for saving girls from sexual slavery and we're building all of this activity on a half-conscious girl's mutterings about a big boat full of cars, but if, and it's a big if, if some girls are brought ashore on Tuesday, I'd like to know where they are taken in the hours of darkness. It could be that some of them are moved on to other towns in the subsequent days, but to know where they go on arrival would at least give the police a starting point."

"Very well Mr Hawkridge, with the usual proviso that we don't want to get mixed up in what is really police business, my operatives will keep a watch on the Royal Portbury Dock until Wednesday morning and follow anything that looks suspicious."

Timmy asked Penny to get Sid Durant, the Production Manager, to see him.

"Sid, there's a car transporter called the Octavio Maru due in at Royal Portbury Dock, Bristol, on Tuesday morning. I believe that there's a chance that Asian girls are being smuggled in for use as prostitutes and have asked Mr Swift's outfit to do some undercover work that night. If I'm right the story could be worked up into a 'true story' television feature. To do this we would need some archive material of small girls on Arabian beaches and shots of the ship's arrival. Will you have someone see if we've got any archive film of one of those ships and if we haven't, send someone down to Royal Portbury Dock quite openly to take some video film of the ship coming in and of cars being driven ashore and parked?"

"OK Timmy, It'd be safer if I get the boys to go down, then we'll know that we've got it right."

Penny, who most times came in when Sid came in, said that Timmy ought to be careful, dabbling in the sex slave business. He should remember what had happened the last time. He had long ceased to be surprised at her ability to listen in on his telephone conversations and to what was going on in his room and still complete her own work swiftly and efficiently. He had a policy of recording every discussion and Penny kept the tapes and transcribed the more important happenings, so he had no objection to her keeping her listening button down and listening. She'd find out anyway. He accepted that his production manager Sid Durant would always know because he was married to Penny. In any case, if they heard him telling Helene that he loved her, who cared, he was willing to shout it from the rooftops.

That evening he told Helene about his conversation with Mr Swift.

"Even as we speak his chaps are in, or on the way to, Bristol with two make-believe BT vans filled with night vision equipment and, we hope, the Octavio Maru is making her way up the Bristol Channel to arrive off Royal Portbury Dock with the high tide. The game's afoot."

## Chapter Eight

THE Confidential Enquiries operatives collected their loaded vans and set out westwards along the M4. The first was driven by Fred Smart, an economics graduate in his late twenties, with Paula Simms as passenger. Paula, an attractive brunette, was a trained economist and also a black belt at Judo. Fred and Paula had spent a while in Bournemouth keeping observation on the Pierre Blanc showroom-cum-garage from which stolen luxury cars were being shipped to France and had been caught up in all the things that had developed thereafter. Fred had been the one who had contact with Timmy and Helene and had enjoyed the experience. It was he who had remarked to Mr Swift, of Helene, that you don't expect beautiful girls like her to be a budding Einstein. In fact all the team who had operated on that case in Dorset had enjoyed the job.

The second van was driven by ex policeman Will Toms and the much younger Bert Smith drove his car behind. Bert was the electronics wizard.

They had been given an outline of what was required and as far as private enquiry agents were capable of being surprised, were surprised. To a man, and girl, they thought this a matter for the police and were concerned lest the police would also be there and take a dim view of their presence. No matter how much Bert Smith professed 'that it was no skin off their noses if the police told them to get lost, they were still getting paid', good investigators don't like wasting their time.

They slept in a small guesthouse in Clevedon and breakfasted early so as to be able to arrive in the vicinity of the docks at the time service engineers usually appear. The Octavio Maru was coming through the dock entrance with barely a metre of space between the vast flat side of the hull and the dockside. Paula, who came from a navy family and loved the graceful lines of the navy's ships, thought that she had never seen such an ugly, top heavy looking ship and thought that if there were any girls on board they must have been seasick because the Octavio Maru looked as if it would roll like a pig. But clearly its box like hull would hold lots of cars and she was impressed with the practiced skill with which the pilot and tugs crews brought the ungainly ship through the entrance and to a berth alongside.

They selected two telegraph poles near the perimeter fence and parked a van under each. They put on their overalls and hard hats and leisurely opened the van doors. They were cautioned by Bert not to do things quickly "Remember, you're supposed to be working for an ex-nationalized company and old habits die hard." They put a ladder against a post and Fred Smart went up and looked around. He thought that it would do, there was no closer site to put the cameras. He noticed a man with a video camera and an assistant, taking shots of the ship. There was no point in positioning the cameras until early evening so they pretended to work, as far as they could see no one was in the remotest bit interested in them. It was decided that Will Toms should take the car round to the other side of the basin and examine possible camera sites there.

No sooner was the Octavio Maru secured than large doors were opened in her side and telescopic ramps emerged and angled themselves down to the ground, at which a crowd of men who had been waiting at the dockside went on board together with a small lorry that seemed to be loaded with cans of petrol. It was not long before the first car appeared at the hole in the ship's side and was driven down the ramp and parked some distance from the ship adjacent to the cars already in the vast parking area, left over from previous shipments, Fred assumed. Soon there was a flood of cars emerging to be parked in neat lines ashore. As far as they could tell there was only the vaguest colour pattern in the way the cars were disembarked or parked, and in places red ones were next to green ones and yellow ones and so on. Paula wondered about the car keys. Did the men who drove the cars off the ship take the keys back to be placed on some vast keyboard or did they leave them in the unlocked car and rely on the perimeter fence for security? If this was so, she would have the place patrolled at night. Did they? The key question was, of course, relevant to the problem of getting the girls out of the boot. If the cars weren't locked then the boots wouldn't be locked but closing them afterwards would make a loud noise on a still night. Added to which it was difficult to distinguish colours in the dark. If red was still the flavour of the month, how would the ungodly sort out the red ones this time round? The more she thought about it the more stupid the whole exercise seemed.

Will Toms returned to report that there was a post from which a distant cover of the parking area was possible and they decided that he should take the second van round and mount a camera on that side. Bert would operate between the two vans setting up the electronics. By dusk the cameras were in position, cables run, consoles set up and recorders connected in the vans. Now all that they could do was sit and wait.

Bert admitted that he hadn't expected the parking area to be lit so brightly but he was sure that the cameras wouldn't be affected.

Just after one a.m. Will Toms telephoned to say that there was movement in the dock basin. Sometime later they saw tiny pin pricks of light down among the parked cars. The cameras were brought into close-up and they could see a figure open a car boot and a smaller figure emerge with some difficulty. The figures moved away and there was another pin-prick of light and another boot was opened and another cramped figure emerged. This was repeated until there were about ten people creeping in single file between the cars and moving towards the dockside. Bert said that he thought that some one had stuck a small patch on each car containing a girl, it needn't be bigger than a postage stamp, and when ultra violet light was shone it would scintillate. It could be a broad beam of invisible light to sweep over several cars at once. Very neat, he thought.

Fred phoned Will and found that he had them in sight and later he said that they appeared to be getting into some sort of boat. He then reported that a vehicle driving on sidelights had appeared at the eastern end of the dock towards which the craft was slowly making its way. One thing that the surveillance team had checked thoroughly was the access to the docks and they knew that there was only one good road out. Bert and Paula took the car and driving without lights, began the difficult and potentially dangerous task of following the van that shortly afterwards appeared on the access road.

The van crossed the M5 at the Gordano service area and made its way along the country road that follows the River Avon, past the police equestrian and dogs center and into the center of Bristol where it passed the Bristol Royal Infirmary, briefly touched the Broadmead shopping complex and turned north along Stokes Croft in St Paul's. Here it stopped in front of one of a terrace of four storey buildings.

Bert drove past while Paula took a quick photograph of what appeared to be a massage parlour. By the time they had turned round and come back huddled figures were being hurried across the pavement and into the house.

Bert and Paula returned to the motorway service area and joined the others who had recovered their equipment and packed it in the vans ready for their journey to London and were relaxing over a snack and a cup of coffee. They were all well pleased with their nights work.

Mr Swift phoned Timmy as soon as he arrived.

"We had complete success Mr Hawkridge, it was just as you thought, someone came in the early hours and opened the car boots and we think that eight or nine girls got out. They got out of the compound by water but my people had foreseen that possibility and one of my chaps was on the other side and could see what was going on. We followed their van to a place called Stokes Croft in St Paul's in Bristol where they were taken into a four storey terrace house whose bottom floor, at street level is a massage parlour. We have a photo of the place. Stokes Croft is a very busy road. So it all fits with what the girl said."

"That's splendid, Mr Swift, a massage parlour in Stokes Croft was one of the two addresses of brothels that our anonymous callers hinted at on the tapes. Did your people say anything about a police presence?"

"Only to say that there was none, neither did they see anyone patrolling the car park during the night. The dock authorities seem to place reliance on the extensive floodlighting system and the high wire fence."

"The question for me," said Timmy, "is what do I do now? I have to do something. The local police down there want hard evidence. How soon can I have a cassette of what your people filmed during the night? I told the police that I thought that the car transporter was the way the girls were brought in and a ship was due from the same place as last time and now we have proof. I've got a friend in the Home Office perhaps I'll have a word with him."

"You should have my report and the cassette by lunchtime."

"There's just one other thing, Mr Swift."

"Knowing you, Mr Hawkridge, I rather thought that there might be."

"It's simply that I think that we're only scratching at the surface of the thing. Look at it this way, someone has got what they think is a foolproof way of smuggling people into the UK. So far we have evidence that, say, sixteen girls have been brought in, eight or nine of which were last night. Now here I admit that I am in totally unknown territory, but how many new prostitutes do you think Bristol can absorb in a year, sixty or seventy? That's about what the present rate of supply would produce."

"Do you think that there is that number of girls wanting to come to England as prostitutes?" said Mr Swift.

"But they don't come to England expecting to be prostitutes, they expect to be welcomed as immigrants and given benefit money and accommodation and jobs like the Pakistan or Bangladesh or Indian grapevine says they will."

"I tend to agree but where is this leading us and in particular, leading me?"

"I believe that the smuggling thing we've stumbled upon is supplying girls to other places in England. What's more, we don't know what else is getting in that way. If I were a crook I'd be bringing in drugs as well. Other people might want to bring in arms or explosives or terrorists."

"And what do you want Confidential Enquiries to do? We're a firm that makes discreet business enquiries on behalf of companies in the Square Mile."

"Come off it Mr Swift, your operatives have never had so much fun in their lives as they had in Bournemouth."

"Alright, what do you want me to do?"

"Will you please keep a watch on the massage parlour in Stokes Croft and see if any girls are transferred to another town. And, secondly, I know that Helene wants to follow up some of the calls on the tapes and I would be grateful if you could provide someone to accompany her on visits in Bristol."

"OK Mr Hawkridge, I'll make the arrangements. I suggest that Paula Simms should accompany your wife, she's a black belt and looks as if butter wouldn't melt in her mouth."

"Thank you Mr Swift, I knew you'd see it my way in the end. Goodbye."

They ran the Royal Portbury Dock videos on their TV that lunchtime. The car park compound was brilliantly lit and showed the man locating which cars had girls and opening the car boot to release them, the girls stretching and then the whole party creeping slowly between the cars to the dock side. It was so clear that it was difficult to understand why the dock security personnel couldn't see what was going on. There was also a picture of the house in Stokes Croft with the van outside and a picture of the van that clearly showed its registration number. A man seemed to be removing a box from the van.

"What are you going to do with it, Timmy?" asked Helene.

"Well, I'm pretty disgusted with the Avon and Somerset police for doing nothing for the second time, Roger could at least have had one of his patrol cars pass by a couple of times during the night but they are the authority down there, so we'll send them a copy of one of the cassettes."

"We can do better than that," said Bill Lawrence who was present with Sid and Penny Durant, "We can send it to them by wire. Leave it to me."

"I'll ring Roger Hardwick and tell him to expect it," said Timmy.

Penny said that the Chief Inspector was on number two.

"Hello Tim, what's the panic?"

"Hello Roger, look, because you said that you had no police to spare, I had a firm of private investigators who work for me in the City, mount a watch on the cars that were landed from the Octavio Maru yesterday at Portbury. They took video film of eight or more girls being helped out of the boots of cars and smuggled out of the port area sometime after one a.m. My people followed the van to a massage parlour in Stokes Croft and got the registration number of the van. All this is on the cassette which is at this moment being transmitted to your headquarters."

"You'll have to give me a moment to digest this, Tim. You say that you paid for private eyes to keep watch at Portbury Dock and they filmed people getting out of the boots of cars that came from Japan and a copy of that film is now being recorded here?"

"Yes, we have it all on tape. Of course I don't know whether the people emerging from the car boots were economic refugees being forced into prostitution, like the girl who was half murdered, or terrorists, or drug smugglers, all I am telling you is where they were taken in Stokes Croft. With luck some of them will still be there."

"I shall have to tell the Chief about this."

"You can tell him from me that we believe that this is a much bigger smuggling racket than getting a few girls for the Bristol brothels. You should remind him also that, again thanks to Liz, you have a man in custody and the names of his two accomplices who I suspect were also guilty of the attempted murder of Ah Ming. That alone should justify raiding the place in Stokes Croft."

"It's not as simple as that, Tim. There are so many dodgy lawyers and stupid do-gooders these days that my Chief has to watch every move that we make."

"Well you could tell him that we are making a twenty five minute video based on what happened to Ah Ming which will include the stuff that was shot last night, Stokes Croft and all. It'll be shown on the national TV and how it ends is up to him. It's his choice."

"You wouldn't Tim?"

"Roger, you know better than I do that this isn't a game, you have to convince your people to act today, this afternoon in fact. I've got people watching the massage parlour and if they see people moving out in a hurry, your Chief will know that he's got an informer in the force, won't he? And it'll all go in our video."

"OK Tim, I'll see what can be done. My secretary is telling me that I'm wanted urgently to see a video that's just come in, yours I hope and I'll make the CC look at it. After all that, thanks, remember, I'm on your side. Goodbye old man, I'll keep you in touch."

"What next?" said Helene when he'd put the phone down.

"What do you mean what next?"

"You've got that Sherlock Holmes look about you, my pet."

"I don't recognize the comparison, I don't smoke a pipe, I can't play the violin, I don't fool about with opium, I don't wear an Ulster overcoat. There's no record of him doing, well I'll tell you what there's no record of him doing, when we haven't got company."

"Oh go on Timmy," said Penny, "it might give Sid some ideas."

"I'll tell you tomorrow, Penny," said Helene. "Now, come on children, the boss wants to speak with Joy and get her to send a pair of reporters to watch the back and front of the massage parlour, doesn't he my sweet?"

"Yes, that's it and they must have video cameras but how they'll conceal them and where they'll park if they use a car, I know not. Penny, get me Joy, will you?"

Late in the afternoon Penny buzzed to say that Joy was on line one.

"Timmy, the police raided that massage parlour in Stokes Croft this afternoon. My young man, Jeremy, was there and says he got some good shots. You'll want those for the film, won't you?"

"Yes. That's splendid news. Did your man see who the police brought out?"

"Yes, he says that they took away more than a dozen darkish girls and three men, the massage parlour staff seemed to be left alone. They also removed a number of boxes. Jeremy, our reporter was thrilled to be on the spot and I'll give him a spot on the local news tonight."

"Tell him well done from me and remember to send us a copy or the original of the video and, by the way, say something nice about the police."

About an hour later Penny buzzed to say that a DCI Hardwick was on line one,

"Hello Roger, good news I hope?"

"Yes Tim, very good news, I went out on a limb and persuaded the CC that we had to take action and the boys from Bridewell raided the house in Stokes Croft this afternoon. As a result we arrested the two men who were named by you and another person took possession of what appears to be various sorts of drugs and detained thirteen Asian girls who we don't quite know what to do with at the present moment except to put them somewhere warm and safe. We brought away all the papers we could find and hope to get a lead on who's behind this rotten business. The CC's called a meeting with the car company and the port authorities and informed the Home Office. They'll go after the ship owners. We want to use your video in evidence, you've no objection, I hope?"

"That's splendid, well done. To answer your question, no objection but the private eyes, Confidential Enquiries Limited, would prefer not to be named," said Timmy.

"Can I assure the CC if he asks me, that your TV video will have a satisfactory ending?"

"Yes, it most certainly will. Thanks for the good news. See you soon I hope. Goodbye."

# Chapter Nine

OVER dinner in the small restaurant round the corner from their house in Chelsea, they discussed their next step.

Helene could remember her list of baddies and goodies.

"We've done something about the men who import girls and they're probably the men who run those places, you know."

"Yes," said Timmy. "Call them houses of ill repute if you don't like saying brothels, Angel. The police have taken action on that one and its ramifications will extend to Japan. Incidentally I've asked Mr Swift to watch the house in Stokes Croft. Perhaps I should stop him now that the police have raided the place?"

"Next there are the men who steal or tamper with cars."

"The police will be happy to deal with those," said Timmy.

"Next there was the man who said that there's a man in the Civil Engineers Department who's taking bribes from contractors."

"I've asked Joy to send in a reporter on some pretext and make voice recordings of the senior personnel."

"Next are the men who are trying to evict old people from their homes," said Helene.

"Hm, now there's something that perhaps we should take a look at," said Timmy, "it could be a small time Rachman wanting to increase the rents extortionately or it could be some giant property tycoon wanting to clear a site for a major property development."

"What's a Rachman?"

"Oh, he was a man who used violent methods to get people out of their flats and houses in North London so that he could put new people in at higher rents. The rent of the original occupants was controlled but not the rent of new tenants. The law finally caught up with him but by then he owned a hundred blocks of flats and several night clubs. As a result, his name, like Quisling, entered our language."

"There's a man on the tape who says his landlord demands money above his controlled rent and does nasty things if it isn't paid," said Helene. "He says he's not the only one to be making these extra payments for non-existent services. I think we should listen to that tape once more. It could be the tip of the iceberg of that sort of extortion in Bristol. We'll do it when we get home."

Timmy said, "I seem to remember that a number of the callers were in the same part of Bristol, some market or other. If they are close to one another it could be a big property developer after the site and that could mean trouble."

"What sort of trouble, the law's the law, even in modern England, isn't it?"

"Yes but it's the difficulty of discovering who's actually behind the nastiness that's the trouble in these cases," said Timmy. "It brings me back to the threatening phone calls that the station has been getting. I can't for the life of me imagine how they got to hear that we had received complaints through the phone-in."

They made their way home and sometime later Helene found the call she had remembered on the Landlords tape.

*"Good evening, can I help you?"* said a student's voice

*"It's about my landlord. "*

*"Yes what about your landlord?"*

*"Well, I live in this house in Knowle West with my wife and two kids. I can't work because of my back and we get housing benefit from the Council. They pay it direct to the Landlord. It was alright under the old landlord but the new one wants extra money for services."*

*"What services?"*

*"Well, when I wouldn't pay he took off the front door lock and anyone could 'ave got in and I had to pay for him to replace it. He called that 'services'."*

*"How much does he charge for these services?"*

*"The rent the Council pays him is £82 a week and he makes us pay an extra £20 a week."*

*"Have you been to the Council about it?"*

*"Yes I went to that place on Airport Road and they told me not to pay it. It's alright for them, they don't get their windows broke and then have to pay for them to be repaired. It's time something was done about it."*

*"I'm sure something will be. Thank you for calling,"* said the student.

*"You won't let him find out that I've called you will you?"*

*"No, we won't tell your landlord."*

"That sounds like extortion," said Timmy, "but we don't know whether the £82 the Council pays is the full rent. In many cases they only pay part of the rent and the tenant pays the balance. What we'll do is get someone to ask questions at the Rent Service office and at this Council office on Airport Road and see what the controlled rents are for two and three bedroom houses in Knowle West. Then, for a start, try and find out who are the landlords who own more than, say, ten properties in the area."

"Will you ask Mr Swift to do it? It could cost a lot of money?"

"No, the first enquiries will be made by Hawkridge Radio Bristol's roving reporter, I think his name's Jeremy," said Timmy. "I'll have a word with Joy in the morning. I've already asked her to have him do a programme on the Civil Engineers Department."

"Some of the people who phoned-in actually gave their names and addresses, why don't you have someone call on those people and have a chat?"

"Good idea, Angel, but who have we got to do it, Joy, Sally, Liz, you, or me? Or perhaps we should ask someone from Mr Swift or my lawyers?"

"I'd like to ask Liz but she's not used to this sort of thing and anyway, she's busier than I am. Why don't I go to Bristol for the day and perhaps one of Mr Swift's men or women could come with me?"

"Angel, why don't I come with you?" said Timmy.

"Because you've a business to run, my love and I can't get into any trouble just talking to people, can I?"

"OK, I anticipated that something like this might arise, so when I last spoke to Mr Swift, I asked him if he could provide an escort if you decided to do anything at the Bristol end and he volunteered Paula Simms. I'd feel better if it was a man, pity that young Will of the Tolbrite Garage doesn't live closer." He went on "We've possibly got the phone numbers of some of these people who you could ask if you could call on them."

He realized that he hadn't seen what progress Bill Lawrence had made in tracing the telephone calls.

He was brought back to the present to hear Helene remark,

"We've got all four weeks tapes now and the final score is 366 made up of sex 57, cars 61, street violence 46, housing 111, drugs 55 and general crime 36. I've asked Bill Lawrence to add the last two weeks to the six tapes containing the first two weeks calls. I believe that we should make an effort to listen and think hard about the more important of these calls. I'm going to spend tomorrow listening once more to the calls about householders being harassed, pick out the addresses and phone numbers and generally get ready to go to Bristol on Thursday. While I'm there I'll try to see Sally Evans and Chuck's wife, Betty."

"That's more than a day's work, Angel, we can probably identify where about twenty of the housing calls came from in addition to those who gave their names and numbers, so to speak. I suggest that you plan on being there on Friday as well. Tell you what we'll do, I'll drive down to Bristol in the late afternoon on Friday and you can decide then whether we stay there to make some more calls together during the weekend, or go to Tolbrite or back to London. Mr Swift's girl can come back to town on the Friday teatime and I'll be your escort. How is that?"

"You are a dear, I too think that there could be a week's work for me in Bristol, but I didn't want to say so, and I don't intend to be away that long."

The next morning he asked Penny to get him Bill Lawrence, Joy Philips and Mr Swift, in that order.

As usual Bill was ahead of the game and produced a table listing the phone calls and where possible, the phone from which the call had been made. There among them were the callers about harassment and property. Most were from public call boxes. Bill suggested that this could either mean that they didn't have a phone and hence were probably poor, or that they were hiding their identity. He said that the caller who had alleged bribes for contracts had been astute enough to dial 141 first.

Timmy asked Bill to give Helene a copy of the list.

He phoned Joy, and explained,

"You won't be familiar with them but there were several calls on the help-line about a landlord or landlords asking for additional rent, over and above the controlled rent, calling it services and threatening tenants who won't or can't pay. Sounds like Rachman rearing his ugly head again. Several calls were from South Bristol. Knowle West was mentioned. I'd like you to have your reporter visit the local council housing office and ask some intelligent questions about their work for a forthcoming radio programme similar to what you're doing in the Civil Engineers Department."

"OK Timmy but you won't forget that we have to do our routine reporting to make your radio station run, will you?"

"If it gives us the bare-bones of material for a half-hour programme it'll be worth it, Joy."

Penny buzzed him and said that Mr Swift was on line 2.

"Morning Mr Swift."

"Good morning Mr Hawkridge, no more murders, I hope?"

"Not so far but it is only Wednesday. Actually it's good news this time. On the basis of the evidence you obtained, the police raided the house in Stokes Croft and took away a lot of girls, two or three men, some drugs and a lot of documents. I've said that they may use your video in court but that you would not wish to be named. I hope that was correct?"

"I heard it on the news and you're correct, in my line of business it's better not to seek publicity. Does that mean that my people needn't watch the massage parlour house?"

"Yes, no, you know what I mean, they needn't watch that brothel. Now, let's discuss another subject. When we last spoke I asked if you could provide someone to be with Helene when she interviews some of the people who called our help line in the four weeks it was in operation and you nominated Paula Simms."

"Yes, I've warned Paula."

"Helene is going to Bristol first thing Thursday morning for two days, would you ask Paula to get in touch with her to agree the arrangements. We'll make the rail and hotel reservations and hire a car and driver to take them around. For your private ear, I think that these interviews and the traveling between interviews will take up a great deal of time and that by the close of play on Friday they may feel that they will have to allocate some time during the following week. I'll be driving down to Bristol on Friday afternoon and your Paula can have the weekend off. Helene can decide if she wants to stay on and resume the task on the Monday or whether to restart later in the week or she may feel that she has enough and she'll tell Paula."

"OK Mr Hawkridge, I'll tell Paula that she's on indefinite assignment."

Helene met Paula at Paddington Station and learned quite a lot about her during the journey to Bristol. She was a very attractive brunette with an enquiring mind who had been drawn to the enquiry agent business because of the problems it sometimes presented. She had enjoyed the work in Bournemouth and Southampton leading to the arrest of several crooks and didn't share her boss, Mr Swift's, reluctance to undertake such work. She was happy to be working once more for Hawkridge Media. Helene had prepared a list of the addresses she wished to visit and had with her, her faithful laptop and a small tape recorder and the six tapes which had been coded by Bill Lawrence's staff to give her rapid access to any specified call. She had told Joy Philips that she would call at the radio station at one p.m. and would like to speak with her and Sally Evans, separately.

She warned Paula that much of what they were to do in following up the phone-in calls would prove to be fruitless. In many cases the calls were from third parties such as a daughter phoning from one of the suburbs about her old mother in the city center, a phone-call that the daughter would probably deny making when asked for further facts. But they must follow up every lead.

The hire car was waiting outside Temple Meads. Helene explained what she wanted and gave the driver the list of addresses, which, with the aid of a street map of Bristol, Timmy and she, in bed and with much giggling, had arranged into what they thought was a logical order to avoid much cross city travel. The driver agreed that it didn't look bad and he would study it while the ladies were making their first call. He took them to their hotel to register and leave their bags.

The first call was to one of the people who had given their names and address and invited discussion. A middle-aged man opened the door. Helene explained who they were and was taken aback at her reception.

"Fine lot of people you are with your promise of anonymity, I told my wife we should never trust no-one."

"What do you mean, Mr Green?" asked Helene.

"Well, that man from the landlord turned up and warned us not to go shooting our mouths off to those radio people or else. You must have told him, how else would he know?"

"You have my word, Mr Green that no one from the radio station has told anyone anything about your call."

"Then how did he find out, then?"

"That we will try to discover, believe me but you'll realize that he could have heard about the phone-in or seen the advertisement in the paper and was simply warning you not to take part. Now please tell us what's been happening to your mother?"

"It's the wife's mother. She lives in Midland Road, off Old Market. She's lived there nigh on forty years, always paid the rent. Along comes this man one day all smiles and says that he represents the new owners and will have to put up the rent. How much asks Gran? Oh at least double says the man. I can't pay that, says Gran. Then you'll have to get out says the man. Gran told us in tears and we said sit tight, but the man keeps coming and won't take her rent, the old rent, I mean, and keeps telling her you're in arrears. So we go to the Citizens Advice and they say that the man has no right to say that but now all sorts of things start to happen to Gran's house, like banging on the doors at night, windows getting broken and slates off the roof. So we goes to the police but they say there's nothing they can do unless they catch the man doing it. The old girl's a nervous wreck."

"That's terrible. Has your Gran had any letters or other documents from this man, does she know where he comes from and who employs him?"

"Yes, Gran got one letter telling her about the rent increase. It came from somewhere near London, I think."

"Do you think I could have a copy of that letter and any other letters about the old rent?"

"Yes, I don't see why not, we've got them here because the old girl can hardly see now, her eyesight's that bad, an' we have to look out for things for her."

He went away and returned with a plastic shopping bag containing some papers.

Helene glanced through them and said,

"These should be useful. We'll give you a receipt for them, take them away and copy the important ones and bring them all back tomorrow."

"OK, I hope you can do something for us, miss."

Their next call was to a house from which a call had been made but that had not given a name or address. Helene knocked on the door that was opened by a large woman.

"Good morning," said Helene "We're making a survey of people who may be having housing problems, do you mind if we ask you some questions?"

"You from the Council?"

"No, we're from London but we've got an office in Bristol."

"You're from them rotten bleeders as is trying to get us out, push off."

Paula deftly inserted her foot in the door space.

"No we're not," said Helene. "Look, we're from the Chuck Williams Show."

"Then why din' you say so?" said the woman.

"We want to see if we can help you, may we come in?"

The woman grudgingly led the way into a dingy sitting room and turned down the radio.

"What sort of trouble are you having?" asked Helene.

"Well, we've lived here for more than twenty years an' always paid the rent. Then the old man as owned it died an' his son wants to put up the rent."

"Is your rent controlled?

"I dunno."

"What sort of tenancy agreement do you have?"

"I dunno."

She put her head out of the door and shouted "Hey, Father, 'ave we got a tenancy agreement?"

A man in his shirtsleeves appeared,

"We may have 'ad all them years ago but I dunno where it is now."

"You are probably covered by the Rent Acts," said Helene. "Go to the Citizens Advice Bureau or to the Rent Service office and they'll deal with your new landlord or tell you how to deal with him. But you must realize that if your rent hasn't been increased for some years he's probably entitled to put it up a bit but not much, the Rent Service will decide."

The man looked doubtful. Helene added,

"Promise me that you'll do that. Go to the Rent Service Office, it's in the phone book."

"Don't worry, Miss," said his wife. "I'll see that he goes."

They made several stops of a similar kind and reached a derelict looking house backing onto Old Market.

Helene knocked on the door. After a while it was opened by a frail looking elderly woman.

"Good morning," said Helene "someone from this house called the radio station about a problem with their landlord and we would like to see if we can help."

"That was my daughter's hubby, I told him not to do it and it would only bring trouble."

"We mean you no harm, we want to know all about it," said Helene. "We're from Hawkridge Radio."

"That's not what that man said the other day, he came here last Thursday and said that we'd better keep our traps shut and don't go sounding off to those nosy wireless people if we know what's good for us."

"We had nothing to do with that, we have no idea who that man is, do you?"

"Yes," said the old woman," he says he's the agent for the people who're buying up all the old houses around here. They made me an offer for this house and I said 'No thank you'. They increased the price they were prepared to pay and I said that I'd been born in this house and God willing, I would die in it. The man said that I should be careful that it wasn't sooner rather than later."

"Have you had any letters or other documents from the man's firm?"

"Well, there's the letters giving the price they're willing to pay me to leave."

"Could we see them, please?" said Helene

The old woman went away and reappeared some minutes later with a bundle of papers.

"My son-in-law says I should get a lawyer but I only got my old age pension and a bit of housing benefit and that don't leave much for things like lawyers."

"You can get free advice at the Citizens Advice Bureau and you can also go to the Council and ask them for help," said Helene, "but meanwhile could we take these papers away and copy them. I'll give you a receipt and we'll return them tomorrow." She added "Have you had any other trouble or damage to the house?"

"Yes, someone has broken a window and tried to jemmy the back door and blocked up the drains. That same day that man came and said he'd get a public health thing and then they'd make me leave and then I'd get nothing for my house."

The next call was at an affluent block of flats.

A well-dressed woman opened the door and asked their business.

"We're from the local radio station, following up the call you made a few weeks ago concerning housing."

"Oh yes, I remember, I was so mad and I couldn't sleep so I got it off my chest by ringing that man, the man who was murdered. I say, he wasn't killed because of my call was he?"

"No," said Helene. "What was your complaint?"

"It's these property speculators who write to me, out of the blue, on fancy headed notepaper offering to buy one or other of the properties that I own and rent out."

"Presumably you treat them as junk mail and simply ignore them?" said Helene.

"Yes, but in each case the house they want to buy is occupied by an elderly tenant, usually a woman, who has been there for years and who's rent is regulated. The speculator says that he is prepared to offer a good price for the house with the sitting tenant. But the price they have in mind would be way below the free market value of the empty house. He's relying on the old tenant dying in a few years when the market value of the house would increase by anything up to fifty percent."

"And your complaint is?"

"Why are these speculators allowed to have access to the Rent Service files? They must comb the files and the electoral roll looking for regulated properties occupied by old people. Like vultures waiting to profit from death."

"I agree with you but what they are doing is within the law."

"Then the law should be changed. You see it's not people like me who belong to the National Landlords Association who get caught, it's the sons and daughters who've just inherited a house with a sitting tenant and sell it to get their hands on some ready money."

## Chapter Ten

WITH a slight sense of shock Helene realized that she was due to interview Joy Philips and Sally Evans at Bedminster Down in half an hour's time. She phoned Joy and told her that they were on their way and asked her if she could arrange for a few sandwiches to be available.

They spoke with Joy over lunch. She had sensibly asked Sally Evans to come in at one-thirty. Joy had little to offer other than to say that she now thought that things between Sally and Chuck had been more serious than she'd imagined. The threatening calls had, if anything got worse since their reporter had started making enquiries at the council offices and she was beginning to be a little scared when she came out of the station at night and had to cross the car park to her car. One of the threats had mentioned her daughter and named her school, so she was now concerned for the safety of her family. Chuck had a lot to answer for, for causing so many stones to be turned over.

Sally Evans was on time. She looked a shadow of her former self.

"I'm sorry to have to ask you questions Sally, but Timmy has asked me to speak to all the staff who knew Chuck and we believe that you knew him better than most of us."

"What do you mean by that?"

"Well, you were his producer and producers usually have a very close relationship with their stars," said Helene, "and we know how close you were to Chuck."

Sally started to cry.

"You don't know what he meant to me, he was so understanding and kind. My husband's a beast and Chuck was going to take me away."

Helene made sympathetic noises and went on

"We know that Chuck used to go into the student's listening room and listen to the tapes and that you were with him, the youngsters called you his girl friend."

"Well I was," sobbed Sally.

"Was there anything about one of the messages that excited Chuck?"

"Yes, he was very excited; he said he recognized a voice and this could be the key to our future happiness."

"Did you recognize the voice or did Chuck say who he thought it was?"

"No, he wouldn't say. He just kept smiling and chuckling."

"I have to ask you this. Where were you on the evening Chuck was killed?"

"I was at home getting ready to come to the studio."

"Can anyone vouch for that, say, your husband?"

"No, I was alone. He had stamped out in a temper. I heard his car start and drive off at about eight o'clock."

"Do you think he knew about you and Chuck?"

"No, I don't think so. He would have killed me if he suspected. Chuck said that his wife knew that we were lovers."

"How was that?" asked Helene.

"They slept in separate rooms because he was out half the night and she had to get up to go to Colston's in the morning. They no longer had anything to do with each other, if you know what I mean and because he no longer tried to make love she put two and two together and decided that he'd found someone else and it was a short step to decide that it was me. Chuck didn't deny it, he said that she said 'Did you decide that because you spend half the night together you might as well go the whole hog and spend all the night together?' Anyway, she's got a man friend. Chuck thought that he was a master at Bristol Grammar School."

"Is that where you think she was the night Chuck was killed?"

"How should I know, if it had been me I'd have met my lover when I was sure of where my husband was, in the studio and on the air, but perhaps her man friend couldn't get out that late, perhaps he has a wife as well."

"Is there anything else you want to tell me?"

"Yes, I want to keep working for Hawkridge Media. I'm determined to make a clean break and leave my husband as soon as I can see my way to do it."

When she had gone Paula remarked that you never know what's going to crawl out from under a stone. Helene decided that they would call on the widow and asked the driver to go to Long Ashton. She found that Providence was a steep narrow road connecting the road to Weston-super-Mare at its bottom end to the road to Clevedon at its top end with two country pubs and numerous houses perched on its sides. Helene was relieved that they had a hire car; parking seemed to be impossible. They left the driver to cope with that problem and went up steep steps to Chuck's front door.

They had phoned ahead and Betty Williams was waiting for them.

"Timmy has asked me to come and see you to say how sorry and shocked we are at Chuck's death, and to see if we can help in any way."

"Well, that's a bit tall considering that you had just sacked him," said Mrs Williams.

"Betty, Chuck virtually sacked himself. He had become difficult to manage and Joy Philips was already planning to axe his phone-in show because she could no longer rely on him not to say something outrageous and get the station involved in costly law suits."

"His producer was supposed to prevent that."

"Knowing what you must know about Chuck and Sally, do you think that Joy could rely on Sally Evans to keep him in check?"

"Oh, so you know, do you?" said Betty.

"We know a great deal, Betty, perhaps much more than you think. I suppose that the police have asked you a lot of questions. Where did you tell them you were the night that Chuck was shot?"

"I don't see that's any business of yours but I was out with a friend."

"A man friend?"

"Yes, and Chuck knew all about it."

"Unfortunately we can no longer ask your husband. Where did you go with this friend?"

"We drove around a bit in my car, talking. We were together at the time Chuck must have been killed."

"I presume that the police have spoken to your man friend?"

"I wouldn't know, I haven't seen him since."

"What, not even at Bristol Grammar School?"

"My, we have been busy, haven't we?"

Helene decided to call it a day and asked their driver to take them to the hotel.

She told Paula "I'll go in to dinner at seven and I won't go into the bar beforehand. It's just possible that Timmy's sister, Liz might be able to join us so don't be put off if you see another person sitting with me."

96

She went to her room and called Timmy.

"Hello, Penny, I'm back from the first day's calls and worn out. Is Timmy free?"

"Hello Helene, I'm so glad you've called, perhaps he'll settle down and do some work afterwards, he's been wandering around the building and every time he passes me he asks 'Any word from Helene?' I'll put you through."

"Hello Timmy darling, it's me."

"Hello Angel did I tell you that I love you?"

"Yes, a million times. Now to work; I've made a few calls and I'm exhausted. You were right, it could be a long job but I think that by the end of tomorrow we'll have a fair indication of what it is that's bothering people about housing. Wherever possible I've collected copies of what correspondence there is and it's not much. I talked to Sally Evans and she admitted her affair with Chuck and excused it because Chuck's wife is having an affair, that's where she was the evening Chuck was being shot. Oh and Sally's husband is violent, suspicious of her relationship with Chuck and was out that night. So that's three people who could have killed him, depending how deeply their passions were roused."

"Yes, Angel, that's interesting, but we mustn't pursue the murderer, that's a police job, but I wonder who actually did it?"

"Oh Timmy, you make me forget a most important bit. The very next day, the Thursday after our meeting at the station at which we discussed the contents of the tapes, on that Thursday one of the baddies who are trying to buy up property in the Old Market area, visited at least three of the houses and warned the occupants that they'd better keep their traps shut and not go sounding off to those nosy radio people or they'd regret it."

"Did he now, you're wondering what I'm wondering, who spilled the beans?"

"And another thing, Sally said that when she and Chuck were having their sneaky listen to the tapes he suddenly said '*I know that voice*' and words to the effect that this could be the break that would secure their future together, poor girl."

"That's interesting, you know the tapes better than I do but as far as I can remember, there's only one call that could ring instant cash registers and that was the cultured voice that alleged bribery in the Civil Engineers Department," said Timmy.

"Yes and you've already got Joy making recordings of the voices of that staff. You don't miss much, do you darling?"

"Yes I do, I miss you, Angel."

"I was wondering who told the property developers?"

"It was probably what Chuck said to the local paper that alerted them," said Timmy.

"Yes, that could be it. Now to more pleasant things I phoned Liz at lunchtime and she said if she can get away, she'll join Paula and me for dinner at seven. I hope she can because it's the next best thing to being with you."

"We are a couple of idiots, Angel, but please don't change. Now I'd better get on with my work and keep the wheels of the entertainment world turning."

"Bye bye lover, tomorrow evening can't come quickly enough."

Liz arrived at seven looking cool and attractive despite having come directly from the hospital. Helene introduced Paula and explained what they were doing in Bristol.

Since she had said most of it to Timmy more than an hour earlier and had been rewriting her notes since, she was able to paint a pretty convincing case against the speculator. She had idly been wondering whether it would be sensible for them to buy the properties themselves with all sorts of promises to the occupants about lifelong occupancy, in order to go head to head with the speculators. She had to remind herself that it was none of their business except to see that the little people weren't cheated.

She had also thought some more about Chuck recognizing the voice. She realized that there was not just one but two voices that put the finger on other people, so to speak. There was the voice that named the man who it alleged made a fortune from drugs and there was the voice that accused someone in the Civil Engineers Department of taking bribes. As regards the latter she reasoned that if an official feels that he should draw attention to a colleague's shortcomings, it is bound to be about a person senior to himself. Simple logic is that if the offender is more junior, then the caller should have remedied the matter himself. So the cultured caller was running his boss in. Perhaps the caller who named the alleged drug baron was an employee of said drug baron, in which case he would be in dire straits if someone threatened to tell the drug baron.

According to Sally, Chuck had instantly recognized the voice and it was reasonable to assume that they had met outside their official work, like at the golf club or the local pub. She reasoned that it might be worth seeing if any senior officers of the Civil Engineers Department or employees of the alleged drug man lived in Long Ashton.

"How is Ah Ming?" asked Helene and, turning to Paula, said, "she's the Asian girl who the ungodly threw into the harbour and started all this."

"She's practically recovered and the hospital is ready to discharge her. I've suggested that she be placed in my care and given the Manor House as the address at which she would be lodged. You will back me up, won't you?"

"Of course, at the very least she could prove to be very useful as an extra pair of hands. Have you seen the policeman lately?"

"I've only seen him once since the murder. We had a drink at the Clifton Hotel. He seemed to be more interested in what you and Timmy were doing than anything that I said. He's a strange man, he seems to brood and look right through you, lost in thought. I can't explain it, I'm used to men looking at me, like you must be, but Roger doesn't look at you, he seems to look through you. I've only seen him a few times in total, he's always been the perfect gentleman, but something's bothering him. I like lively people who make me feel better for being with them, like you and Timmy. You don't know how lucky you are."

Paula was nodding.

"I think we both do, Liz," said Helene. "Did I say that Timmy's driving down tomorrow evening and then we'll decide where to spend the weekend, here in Bristol, at the Manor House at Tolbrite or back in London, depending really on Timmy's Sherlock Holmes feelings and how much work he brings with him. I expect that we'll compromise and drive down to Dorset in time for dinner on Saturday and back to London on Sunday evening. When are you free this weekend?"

"I'm on call the whole weekend and won't be able to go home. If you're about I might be able to slip out for an hour for lunch on Saturday. This hotel is convenient."

The next morning Helene and Paula started their round at nine a.m. reasoning that no one would welcome earlier callers.

They went to a house near Old Market at which there had been no response to their knocking the previous day. An elderly woman came to the door; leaning heavily on two sticks and opened it a few inches on a heavy chain.

"I've already told you, I'm not selling."

"We're not interested in buying," said Helene.

"Then what do you want? If you're selling something, I don't want that either. I got no money."

"We want to talk to you about the people who are trying to get you out of your house. We're on your side we're from the Radio station."

"Oh, you're from that lot. Had the man from the other lot round here this morning already, telling me not to speak with you or else. I told him to push off."

"Have you got any letters or other papers from the other lot that we can see, please?"

"You'd better come in." She laboriously undid the chains and opened the door, at which point a man appeared behind Helene and Paula and attempted to force his way into the house. He pushed Helene, who lost her footing and fell back against the wall, and he knocked the old lady over. Paula reacted quickly, took hold of the man's arm and with one deft movement turned him round and pushed him across the pavement. Helene was beside the door helping the old woman up, leaving Paula outside with the man who turned and lunged at her, only to find his arm grasped and pulled and his off-balanced body thrown to the ground with his arm pushed up between his shoulder blades. He was still being held thus when the police car arrived.

Paula explained that the man had assaulted her and Helene Hawkridge and the householder when he had attempted an unauthorized entry into the house. Several of the onlookers confirmed that the man had knocked the other women down and had twice attacked this young woman. Helene confirmed that the man had attempted to force his way into the house and had assaulted the old lady, herself, and Paula. The policemen put handcuffs on the man. Names and addresses were taken and Helene stated that she would prefer charges for assault.

The old woman was delighted and cackled with mirth.

"Just like on the telly and here on me own doorstep, just wait till I tells me friend Dora."

"Well done Paula, you just gained two admirers. You realize that probably we'll have to come down to Bristol for his trial but it'll be worth it for the renewed hope it will give to the people he's been bullying." She turned to the old lady,

"Now Mrs, I don't think you told us your name?"

"Mary Robinson, just like the jam people."

"Now, Mrs Robinson, what about the papers you were going to show us?"

She invited them into a room and went over to a heavy bureau and after a great deal of searching accompanied by wheezes and heavy breathing, produced a thick file of papers relating to the house.

"This is they," she said. "It's all here, my late husband used to say 'you must keep the records in date order, Mary.' He was a great one for keeping records."

"May I take them away and copy the important ones, they might be very useful. I'll bring them back this afternoon. One last thing, Mrs Robinson, that bureau over there in the corner where you keep the records is probably worth a lot of money. If anyone comes here and offers to buy it say No in a very loud voice and get an expert to look at it, it would be worth paying for someone to give you a true valuation because the bureau is probably worth several thousand pounds."

"Well I never, today's my lucky day, thanks to you two."

Helene rang Joy and told her what had happened and added,

"Joy, there are a lot of people who have been intimidated by the man who was arrested today. Let's tell them about it on the local news, it'll cheer them up that someone's fighting back on their behalf, Say something like Quote: *A man who has been using heavy handed methods in trying to persuade elderly householders in the Old Market area and other parts of the City to sell their properties, was arrested this morning when he assaulted three women while attempting to force an entry into one of the houses. He was overcome and held until the police arrived by one of the women who is a black belt at Judo*: Unquote.

"Are you alright, Helene?"

"Yes fine, but I expect that we've stirred up some more trouble. You must be extra vigilant going to and fro to your car. I'll tell you how we're getting on later."

She turned to their driver. "Will you take us next to this address in Stokes Croft please?"

She explained to Paula that she had had enough of housing for the time being and thought she'd try prostitution next. The driver was suitably puzzled. He knew who she was and who she was married to and she was going to try prostitution. She then added, "We had fifty seven calls about prostitution and this is the closest to where you were the other night." The driver relaxed, she was only going to ask questions about prostitution. She should ask a taxi driver.

The driver put them down nearly opposite to the massage parlour. The house had four storeys, arranged as four flats and Helene had no idea which one she wanted. She phoned the number that Bill Lawrence had assigned to this particular message and asked to which floor the number referred, A puzzled voice said "Third" so they walked in and up the stairs to the third floor and rang the bell.

A middle-aged woman opened the door on a chain.

"Good morning, we're from Hawkridge Radio Bristol and we'd like to ask you some questions, is it convenient now?" said Helene.

"What sort of questions?"

Over the woman's shoulder Helene could see a crucifix on the wall.

"Someone telephoned our station about the goings on in the massage parlour across the road. We think that there is great wickedness there and are collecting what evidence we can. Can you help us? Can we come in?"

The woman unclipped the door chain and stood back for them to enter, replacing the chain as they did so.

"I know that this could be a bit embarrassing for you but why did you phone?"

"Because what they were doing is wicked and at last the police came and took them away."

"You and I might not like the idea of people going in to be massaged but it's not against the law."

"Many things are within the law but are wicked in the eyes of the Lord, like people living together who aren't married, and having babies."

"Yes I agree with you," said Helene, silently asking forgiveness since she and Timmy were living together with only a civil marriage license. In her heart she wouldn't consider herself properly married until they could get to her home in Burgundy in the summer for what Timmy half jokingly called a proper church wedding, with white frocks, top hats and buckets of champagne. "What wickedness have you seen?"

"It's what went on upstairs or one could say, what came off upstairs. I've seen girls and men embracing with no clothes on and the girls had brown bodies. You never saw a white girl except them downstairs. Upstairs all I saw were brown girls and they never came out for walks or shopping."

"Did you ever hear noises in the night?"

"The lights are on till all hours and men are still going in and out. I think the people who run it make them keep quiet. I was awake the other morning when a white van pulled up and a lot of girls got out. The men from the van carried their things inside in boxes, perhaps they'd been out for a picnic but it was about three a.m. when they got here. I heard them and got up to look out of the window and looked at the clock at the same time."

"Since then have you seen any girls leave the building in the white van?"

"I wouldn't swear to it but two or three nights ago, I heard a noise and got to the window just as a girl got into the white van that then drove off. I had a feeling that the one I saw was the last of several girls and the man on the pavement pushed her roughly to make her get in, it was as if she didn't want to go. Since then the police came and took a lot of girls and some men away. About time, I say."

"Do you ever see policemen near the massage parlour?"

"Sometimes a police car stops there and an officer goes in for just a moment and comes out laughing."

"That has been most helpful and I hope that we might call on you again in the near future," said Helene. "Thank you."

They were duly let out and heard the chain put in place behind them.

# Chapter Eleven

HELENE wondered what progress the police were making in the case of the attempted murder of Ah Ming and the attempt to get at her in hospital. The police had the man who the Securifirm guards had captured and according to Timmy now had the other two men who had been seen riding in a car the night of the attempt at Southmead Hospital. She hoped that they would provide an opening to get the men behind the dirty business. She made a mental note to ask Timmy if there was anything they should do about this.

She had also realized that with her blonde hair she was rather easily recognized.

The remaining major subject of calls had been drugs and the only matters of substance had been the names of two or three public houses where it was said drugs could be readily bought and the name of a man who was said to be the banker. Since she had decided that the caller might be one of his employees she had looked him up but that was as far as she could go. She wondered if he had a family, a nice wife and children who had no idea where the money came from. This could be a job for Mr Swift.

She decided that she'd go back to the radio station and check up on the photocopying, have a sandwich with Joy and then take the borrowed documents back to the houses from which they had been taken. She would then go back to the Grand Hotel, dismiss the hire car, have a nice long bath and wait for Timmy to arrive. She outlined this programme to Paula and half proposed that she should leave for London before lunch, but in no way, Paula would see the thing through and collect her luggage when the car dropped Helene at the hotel. The driver's final duty would be to take Paula to Temple Meads railway station.

They drove to the radio station and Helene handed over the final set of documents for copying during the lunch hour. She and Paula told of Paula's citizen's arrest and asked Joy to use her contacts to find out what the man had been charged with. Joy said that the crime reporter in the Western Daily Press was a friend of hers and a most useful ally. Helene stressed that all information was valuable, if someone who was in custody was released on bail, we wanted to know the lawyer used and who instructed the lawyer and if necessary, who instructed the instructor. While on this subject she wondered what had been done about the white man and the two black men who had attempted to get at Ah Ming. They were in custody, or had they been let out on bail? If so we wanted chapter and verse on who got them out. Changing the subject she asked Joy to use her business contacts to identify the senior employees of the alleged drugs man. The local press should know what there was to know, even if they dare not print it.

Joy promised to do her best but added, somewhat plaintively, that she had a radio station to run.

Helene and Paula spent the afternoon returning the borrowed documents and Paula was delivered to Temple Meads in time to catch an express to Paddington and her home.

Helene was in the foyer when Timmy arrived. She looked gorgeous in a form hugging cream frock, sheer tights and cream shoes. He hardly had time to hand his car keys to the Hall Porter and she was in his arms "Oh Timmy, I have missed you so."

"Angel, I missed you too but it was only for one night."

"Yes but it's only the second time we've been apart since you-know-when."

"I know. Now put me down. I'd like to wash, then a drink and a leisurely dinner during which you can tell me all about it and then bed. I dropped my bag outside. Ah here it is, come on Angel we're holding everyone up."

While he washed, she told him in a torrent of words about the calls she and Paula had made and how Paula had dealt with the man who had tried to intimidate Mrs Robinson and how they now had copies of the letters and other documents that the property speculators had sent to the occupiers of the various houses and what she had asked Joy to do, adding that the copies of the documents that she had collected had yet to be studied.

"Hold on Angel," said Timmy. "Give me a chance."

Undeterred Helene ploughed on.

"We've got to sit down with these papers and the tapes and the other bits of information we've gathered up to the present time and have a good think."

"To be absolutely honest, Angel, I'm not entirely sure what we're trying to achieve."

"Well, for a start, there's the murder of Chuck, who did it?" said Helene. "Then there are the girls being smuggled into England for you know what and thirdly there's the old people being swindled out of their homes. Surely that's enough?"

"I agree, but why us?" said Timmy. "I agree that we have a sort of moral duty to see that the person who killed one of our employees," he paused and thought, "I suppose that he was an ex-employee, is apprehended, but that's really a matter for the police. Equally as citizens we have an interest in preventing the sexual exploitation of those unfortunate girls and the harassment of old people and we have just spent a great deal of money having Mr Swift photograph them in the act, which evidence we have given to the authorities and which they have used in apprehending the baddies. Then there's the effort you have made in collecting documents. The question remains, why us?"

"You know very well, Why us? It's because it's not in your nature, nor in mine, to stand idly by and see less fortunate people suffer," said Helene. She grinned at him, "added to which it gives us material for a real-life TV documentary."

"You know, every day I find a new reason for loving you, I couldn't have put it better myself."

"I know."

"What do you know, Angel?"

"That you couldn't have put it better yourself, my love. Now, let's be serious, what are we going to do this weekend? Liz is on duty the whole weekend but will try to come here to lunch with us tomorrow. We could make a few calls in the morning have lunch and then go down to your parents in the afternoon and back to London as usual on Sunday."

"What sort of calls did you have in mind?" asked Timmy, artlessly.

"The local reference library first, then the local Chamber of Commerce and the University library next, and last perhaps the Council House."

"What on earth do you expect to find there?"

"At this moment I don't know but it should give us a better feel for local politics and rivalries," said Helene.

106

"I can think of better ways of spending my time with you but we'll do as you suggest, after we've been out to the radio station, had a small tour round the Old Market area and visited Roger Hardwick out at his police headquarters."

"But that'll take up the whole morning."

"Yes, Angel, that's what I thought."

The following morning they phoned the police headquarters at Portishead, Roger Hardwick could see them at ten o'clock.

They circled the Old Market area while Helene pointed out the houses that she had visited. It was clear that there was not only one, but two potentially valuable sites which only required the removal of one or two houses to enable development to go ahead. Looked at objectively if the development was done as well as that which had already occurred in the vicinity, it would be a good thing for Bristol. But not at the price of old people losing their homes, run down though some of them appeared to be.

On the way to the police headquarters at Portishead Down they passed the dock where hundreds of cars remained, and were shown into Detective Chief Inspector Roger Hardwick's room at precisely ten a.m. He expressed his pleasure at seeing them and asked how he could be of assistance. Timmy said,

"You know that as a result of the phone-in we are in possession of a lot of information about suspected wrongdoing in your area. We condensed it down on to six tapes and you were with us when Helene gave her summary of results. You took away copies of the master tapes and the six tapes."

"Yes and I've been listening to them whenever I have a moment," said the DCI.

"All of this started because we became aware that an Asian girl called Ah Ming had entered the country illegally, been forced to become a prostitute and then nearly murdered and some men tried to finish the job at Southmead Hospital. We obtained the names of the men concerned and passed the information to the police, suggesting that these might also be the three who had beaten Ah Ming and thrown her into the harbour,"

"And?"

"We wondered whether these men have been charged with attempted murder?" said Timmy.

"I don't know, I'll look into it."

"Next. We didn't know it at the time but the disc jockey, Chuck Williams and his producer, Sally Evans, had been listening to the tapes each day. Chuck heard one message and is reported by Sally to have said 'I recognize that voice etc' and to have made a phone call. Some days later he is murdered. We know now that Chuck and Sally were lovers and planned to live together. Sally's husband is stated to be a violent man. We also know that Chuck's wife, Betty, was having an affair, believed to be with a schoolmaster. That's several people with a motive for killing Chuck."

"And?" said the DCI.

"It occurred to us that the call that Chuck made must be on someone's phone bill. Have you checked Chuck and Sally's phone bills for calls made?"

"I don't know, I'll ask the officer in charge of the case."

"Next. Helene and a friend were calling on an elderly woman near the Old Market yesterday. A man   attacked them. They were there because the owner has been put under pressure by a property speculator who wants to develop the site. Helene's friend happens to be a black belt and made a citizen's arrest. Helene told your officers that she insisted in pressing charges for assault. We'd like to know if the man has been charged for assault. If he has been released on bail, who posted the bail? It might give us a lead to who's behind the intimidation."

"I don't know, I'll look into it."

"My final question is what have you been able to do, if anything, about the prominent citizen who was named as a drugs baron?"

"Of all your preposterous questions, Tim, that's about the limit," said the DCI, "this is the county police headquarters, not a radio studio."

"I admit that my last question was a bit of a cheek, sorry. But you might like to know that we have a witness who says that two or three nights before the last shipment of girls arrived at the house in Stokes Croft, some girls were loaded into a van and taken elsewhere. The same witness has seen police officers calling at this establishment."

"Timmy, you must understand that it's only because we're old friends that you got in here at all and there is no reason why I should answer your questions. I'll do what I can because of your assistance to the forces of law and order in the past but you must realize that you're playing a dangerous game my friend and someone could get hurt."

"It's simply that the bulk of the population seems to have forgotten or have never been told by their parents that the maintenance of standards in our public life is a duty for everyone and not just for the police," said Timmy. "Remember what Edmond Burke said, 'the sure way to ensure the triumph of evil is for good men to do nothing' or words to that effect. Look Roger, we didn't come here to give you trouble we simply wanted the sort of information that we thought your press office would give to the daily press. It is good of you to see us and thanks for your time."

"Was that wise?" asked Helene as they drove back en route to Bedminster Down.

"Was what wise, Angel?"

"Annoying Roger, he and the police can make things awkward if they choose."

"I did it quite deliberately to test where his loyalty lies, if he's an honest copper, he'll be sending out an olive branch. If he has some sort of interest elsewhere, the game could get interesting. Remember he is one of the few who knows what's on the tapes."

They went to the radio station and found Joy in reasonably good form. She confirmed that both she and Sally had made statements to the police and had signed the typed versions. There had been no follow up. Helene told her about the house calls that she and Paula had made in the past two days and that she would study the copies of the documents Joy had made in the coming days. She added that she had been impressed by Paula and might ask her to make some follow up enquiries on her own. One thing they could be sure of, Paula could take care of herself. Perhaps Paula could help Jeremy, the young reporter?

"We'll see," said Joy, without much enthusiasm.

Back at the hotel, Liz arrived breathless and kissed them both. Over lunch Helene told her all that had gone on during the past two days and played her the tape of their interview with Roger Hardwick. Her reaction was, "I don't expect he knows who's been charged or released at any one time, remember his authority covers all of Avon and Somerset." Helene thought that a reasonable comment and also wondered, girl like, if there remained any chance for Charles T Howard, the US Treasury agent, from Virginia USA. Timmy thought good old Liz and aren't they the most gorgeous pair.

Liz went happily back to the BRI. They packed, paid their bill and drove off.

"I know I've said it before" said Helene "but sitting here beside you as we drive along is a most pleasant experience. This is the second time we've been this way, last time I drove. Now I can pay more attention to the Somerset countryside. I also want to mention one thought."

"Only the one Angel, what's that?"

"Well, if you think of what Chuck is supposed to have said about the key to their future together, he must have had a substantial sum of money in mind, mustn't he?"

"Yes, I suppose he must," said Timmy.

"And there were only two names or clues to what might be well-off people, directly mentioned on the tapes?"

"Yes."

"Well then, which was most likely to be able to produce a pot of gold, a city Engineer or a drugs baron or an assistant drugs baron?"

"You mean an innocent assistant to a drugs baron. If he was an assistant drugs baron he'd probably go to jail with his boss. To answer your question about their ability to pay, it would be a drugs baron, without a doubt. And he'd be the most able to get someone to shoot a bothersome radio disc jockey as well," said Timmy.

"So what do we do about that?"

"Angel, at the present moment I haven't a clue, except a determination not to get you shot or" as an afterthought, "to get shot myself."

They arrived at the Manor House and were hugged by Margaret.

"Did you have a lovely time in Bristol? Did you see Liz? Is she keeping well?"

"Yes on all three counts Mother and we had lunch with her today so our news is bang up to date," said Timmy, "and now may we come in?"

When they came down,

"And what about you two, you haven't been dealing with nasty people again, have you?"

"One or two," said Helene. "Timmy virtually made the man you call Liz's policeman take action and arrest the men who were smuggling those Asian girls into Britain."

"Didn't he want to do it?"

"Well, it was a bit difficult to make them act quickly but they did in the end."

"What are you going to do now?"

"Nothing for the present, I think that we let things take their course for a week or so," said Timmy. "But the future of Ah Ming is likely to become a pressing issue in the not so distant future."

"We'll have her here if that's what Liz wants," said his mother. "That's that then. Come on, the Sergeant will get us some tea and you can tell Daddy and me all about it."

After tea they repaired to the library and sorted through the pile of documents that Joy had copied from the householder's originals. They read each one and selected the important ones, which they put in date order for a much closer scrutiny.

Each property had received three or four letters. They were on embossed notepaper headed Labgrove Estates with a list of directors. The first stated blandly that the writer's company was willing to purchase the property should the occupant wish to take advantage of the present favourable property market conditions. The second was a hastener pointing out that generosity such as that offered for an old property could not be expected again. The third was in the same vein adding that the writer understood that considerable demolition and building work was shortly to take place adjacent to the property and would be expected to much reduce its market value. The forth said the same, pointing out that although every effort would be made to minimize it, demolition and building would likely interfere with access to the property and services to the property, might affect its stability and would adversely affect its market value. Sell now was the message.

They decided that an investigation of Labgrove Estates might show dividends and that this would be done as a matter of urgency, commencing Monday.

"How do you intend to go about it, we'll have to be careful?" said Helene.

"I think that we should do the obvious thing and look into the directors, most will be people who know nothing and do nothing except attend an annual board meeting and collect their pay but one or two of them will be the men who run the thing. We'll try to identify them and put them under a magnifying glass, what other directorships do they hold? Have they ever been bankrupt or associated with a company that went bankrupt? What overseas interests do they have and where? What is their lifestyle? Where do their children go to school? How often do they go overseas? And so on. Then we invite Mr Swift to think about what we've discovered."

"You don't think that we should ask a banker like Peter Davenport to prepare a report?"

"No, my love, not on this one and in any case he'd simply ask someone like you to do it. Probably he would ask someone far less able than you and certainly not as beautiful."

"But they'd have access to all the bank's records and experts," said Helene.

After dinner they put on their warm coats and Wellington boots and walked across the park to the Tolbrite Arms. The night was dark and a blustery wind blew leaves around as they walked. The locals had got used to their dropping in when they were down and there was a chorus of good evenings and hello's.

"Hello Mr Trowbridge, nice to see you, how's trade? Two Bouchier red's please."

"Not so bad, don't get so many trippers of an evening but the lunch trade has held up fairly well, quite a lot from the offices in Poole and Bournemouth."

"That's a good recommendation for Mrs Trowbridge's cooking," said Helene.

"Hello Tim," said young Will, looking at Helene. "Thought you'd be down this weekend, solved the murder of that disc jockey yet?"

"I'm over here Will," laughed Timmy, "is it Gloria's night off? In answer to your question, no we are still baffled. He lived up an ill-lit country road. A voice phones and says it's the BBCTV; we'll be there to interview you at eight-thirty. At eight-thirty there is a knock at the door, the victim goes cheerfully to open it to be interviewed and bang, he's dead."

"You know, Timmy, every time we think of Chuck's murder we say 'it's a matter for the police'. If they've shown as much initiative on that as they have on the other things on the tapes, then the murder will never be solved," said Helene.

"What's this about tapes, have you got another lark going?" asked Will.

"Sort of," said Helene, "and we nearly sent for you to look after me in Bristol last week, but Timmy got a girl instead."

"Tim always was a spoilsport. You ask Liz," said Will.

"If we wanted someone to make enquiries for us in Bristol would you be able to get away for a day, Will?" asked Timmy.

"Would Helene be there?"

"No she wouldn't, but you could take Gloria with you and, of course, you'd be on expenses."

"Those words are music to my ears, it's barely three months since you took me off the gravy train and Christmas is coming, so when do we go and what do we have to do?" said Will.

"I want you to go to where the murder took place and ask at every house in the road and in the two pubs at lunchtime, whether anyone saw or heard anything peculiar on the night the disc jockey was killed. The more awkward people are the more awkward and persistent you're to be, got me?"

"OK Tim, I'm allowed to be awkward, what sort of place is it?"

"Helene's been there," said Timmy.

"The road is country like and narrow," said Helene "It's quite a steep hill and houses are perched on both sides. On the right hand side, going up, you have to climb up to the houses and on the left hand side you go down to the houses. It's called Providence and is in the village suburb of Bristol called Long Ashton. The disc jockey's house is near to the top, on the right hand side and the killer should have been visible from nearby houses. Also, the killer must have had transport, the turn into and up Providence is difficult and parking in the narrow road is near to impossible. That could be the key."

"If it takes a long time do we stay the night on expenses?"

"Yes, but I hope that you don't because you don't want to get into your future father-in-laws bad books and I might have other things for you to do later. Anyway, if you think about it, it's better just to drive home in the evening and perhaps have a meal on the way than to wake up in Bristol and know that you're both going to waste the best part of the morning getting back to Tolbrite," said Timmy.

"What's my cover story?"

"Oh, I don't know at the moment. I'll have to think about that," said Timmy.

"Timmy'll give you a letter from Hawkridge Radio Bristol saying that we are concerned at the lack of progress in catching the killer," said Helene, "and asking the reader to search their memory for what they remember about that evening and discuss it with our representative Mr William Conway and his partner. You should leave a copy at every house but make sure that you talk to the people and draw out everything they might know."

"That's a good idea, we'll give you a letter," said Timmy.

"It's not your night for original thinking, is it lover?" said Helene.

"How do I get these letters?"

"I'll arrange for a hundred copies of the letter to be at the Radio station at Bedminster Down from Tuesday onwards," said Timmy, deciding that it was time to stop fooling. "You decide which day you can go to Bristol and go there to freshen up after your journey and collect the letters from Joy Philips, the station manager. You can see Long Ashton from the radio station but it's rather a long way round to get there."

Will came out with them when they left and Timmy gave him a hundred pounds for wages and a fifty pounds advance on expenses. Will said that he'd report next weekend.

As they walked back across the park Helene remarked that with a little encouragement Will might turn out to be the general handyman-cum-clerk of works for the Manor House Trust. She added,

"There's one joker in the tapes that we haven't done anything about."

"Oh but we have," said Timmy, "you're referring to the alleged drug baron, I presume?"

"Yes, what have we done?"

"Well he would seem to be the one person with enough wealth and underworld connections to be able to quickly commission Chuck's killing. So now we've got Will going to ask questions about the killing. The other thing is that I have a conviction that the girl smuggling has something to do with drugs and if we can shut down one, the other inescapably follows."

"Yes, but is that enough, Timmy, surely he'll find a new source of supply?"

He grinned at her. "I had thought of ringing him up and saying something like 'there are rumours that you are the banker for drug rackets in Bristol and it's suspected that you bring the drugs in through the Royal Portbury Dock. I think these rumours are scandalous and so, as a public duty, I'm going to broadcast to the world that the rumours that Mr so and so is a drug racketeer are not proven."

"What do you think would be his reaction?" said Helene.

"Probably to have me shot as well."

# Chapter Twelve

ON MONDAY Helene started her enquiry into Labgrove Estates. There were ten directors, one of whom acted as Company Secretary. The list of directors included a Labour Peer, a Conservative Member of Parliament and an ex-Conservative MP. They each had directorships in reputable companies that she knew. Of the seven other directors, five featured elsewhere in the Directory of Directors but not in companies that she knew and three of that five were in the current Who's Who. There were two who were not included anywhere and one of these was the Company Secretary who had signed the letters sent to the Bristol householders. Labgrove Estates was not listed but was registered with a nominal capital.

She was conscious that the English half of her was inclined to accept that people included in Who's Who were naturally honourable and to give a nod to those in the Directory of Directors, while her French half, her mothers half, argued the bigger the entry in Who's Who, the bigger the liar. To prove her point Claire-Marie would point out that all the really long entries were well known actors on the London stage.

For the time being, Helene was English. That left the two who were not included anywhere. Since the Company Secretary signed the letters, Helene decided to start with him and telephoned Mr Swift. Yes, he would be delighted to come over.

Mr Swift arrived within the hour.

"How can we be of assistance, Mrs Hawkridge?"

"You know about the phone-in run by Timmy's radio station in Bristol and the disc jockey who was murdered and your operators detecting that girls were being brought in by the car transporter."

"Yes."

"Well, several of the phone-in calls were from old people who are being harassed by a property company that wants to get them out of their houses to free sites for development. Their letters are only mildly threatening but their agents have caused damage to the properties and one actually manhandled me and, oh, of course, you already know, Paula will have told you."

"Yes, I rather think that she enjoyed it."

"Timmy and I are determined to see that the old people are not bullied in ignorance into doing what the property developers want and so we want to know all about a company called Labgrove Estates and who is actually behind it. You'll see that the company doesn't have a telephone number, only an address in Portman Square."

"That's hardly our usual line of business."

"Oh but it is," said Helene, "the company has ten directors, here's the list. Three of the directors are politicians and three of the others are in Who's Who. Two of the rest are in the Directory of Directors leaving the one who acts as the company secretary and one other. I've under-lined them in red.  We would like to know more about them and that, I would suggest, is in your line of business," said Helene.

"That's different," said Mr Swift.

"Because it's easiest, we suggest that you start with the company secretary, then the other man who isn't in the works of reference that I've consulted, and then we'll work our way up from there to the two who are in the Directory of Companies but not in Who's Who. After that check the three who are in Who's Who until we reach the Life Peer.  What we want to know is where do they live? What is their lifestyle? Would their earnings appear to support that lifestyle? Does the wife work? Where do their children go to school? How often do they go overseas? Where do they go? What other directorships or offices do they hold? Have they ever been bankrupt? Who are their friends? Who are their enemies? Is that enough for the present?"

"It might take a little time because we'll have to tread warily. I've got just the chap who loves this type of investigation. Do I report to you or Mr Hawkridge?"

"You can report to either of us, as convenient."

"Have you told the police about this particular investigation?"

"No Mr Swift, we haven't. Last Saturday Timmy and I went out to the Avon and Somerset police headquarters at Portishead and asked the Chief Constable's staff officer what was going on. It finished up a little unfortunately but I think it was a dismal report, here, we taped it, you can hear it for yourself."

Mr Swift listened to the tape.

"Your husband is a remarkable man and I can quite understand why he has been so successful in business but in business they only metaphorically stab people in the back. The sort of people he's now tangling with stab people for real and he must take care. Please tell him that from me and now I'll get along and put your enquiry in hand."

"Goodbye Mr Swift and thank you, we're both very grateful for your help."

She passed on his warning at lunchtime and showed Timmy the memo that she had prepared for young Will to distribute in Long Ashton. Timmy read it and asked her to send it to Joy.

On Tuesday Joy Philips phoned to say that her young reporter has completed his assignment with the Civil Engineers Department of the Bristol Council. The Deputy Chief took him round to speak with all the divisional heads. He was given a good reception and had put together an interesting story that she thought would be well worth broadcasting.

"That's excellent, Joy," said Timmy, "perhaps your reporter should do the same thing at the other major departments of the Council. It could make an interesting series. He's already asking questions at the Housing Department, isn't he?"

"Yes and we have a problem. He was approached and threatened by two men as he left the office in Airport Road. They must have been lying in wait for him. They told him that they knew that he was from that so-and-so radio company and that we'd better forget all that we had been told if we knew what's good for us. If they saw him again in Knowle West it'd be a hiding, not words that they'd give him. We often encounter hostility of one sort or another but Jeremy says this was different. I think that he was badly shaken and I'm not sending him back there. Someone in the Housing Office must have tipped them off, mustn't they?"

"Yes, it looks like it. Sorry about that, Joy, don't send him back. I'd like him to record his impressions including what the men said and what they looked like," said Timmy.

"What shall I do with the Civil Engineers tape and this Housing tape when it's done?"

"Send them to Bill Lawrence I'll warn him that they're coming. You have my word that you'll have the originals back after we've done the voice analysis exercise."

"Shall we take a copy of the Civil Engineers thing before I send it?"

"I suggest not, I don't know much about it but I feel that the less we do with the tape before the analysis, the better," said Timmy. "One other thing, Joy, I know that Helene has told you that I've asked a great friend called Will Conway to canvass the part of Long Ashton where someone might have seen something the night Chuck was killed. You've got the letter that he's to distribute, haven't you? Good, He'll report to you on arrival, probably with Gloria, his girl friend. A word in your ear, don't underestimate ex-commando young Will, several people have, to their cost."

Young Will and Gloria arrived at Bedminster Down in a blue BMW car, which he parked expertly beneath a no parking sign. He and Gloria were taken in to meet Joy Philips.

"Good morning, we've come for the letters that my friend Tim said you'd have ready for us."

"Yes, here they are, did you have a good journey?" said Joy, making conversation.

"Not bad but the roads aren't as good as they should be considering what the tax and the petrol cost. Now in France where we went with Timmy and Helene chasing those crooks, they really have got roads suitable for modern cars."

"Oh yes," said Gloria, "but it was ever so scary when the crooks pulled out their guns at Timmy."

"Yes," said Joy "I heard something about it but they didn't tell me the full story."

"Just like old Tim," said Will, "he was always the quiet one when we were kids but he was always the one who got things done. Tell me, the chap as was murdered worked here, didn't he?"

"Yes," said Joy, "have you ever been round a radio station?"

"Oh no," said Gloria, "could we have a little look."

"Of course, but you won't find it very exciting. I'll lead the way."

They made a brief tour of the building and were nodded to by earnest young people wearing earphones or carrying clipboards or chatting quietly into microphones.

At the end, which Joy made sure was near the main door, Will said,

"Thanks a lot, that was very interesting and I know how busy you really are, so we mustn't spend all day chatting. Could you tell us the way to this place, Long Ashton?"

R J Daniel

Joy took them to the rear of the building and pointed across the valley, saying,

"It doesn't look far, but you have to go the long way round to get there."

She didn't dare to mention the narrow lane called Yanley which joined the A38 a couple of hundred metres from the radio station and which went directly to Long Ashton. Only fools and experts at backing their cars for hundreds of metres in order to find a place where a hay wagon or a tractor or a herd of cows might pass drove that way.

They made their way to Long Ashton, avoiding the modern by-pass that now took the traffic for North Somerset and Weston-super-Mare. They passed the ancient church and an equally ancient inn called The Angel and some distance further on came to a sign half hidden in someone's hedge that said Providence at the bottom of a road that sloped abruptly up to the right. Even Will had some difficulty in making the turn first time. He explained to Gloria,

"I was afraid the exhaust pipe would hit the ground. The bloke that brought it in for repair wouldn't like it. What we'll do is go right up to the top keeping an eye open for the place where the man was shot, you've got the number, haven't you? And look for places where someone could have parked a car in the dark that night. Then we'll turn round and do the same thing coming down again. Then we'll find somewhere to park the car and start talking to people."

Will took the hill at a steady speed as suited the gradient and the narrowness of the road and Gloria muttered, "It'll be on the right."

Eventually they found the house above the second of the two inns which each seemed to be perched precariously on the hillside. The house had a drive that sloped steeply upwards beside the house to a garage at the rear and steps that went up even more steeply to a center front door.

Will wondered what was behind the houses on the right hand side, presumably they had gardens, did they slope up even higher, was there another road beyond and could the murderer have come that way, down the garden path and round the side of the house and got away the same way? He began to appreciate that this detecting business wasn't as simple as it looked but it was more fun than repairing cars.

They approached the top without seeing anywhere that a sensible person could have parked a car without blocking someone's drive. There had been a short bit of level outside one of the pubs, with two cars parked on the left hand side but he bet that those spaces would have been occupied on the fateful night. There were no houses near the top of the hill where the road made a lazy S bend between two parts of a golf course. They were now out in the country. Will turned left towards Clevedon and pulled on to the verge.

He said, "I wonder if this is where the murderer parked? If you think about it, most of the movement of the residents in cars and on foot would be down the hill towards the village and back again because down there is where the shops and the buses to Bristol are. Only the occupants of the few houses at the top would go past the Williams' house and then mostly in cars."

"Except if they walked down to the pub," said barmaid Gloria.

"That's true but it doesn't alter what I was about to say, I reckon that we start by talking to the people in the houses just down below here, above the murdered man's house. Come on we'll leave the car here."

"You remember what we agreed, you don't you go wandering off on your own, we stick together, eh?" said Gloria.

They locked the car and walked down the hill to the first house, being narrowly missed by a car coming round the bend in the hill, the driver of which was clearly surprised to find someone crazy enough to walk in that part of Providence.

They knocked at the topmost house.

An elderly man opened the door.

"Good morning," said Will. "We're from the radio station, Hawkridge Radio Bristol. It was our man Chuck Williams who was murdered just down the road and we think that the police could do more than they seem to be doing. Here is a letter from our owner asking for your help. Can I ask you some questions?"

"I don't see how I can help you, my wife and I were in all that evening watching television and we didn't see or hear a thing. Our lounge is at the back."

"You must have got up to make some cocoa or put the cat out or something," said Will.

"We certainly got up to do something as you so delicately put it," smiled the man, "but I'm sorry we didn't see or hear a thing." He closed the door.

They went to the next house and rang the bell. A harassed looking youngish woman came to the door with a baby in her arms.

"What is it, we don't want any, go away."

"Good morning," said Will, "we're from the radio station where Chuck Williams, worked. You remember, the man who was shot in his doorway down the hill. Here's a letter that explains it, can we talk to you and did you or your husband see or hear anything the night he was killed?"

"What, with two bleeding kids and a husband on nights, fat chance. I gota job to hear myself think."

"Was your husband at work that night?"

"Corse he was."

"What time did your husband go out?"

"About half past eight, he has to be on duty at nine."

"Which way does he go? He goes by car I assume?"

"Up the hill, of course, he works in Clevedon."

"And he didn't see anyone that night?"

"Look, the police already asked us all this, why don't you ask them?"

"Did the police interview your husband?"

"'Corse not, he was in bed, same as he is now. They asked if he went down the hill and I said No, so they said don't bother to disturb him and went away."

"I'd like a word with him when he wakes up, would two o'clock be alright?"

"Suppose so, but don't blame me if he's in a temper."

She closed the door.

They crossed the road to the bungalow next door but one above the Williams house and knocked on the door.

"Good morning," began Will.

"Push off," said the elderly man who opened the door, "we don't want Jehovah's Witnesses around here, there's enough churches and chapels and do-gooders already."

122

Will began to realize that he had to earn that hundred pounds that Timmy had given him.

"We're not Jehovah's Witnesses," said Will, "We're from the radio station."

"Then why didn't you say so?" said the man.

"Who's that, George?" Came a female voice from within.

"Some people from the radio, mother."

"Here's a letter from the owner," said Will, "asking for your help in trying to find out who killed your neighbour Chuck Williams. We're not happy with the police effort so far. Did you or your wife see or hear anything that evening?"

"Bring them in, George," said the voice.

"I told it all to the police, why don't you come in and speak to the wife?"

He led them into the front room on the right where an elderly woman sat in a chair inside the bay window.

"These young people are from the radio, mother. They want to ask some questions about the night of the murder."

"Why don't you put the kettle on George? I'm sure they won't say no to a nice cup of tea."

Oh Lord, thought Will. "One sugar for me," said Gloria.

"Now where was I?" said the invalid. "Oh yes, the night of the murder I was sat here in the dark like I always do, looking out, when I saw this man, I think it was a man, it walked like a man, go past walking down the hill. To my surprise the figure turned into the Williams' and climbed the steps to the front door. I knew she was out, she goes off in her car well before eight o'clock most evenings, perhaps she takes night school, she's a school teacher, you know, now where was I?"

"The man had just climbed the Williams' steps," said Will.

"Yes, and he paused, I could see him silhouetted against that street light down the road, and then he disappeared behind that bush in next doors garden. He must have knocked on the door or rung the bell. George, do the Williams' have a knocker or a bell?"

Her husband came in from the kitchen, holding a tea towel and asked "What was that you said?"

"Oh, it doesn't matter. Now where was I?"

Her husband disappeared again.

"The man had just knocked at the Williams' door," said Will.

"That's right. Anyway I saw the glow as someone I suppose it was that Chuck Williams, opened the front door. Next thing I heard a bang like a car back-firing and saw this man going down the steps and up the hill."

"Could you see how big this person was, were they tall or fat or anything and was the coat they were wearing light or dark?" Will asked.

The man brought in a loaded tea tray. She said,

"I could tell that he was quite tall because his head just reached the bottom of the street light. He paused near the top of the steps, you see."

"You mean if I drew a line from where you were sitting to the street light bulb it would just touch the top of his head?" asked Will.

"Yes, but he had a hat on," said the old lady.

Will turned to the man "Do you have a hat and a tape measure that I can borrow for a minute?"

He was given a brown trilby hat that fitted him well enough and a tape measure.

"Oh, you look nice in that, why don't you get one to wear at home?" said Gloria.

Will brushed aside such frivolous chatter.

"I'm going to climb up the Williams' steps the way the murderer did. I want you to tell me when I am in line with the street light and then we'll see if the top of my head is where his was on the night of the murder. It would be better if we could do it at night but we can't wait till then. Does this window open?"

"Yes," said the old lady.

"You'll get a cold mother if you let him open that window," said the husband.

"Don't fuss George, this is important."

Will opened the window and satisfied himself that the old lady was sitting where she had been on the night in question.

"Now here's what we'll do. Gloria you stand outside the window and tell me when this lady tells you that I'm in line between her and the lamppost. Then I'll stand up straight and the lady will tell us whether I'm too low or too tall. If I'm too low we'll find something to stand on and it'll mean that the murderer is a very tall man. Got it?"

Will put on the hat and he and Gloria went out after opening one of the bay windows. He climbed the Williams steps and after what seemed to him to be a lot of unnecessary *a little bit back and a little bit forwards* was judged to be in line with the unlit street light. He was judged to be too low and found a piece of paving stone to stand on. He was too high. Eventually a one- inch thick plank of wood got it right. The murderer was an inch taller than Will's six feet.

"This could be very important evidence and my boss might ask you to do it all over again with proper instruments, you wouldn't mind that, would you?"

"You have to remember that my wife is ill," said the man.

"Be quiet George, I haven't had as much fun in years. I'm doing something useful."

They drank their tea and left after thanking the old couple for their help.

They called at the houses on either side of the Williams' house but no one answered the door so they pushed copies of the letter through their letterboxes.

Will decided that they had done enough to justify a break for lunch and they climbed the hill to their car. He was able to see that there appeared to be a golf course behind the Williams house and those above it and what seemed to be a nursery behind the houses on the other side.

"It'd be simplest if we just went straight on along this road until we came to a pub that offers Good Food but I expect that Tim would want us to carry on our investigation while we eat, so we'll see what they have to offer in the pubs on Providence."

"I don't mind where we go as long as it's got a clean loo," said Gloria.

Will turned the car round and drove down the hill. The parking spaces were full at the top pub, the Miners Rest, and when they reached the lower one, The Robin Hood, the road was obstructed by a large refuse collection lorry that they just managed to squeeze past. They went to the bottom of the hill and turned right and eventually came to an inn called The Bird in Hand where they found a parking place. Gloria remarked to the landlady that she could understand why it was called Long Ashton and was told that it was the longest village in England and that her pub was thought to be older than that other one near the church.

After lunch they went back to their parking spot on the Clevedon road, locked the car, and walked down to the night shift workers house.

An unshaven man in his shirtsleeves opened the door. Children were crying in the background.

"Are you the people from the radio?"

"Yes," said Will "if we could ask you a couple of questions about the night that Chuck Williams was killed?"

"I can't see as I can help much, I had to go to work."

"What time did you leave the house?" said Will.

"I got the car out at half past eight on the dot."

"Your wife said that you always go up the hill. Did you see any one that night?"

"No, it was deserted as usual. It's pretty lonely up here, 'specially in the winter."

"You didn't see anything?"

"Well there was an Audi parked just around the corner at the top."

"That's where we're parked," said Gloria.

"Did you think that was unusual?" asked Will.

"Not really, I thought it was a courting couple, the wife and I used to stop there a lot before we were married."

"Was there anyone in or near the car that night?"

"No, come to think of it, I got the impression that it was empty. I noticed it because those four interlinked circles reflected my headlights against the dark paintwork of the car."

"So it was a dark coloured Audi?" said Will.

"Yes and it was a Y registration, that showed up as well. I've got a thing about looking at the year of cars."

Will thought that there's no accounting for taste, he had a thing about looking at girls.

"If my boss wants us to write this up and someone from the radio wants you to sign it, you won't mind will you?"

"Be glad to help, we can't let murderers get away with it."

They went down the hill knocking at doors and distributing copies of the letter but no one had seen or heard anything that night. At about four o'clock in gathering dusk they trudged back up the hill and got into the car. It was nice to sit down. Will phoned Joy Philips and reported some success and that he intended to go back to Dorset, he hoped that she had no further instructions. She hadn't, so he squeezed Gloria's knee, put the car in second gear and drove back to Tolbrite.

# Chapter Thirteen

MR SWIFT phoned Helene.

"Good Morning, Mrs Hawkridge, I thought that I should report on the first stage of our enquiry into Labgrove Estates."

"Hello Mr Swift, any luck?"

"Afraid not, we've drawn a complete blank so far."

"Not unexpected in this sort of case."

"These people seem to have been extraordinarily careful."

"Tell me," invited Helene.

"The address in Portman Square is an accommodation address. The house is divided into flats one of which is occupied by the owner, Mr Awnsred. There is a small office in the basement that handles letters for over twenty companies. A young woman does this and apparently does secretarial work for Mr Awnsred. I sent one of my more engaging young men in as a courier delivering a letter for Labgrove Estates and he asked her what she would do with it. She said send it on in one of the envelopes the company provided and suiting the action to the word, she pushed our letter in one and sealed it. The envelope was addressed to P O Box 15683 London EC1. "Who do you write to when you run out of those envelopes?" said my bright young man. "Why, PO Box 15683, of course," said the girl "and they send me a packet of fifty by return. I think somebody does them on a word processor."

"My young man left the door open by saying that he hoped that he would have some more things to deliver there and the girl made encouraging noises."

"What do suggest that we do next?" asked Helene.

"I've got someone preparing a big chart on which we'll enter each board members name, age, address, seats on company boards, and past boards, financial interests, wife, children, mistresses [if known] and so on. It's sometimes surprising what looking at it all en mass can tell you."

"What about Companies House which keeps records of all private and public limited companies in the UK and the names of all their directors and office holders?"

"I've put the ferrets in there, looking for their balance sheets, assets and investment capital as well. The records should also show who the major shareholders are, the powers behind the Board, so to speak."

"Any leads?"

"Not so far but you'll already have noticed that one of the two directors we agreed to start with is called Andrews and my devotion to crossword puzzles tells me that's an anagram of Awnsred, the owner of the house in Portman Square, so we're going to find out a lot more about that particular gentleman."

"But surely that would be too simple after all the cloak and dagger stuff with the correspondence?" Helene said.

"Yes, that struck me too," said Mr Swift, "but you'd be surprised at the number of swindlers who come unstuck because of a small act of meanness. I'll keep you posted. Goodbye."

The next day they spent together with Bill Lawrence and some of his team who had just returned from a week in Qatar on the commercial radio station project. The Emir's son Sheikh Abul had been at Winchester with Timmy and David and had asked Timmy to advise him on opening a commercial radio station in the Gulf Emirate. This had involved picking the location, buying the equipment, setting up the organization, training the staff, getting advertising and scheduling the programmes. Timmy and Helene had been there in the autumn and had got the project started and now big money, Qatar money, was being spent. Bill's earlier skepticism had been replaced by a guarded optimism. He said,

"I don't know how Sheikh Abul does these things but the top floor of the Empress building is now vacant and the builders are in, modifying the internal structure in accordance with our requirements. The Deputy Minister has been put in charge and Salaman, the sheikh's nephew is in charge of the Qatar Broadcasting Service. They are working well together. We've ordered all the equipment from our suppliers for delivery in Qatar with a requirement that the added cost for delivery, installation and warranty in that country be separately shown. So far as I can see the cost mark ups are reasonable and the delivery promises will support our completion programme." He continued,

"I had a lengthy session with the French architect on the changes we're making and particularly the radio transmitter mast we're putting on the top. He showed me his calculations and plans for extra reinforcing of some of the internal walls. It's fortunate that the building has a central core around the lift shafts and services duct and this is the structure that will support the mast. The architect is quite relaxed about it. Salaman has earmarked some of his engineering staff and they will be formally seconded to the new station for training and to watch the installation when we give the word. Peter Bailey, our man on the spot is organizing classes in basic electrics and electronics to make sure that these secondees are up to it. He's also learning Arabic."

"Good for him," said Timmy.

"All in all a most satisfactory technical situation," said Bill, "which comes from having money to spend and the Ruler's support. He sends you and Helene his warmest greetings and prays that you will visit him soon."

"That sounds fine, well done Bill," said Timmy. "I notice that you said that the technical situation is satisfactory, does that mean that the administrative situation is not satisfactory and how are the advertising people shaping up?"

"That's more in the hands of the locals than us and our friends are having trouble with a sheikh called Salem who is doing his best to scare people away from working for us on religious grounds. His main spiel is that advertising is against Allah's teaching but occasionally he breaks into a tirade that advertising will be commercial colonization and makes anti-American and anti-Western comments. I think that people like Salaman and the Sheikh Abul's brothers don't take his threat seriously enough, I think he's dangerous and so does the Deputy Minister."

"Uncle Salem is dangerous," said Timmy "He supports Islamic fundamentalists and actively recruits what he calls martyrs to go to Afghanistan for training, the better to attack the West. He lost his cool when we were in the room in Doha and said that their leader would attack the Americans in their own country and where it would hurt most, in their pockets. He forgot that Helene could understand what he was shouting."

"Well they certainly did, didn't they? Did you do anything about Salem at the time?" asked Bill.

"Yes, Helene prepared a report of what he said and we gave it to the Foreign Office. They thanked Helene and as good as told us that as outsiders we would not understand these things and the Middle East is full of cranks sounding off against the West. Outbursts like Uncle Salem's should be ignored. So we gave a copy to a US diplomat who, we understood, had a more open mind about the contribution that Joe Citizen might make. Then came September 11th and now they all believe what Helene said."

"Well they had a lot of sailors killed when that destroyer was damaged in Aden harbour and there were the bomb attacks on US Embassies in Africa, so they had proof that these extremists meant business long before the World Trade Centre proved it up to the hilt."

"Back to work," said Helene, "we must do all we can to drum up advertisers and prepare outline programme schedules acceptable to the more moderate religious leaders. I think we should go out again and try to help them, although we really can't spare the time."

"I think you're right, Angel, we can't go this side of Christmas, let's plan on going in mid-January, by which time we'll have Bill's next status report and Charles's outline plan for advertising."

"I had a private word with the Deputy Minister as we were waiting for the plane. I mentioned the Ah Ming episode. He said that he was sorry but it will take generations to change the way his people treat women and girls and he strongly advised you not to raise the matter with Sheikh Abul or anyone else in Qatar. He actually said please don't."

In the late afternoon Penny buzzed through to say that Mr Conway from the Old Forge Garage at Tolbrite wanted to speak with him.

"Put him through, please Penny. Hello Will, Tim here, did you go to Long Ashton?"

"This call is on expenses, Tim, isn't it?"

"Yes Will, this call is on expenses. How did you get on?"

"I decided to road test a BMW that we had in for repair and took Gloria like you said and we collected the letters from your manager Joy Philips who showed us round the radio station."

"Good, did you find a road called Providence?" asked Timmy.

"Yes, and I had to be careful I didn't bang the exhaust getting into it."

"It was as bad as that, eh?"

"Yes, this call is on expenses, isn't it Tim? The old man can't mend cars any more but he can still read telephone bills."

"Yes Will, you're covered, why don't I have my secretary, the lovely Penny, reverse the charges to put you out of your misery?"

"Does she ever come down to Tolbrite?"

"Will, what did you want to tell me about Providence?" said Timmy.

"Oh yes, well I feel very pleased with myself. The Williams' house is at the top of the hill so I reasoned that any sensible murderer would come down the hill from the main road that crosses it at the top and escape up the hill afterwards. Since all the traffic is down the hill into Long Ashton's one and only main street, it seems that the police asked everyone if they had seen anyone going up and down the hill below the Williams' house and didn't ask anyone if they had seen anyone going down and up the hill above the Williams' house, are you with me so far?"

"Yes Will, I'm with you."

"We parked on the verge of the main road at the top and walked down the hill nearly getting killed in the process. We talked to the people in the houses above and below the Williams and struck gold in two of the houses above. One was a night shift worker who left his house at eight-thirty and drove up the hill to the main road at the top where he turned left for a place called Clevedon where he works. His headlights showed a dark coloured Audi parked where we parked today, registration Y something. The car was empty. He didn't tell the police because he was asleep in the daytime when they called and they asked his wife if he drove down the hill. When she said 'No', they closed their little notebooks and left."

"Well done, we must see if any of the players has a Y reg. dark coloured Audi."

"The next bit's even better, Tim. We found an old couple, Mr and Mrs Green who live next door but one above the Williams' house. She's an invalid and at night she sits in the bay window looking out with the light out. That night she saw a figure come down the hill at about eight-thirty and climb up the steps towards the Williams' front door. The figure stopped in a direct line with a streetlight further down the hill and the top of his head cut off some of the light. She then saw the glow of an opened door, heard what sounded like a car backfire and the man then walked down the steps and up the hill."

"Where he presumably drove off in the Audi," said Timmy.

"Yes, but I haven't finished yet, Tim. So I did an experiment with Gloria's help. While the old lady looked, I stood in the exact spot that the murderer had stood in, and had to be on a one inch plank to just cut off some light, well I would have cut it off if it had been lit. That means that the murderer's six foot one inch tall."

"That's absolutely brilliant, Will, well done."

"I told them that you'd probably write something and ask them to sign it. They said OK they would."

"It sounds to me that we had better write something together next weekend and then if you can spare the time, you should be the one to get your friends to sign them. Will the BMW still be in for repair?" said Timmy.

"Never under estimate the resourcefulness of a Commando."

"As if I could ever," said Timmy.

"There is one other thing. I asked the old lady and her husband, called George by the way, if she had told her story to the police. She said they didn't ask her. It appears that they came to the door and asked George if he had seen anything and he said 'No'. He said that his wife was an invalid and was asleep in bed so they said that they wouldn't bother her and went away."

"Sometimes it doesn't pay to be kind," said Timmy.

"If I could find the time to go to Long Ashton next week would it be on the same basis as this week, Tim?"

"Yes Will, I'll give you another hundred pounds. What a pity that so much of it will go in Income Tax?"

"What's that? Goodbye Tim, see you at the weekend."

Timmy buzzed Penny, "Did you get that Penny? Type it up and put two copies in my weekend bag."

"I'll let you and Helene have the copies tonight since you have to prepare statements for two separate parties to sign, remember?"

"I was only checking that you were on the ball."

"Yes I was. Don't you think that it'd be a good idea if I took the letters to Dorset to give to this commando at Tolbrite?"

"I'll tell Sid."

He called Joy Philips in Bristol.

"Hello Joy, Timmy here. What did you think of my friend young Will?"

"A bit of a rough diamond but he seemed to be quick on the uptake. How is it you know him?"

"It goes right back to my childhood. My brother and I were away at school and when we came home for the summer holidays we played on the family estate. There was this village boy who seemed to treat the place as his own and after a few skirmishes we sort of accepted him as a playmate. That was Young Will, so called because his father was the village blacksmith, Old Will. He taught me more than I can ever repay about the countryside and animals and how the other half live and we've remained friends ever since, more so with myself and Liz. David was nearly three years older and that's a lot when you're eight years old."

"That's nice," said Joy. "He phoned me before he went back to Tolbrite and said they they'd had some success with your letter."

"They did. I won't tell you why but for each of the following people, I'd like to know the colour and make of the car they drive and their height. Got that? What sort of car and the height of Betty Williams, Betty Williams lover and Sally Evans husband?"

"I've no idea who Betty Williams has been seeing, but I can give you her height. Betty, Sally and I are all about the same height, about five feet six inches. Betty drives a red Ford Fiesta and Sally drives a silver Rover. Sally's husband is big, he's over six feet and he likes fast cars," said Joy.

"Thanks, we'll have to think how to find out who Betty was with that night."

"I suppose the police will know, you could ask that Roger something who came to the meeting about the tapes," said Joy. "Come to think of it, he's very much like Sally's husband in build, tall and athletic looking."

Before he and Helene left that evening Penny presented him with two statements for the helpful people in Providence to sign. She had correctly extracted what was required from young Will's telephone report. Timmy read them aloud to Helene and said,

"You're a jewel, Penny, I hope Sid realizes it."

"I tell him often enough," she grinned at Helene. "I've volunteered to personally deliver these to young Will at the garage but Timmy won't let me."

"Penny dear, Timmy's protecting your virtue. Will lurks under the cars he's repairing until he sees a neat pair of ankles when he comes out and engages the owner of said ankles in cheeky conversation. Gloria, the barmaid whose father's the landlord of the village pub, keeps a close eye on him. There's really no harm in him and he'd defend the Hawkridge's to the death, which says a lot for both him and for Timmy's family."

The next morning Timmy sent for Sid Durant, his production manager. Penny let him in and hovered just inside the door. Timmy accepted this; she might as well hear what was said directly as extract it from husband Sid later.

"Sid, how are you getting on with the smuggled girls film?"

"It's nearly ready for you to see. I've got all the material and it's a matter of final editing and dubbing in the commentary."

"You've managed to find some video shots of small girls being brought ashore with their pathetic little bundles on an unnamed Arabian shore with skyscrapers in the distance?"

"Yes."

"And you've made sure that the background city can't be recognized because that could foul up our operation in the Gulf?"

"Don't worry Timmy, it looks like anywhere between Bombay and Port Said and it's ever so slightly out of focus."

"How does it run?"

"It starts with Ah Ming being thrown into Bristol Harbour, rescued and rushed to hospital. Then there are the attempts to get at her with mention of putting in the Securifirm guards because Liz recognized the danger. Helene under-standing her dialect and you figuring out that the girls might be smuggled in through Portbury. I've put in shots of Liz and Helene. We then go back to the beginning of the Ah Ming trail, the little girls on the beach, then typical Arabian households, then the port of Jeddah, then the Octavia Maru in the Bristol Channel and entering the Portbury Dock, then the doors opening and streams of cars emerging and being parked in rows in that vast space. You employ Confidential Enquiries Limited to photograph the car park at night and we show the shadowy figures emerging from the boots of cars which twinkle, and the boat on the dock and a white van driving away and arriving at the massage parlour in Stokes Croft in Bristol. We then show the police raid on said massage parlour and the men and girls being taken away. I've consulted the lawyers at every turn and I think we're alright."

"It's a shame really but for political reasons we will have to consult our friends in Qatar whether we should publicise the Hawkridge Media connection, otherwise we'll have to market it under another one of our names. Whether any UK TV channel will have the courage to screen it after there was all that bother about the programme about the Saudi Arabian princess, we'll have to see; but I'm sure there'll be a market for it in the USA."

"Will you clear it with the Bristol police?"

"At every step we've told the Chief Constable's staff officer of our suspicions. Since they raided the brothel they are now chastising the car company, the Port of Bristol and the ship owners, so the trade is shut down for the present. Helene and I went out to their headquarters at Portishead Down, and asked for information about the men who had been arrested, one of which was for an assault on Helene. He said that he'd do his best as a favour to us. What he really meant, I suspect, was a favour to my sister Liz who he fancies. His parting words were you're playing a dangerous game, my friend."

"He could be right, Tim, you'd better watch your back."

"I know, but somebody's got to stand up for decency and law and order. What do you think our grandparents would say if they learnt that there are now areas of our great cities where the police don't go but leave it to the gangs to sort themselves out and in so doing, terrorize and extort money from the ordinary people?"

Later in the day Timmy asked Bill Lawrence to see him.

"Did your experts make anything of the voice prints from those Bristol tapes?"

"Yes and no," said Bill. "The man who said that there was someone taking bribes in the Civil Engineers Department was certainly the Deputy Director who showed Joy's reporter round, which means that the man on the take is the boss man himself. So we looked at what major civil engineering work is going on at present and, frankly we can't see the well-known companies who are doing the work near Temple Meads doing that sort of thing. So it's possibly something in the planning stage and that could tie in with the men who are harassing the old ladies round the Old Market."

"It could give us a bit of a lead," ventured Timmy, "say that we go to him at his home and say we know he's the whistle blower. We explain that we will at all costs protect his identity but we need hard facts. We're after the property developers. That's who we need information about and if we bring them down and that brings down his boss, so be it, he won't be blamed."

"Sounds worth a try," said Bill.

"If I can find the time I might go down and call on him. What else have you got?"

"Well, we had to voice print Chuck, so we decided to voice print everyone at your Wednesday meeting including you and Helene and Joy and the policeman. It's not conclusive but there's a resemblance between the DCI's voice print and the whistle blower on the drug baron. I can't be a hundred percent sure but if he was trying to disguise his voice it would explain it."

"That's another reason to visit Bristol. It gets curiouser and curiouser as Alice might have said."

He and Helene compared their day's events over dinner. The only explanation they could see for the DCI's call, if it was he who had called, was that the official channels hadn't a shred of hard evidence against the man and the caller hoped in some vague way that the media could expose him. Timmy decided that on his next visit to Bristol he'd have a very private chat with the DCI.

Helene said, "Changing the subject, Timmy, it's time we went firm on our arrangements for Christmas and the New Year."

"Yes Angel, I've told my parents that we're going to your mother for Christmas and they fully agree that we should. They'll have Sally-Ann and the children and David if he's not on duty, and Sally-Ann's parents from the good old US of A. What we've still to do is to persuade your Mama to come to Tolbrite for the New Year."

"I can't understand why she's so indefinite about it, it can't be another man."

"I think that it's another woman, your old nanny, Matilde," said Timmy, "and she's silly, Matilde must come too, as her companion, mother said so."

"Mathilde won't be a nuisance, Timmy, she's a dear."

"If she brought you up, my love, she can't be bad. That's settled then."

"Just like a man. That's only the tip of the Christmas iceberg. What about the presents for everyone, have you any ideas? Has Sally-Ann told you what the children are having so that we can complement what they're doing and what about your parents? They've been so good to us."

"David usually drops a few hints about the children's presents. I've always been careful not to give them something better than their parents can afford. Father and David usually get a case or two of their favourite whisky and mother a few bottles of scent from Harrods. I also give presents to the staff from all of us. This year we'll have to include something for Sally-Ann's parents, the Maiers."

"Over the years your mother has probably always put you children and the estate first and herself last. She always looks smart and I can guess what an effort that must be. You can do your usual thing for your father and David but this year your mother doesn't get a few bottles of scent, I'm going to invite her up here for a few days and take her on a shopping spree. She won't know it but that's what it'll be."

"I think that's a lovely idea, Angel, but she's not stupid and she'll see through you in the first shop."

"Don't you believe it my love. I'll say that it's in preparation for our church wedding next summer in France, that sort of thing. She knows we can afford it. I'm more worried that she'll think that I'm being critical of the clothes she already has, hence the going to a wedding ploy."

"How do you know she won't simply put it away until next July?"

"That's where Claire-Marie comes in. She spends a great deal of money on clothes. You've seen her, she's beautiful and glamorous. In Tolbrite she'll look like a film star. Any woman seeing her will look through her wardrobe and put on the best thing she's got. I'm going to see that your mother's in the same league, it won't be Parisian but I'll see that it's the best value and style that London can offer."

138

"That's splendid, why didn't I think of doing something like that years ago?"

"While we're on the subject of Christmas, how are we going to get there and how will we come back and what about Mama and Matilde?" asked Helene.

"One thing at a time Angel. Although most of my headquarters staff will be on leave over the Christmas and New Year period, I must go into the office in the mid-week, say on the 28$^{th}$, 29$^{th}$ and 30$^{th}$ December. If we hire a plane we could fly over on the afternoon of the 23$^{rd}$ and come back on the morning of the 28$^{th}$. The plane could then go back and bring your mother and Matilde to Bournemouth on the 30$^{th}$ and take them back on the 3$^{nd}$ January or whenever they liked. Or they could come back with us on the morning of the 28$^{th}$ and have a couple of days in London, or you could stay with them and come back on the 30$^{th}$. Claire-Marie and Matilde can be our guests in England for as long as they wish, darling, but they must decide soon or we won't be able to book a plane."

"I'll talk to her when we get home and tell her that she's got to come to discuss the wedding arrangements."

"That at least is one occasion at which we should all be in one place."

Later in the evening Helene told Timmy that her mother would go for Plan B, to return with them on the 28$^{th}$ and spend a few days in London before going down to Tolbrite for the New Year. And she and Matilde would go home by Air France because she wanted to do some shopping in Paris on the way home. "Be sure and tell mother," said Timmy.

"I already have," she assured him.

The next day Penny buzzed to say that Mr Swift would like a word with him.

"Hello Mr Swift, what's new?"

"Good morning Mr Hawkridge, nothing much, I phoned to see if you have any more information about the situation in Bristol. It's the men behind the rotten trade that we want."

"No I'm afraid not, we must be patient. We're getting on with our TV film about Ah Ming and this slave trade, which includes the night time shots that Confidential Enquiries took. The script, which has yet to be dubbed in, mentions that you took the shots. Do you want the film to acknowledge your part or would you rather remain confidential? It's a difficult choice for you eh?"

"Leave us out of the finished version, please for the present. We can always admit that we did it if anyone asks."

"How's the Labgrove Estates paper chase going?"

"My young man who's getting friendly with the young woman in the office downstairs says that occasionally letters come addressed to Mr Andrews. The young woman sent the first one back *'Not Known at this address'* and a day or two later, Mr Awnsred told her that he would deal with any letters that came addressed to Mr Andrews. My man is now trying to find the origin of the letters that Labgrove Estates sends out."

"Any luck at Companies House?"

"Some, we find that a Mr S.A.Andrews is a director of a big building supplies company in Slough. I expect that we'll find that Mr Awnsred has the initials S.A."

"What next?"

"With your wife's help we're looking at the directors of middle ranking property development companies to see if they have any common directors with the company in Slough."

"Let me give you a very long shot, look for a firm started or run by someone called Hardwick or whose wife's maiden name was Hardwick."

# Chapter Fourteen

TIMMY and Helene took their usual route down to the Manor House on the Friday evening. They were hugged on arrival by Margaret and enjoined to hurry down for a drink with Daddy. The General kissed Helene and shook Timmy's hand. "Good to see you both, did you have a good journey down?"

"Yes Father but the traffic doesn't get any less. Is all well with you and the estate?"

"Nothing we can't cope with. We've got young Will Conway looking into the Vicar's heating, the Vicarage, I mean, and he seems to be making a sensible job of it."

"We wondered if he might be a good chap to make the official Mr Fix-it for the Manor House Trust," said Helene with a smile at her mother-in-law.

"Well he's done most of the small jobs that we've had done to date," said she, "and what's so refreshing is that he's always so cheerful."

"That's his training in the services," said the General, "never let 'em get you down."

The next afternoon Timmy and Helene walked across the park to the village and to the garage where young Will was leaning into the opened bonnet of a red Volkswagen Golf.

"Hello Will," said Timmy, "this is me, over here, stop looking at my wife."

"Hello Helene, if you ever get tired of him I'm always here," said Will.

"And tinkering with the lovely Jane's car too," said Timmy. "How is she?"

"Still stripping six nights a week at the Half Moon Club and staying the same nice girl," said Will. "She's well rid of that rotten husband of hers. Bye the way I'm pleased to admit that I was wrong when I told you that the man who killed him had been sentenced to twelve years, it was fifteen. They were all a rotten lot."

"As promised we've brought you the statements that we'd like you to get the people who you spoke to in Long Ashton, to sign.

They're quite short and the folk should raise no objections. Do you think you can get away one day next week to get them to sign?"

"We could do it one afternoon when we know the chap on night shift will be awake. The old lady will always be there, poor thing."

"OK then, here's your fee and expenses."

"You don't need to give me all that, Tim, it's only a small job and I sort of feel embarrassed. But not much, I hasten to add."

Helene grinned at him. "Take it while you can Will we're always grateful for your help."

"Well, if you force me," said Will.


Liz arrived mid-morning on Saturday. She was not alone; she had a passenger; a very scared looking Ah Ming. Lady Hawkridge walked down the steps and opened the car door with the Sergeant hovering protectively behind. Liz walked round from the driver's side.

"Come on Ah Ming, this is my mother and where I live, out you get."

Liz picked up a small bundle from the back seat and gave it to the Sergeant. "These are her total worldly possessions and they're what the hospital gave her."

"Is Helene about?" asked Liz. "Oh, here she is, thank God, Helene, please tell Ah Ming that we've arrived at my home and she's got nothing to be frightened of."

Ah Ming's face brightened as Helene approached and spoke with her. She climbed out of the car and stood submissively with her hands folded while Helene told her who these people were, Lady Hawkridge, the wife of the man who owns this house, Doctor Liz who you know and trust, she is the daughter of Lady Hawkridge, Mr Timmy who is my man and is the son of Lady Hawkridge and this is the Sergeant who is the boss servant.

There was a silence that threatened to become awkward. The Sergeant took charge,

"If I may, I'll take Ah Ming through to Mrs Holmes and we'll show her the room she might have and we'll give her something to eat, poor waif. If we need help I'll ask Miss Helene." With which he took Ah Ming by the hand and away to the kitchen.

"Poor little soul," said Margaret, "we must all seem strange to her."

"You have to realize that no one has ever been kind to her before," said Liz, "she's been abused in every way since she was a small child and is terrified that she'll be sent back to where she came from and the whole ghastly business will start again."

"What do you intend we should do with her, are you sure that she doesn't have to go back to Bristol with you?"

"Actually Mummy, she's been released into my care, thanks to the influence of Roger Hardwick, and she could stay here if you and Daddy don't mind. You don't mind do you?"

"It's all very difficult. The person who'll have the most bother is Mrs Holmes. It's not as if the girl speaks our language."

"If you have a problem you can ring Helene, can't she Helene?" said Liz.

"Yes. Ring whenever you like at the office or at home. If it would help we could take her back to Chelsea with us, but we are out all day and it wouldn't be as good for the girl as being here and having people about, even if they can't speak her language."

"I quite agree," said Margaret, "she shall stay here and we'll all do our best to see that she's not scared any more."

And thus it was that Ah Ming came to the Manor House.

On the way back to London on the Sunday evening Timmy said,

"There are four things outstanding. First, who murdered Chuck Williams? That's up to the police. Then there's the matter of the drug baron. I'm inclined to think that was a disgruntled employee having a sick joke, but I'll keep an open mind. Thirdly there's the harassment by the would-be property developer. Perhaps the alleged bribery of a top City official will give us a lead there and lastly there's the matter of a landlord or landlords who extort money from tenants. It must have been their thugs who scared off Joy's reporter and that could indicate that we've hit upon something serious."

"What do you intend to do about it?" asked Helene.

"We must go to Bristol one day this week to tackle the Deputy Civil Engineer. We'll see if we can find out who it is that's bribing his boss, if, indeed his boss is being bribed."

"What will you do then? I mean, how does that help us?" asked Helene.

"We decided the other day, my pet, that any bribery, if there is any bribery, probably relates to a development that will occur in the immediate future, like those sites near Old Market and we might find out, from the top down so to speak, who is really behind the attempts to get those old people out of their houses."

"What about the bad landlords?"

"That's a different kettle of fish, the very lowest level of crime, to extort money under threat of physical injury from poor people. It's a protection racket and we have to tread warily. They're the people who've been making threatening phone calls to Joy," said Timmy.

"You won't do anything silly, will you?"

"That's the problem. We need hard evidence and one way to get it might be to organize another phone-in specifically inviting people who are paying extra rent or protection money or the like to give us the facts with the same rules as before that they don't need to give us their names, just the name of the extortionist."

"Well, I don't think you should do anything about that without first discussing it with Mr Swift and Roger Hardwick," said Helene, "but having lunch with the Deputy thingamybob sounds civilized and safe. Anyway, I've decided that I quite like Bristol. What day could we go?"

"Let's plan on Wednesday, that'll give Penny time to rearrange my diary and Sid might have a rough cut of the smuggled girls' video. We'll go by train and get a driver to meet us."

"How do you know that the Deputy thingamybob will be in Bristol that day," asked Helene "and how do you intend to meet him. You can hardly arrange to breeze into his office and say 'about this bribery thing', can you? If he's home, do we wait until late evening to tackle him?"

"You're quite right we'll invite him to lunch and do the thing in a civilized way. Perhaps we should have Joy do the arranging, say that her chief was impressed with the recordings that Jeremy made and so on and that I would like to invite him to lunch at the Grand Hotel, would Wednesday be suitable? She could say that her chief will be instantly recognizable because he'll be with a stunning blonde."

"That sounds more like my Timmy. Flattery will get you everywhere and it might be a brunette, as well."

Joy contacted the Deputy Civil Engineer, a Mr Earnshaw, and he said that he would be pleased to accept Timmy's invitation to lunch at the Grand at 12.30 on the Wednesday.

Helene phoned Liz and invited her to join them if she could get away.

Thus it was that when Mr Earnshaw entered the dining room at the Grand he was confronted not by one attractive girl but two. He was elderly and Timmy judged him to be close to retirement. Timmy stood and made the introductions saying, "I know you won't mind my sister, Doctor Liz Hawkridge joining us, she's at the BRI."

"I want to thank you, Mr Earnshaw for the excellent job you did in helping our reporter make his programme about the work of your Department. We are so impressed that we're going to make a series about the work of other Council Departments."

"I was pleased to be of assistance," said Mr Earnshaw.

They ordered and the meal proceeded with the sort of general conversation such occasions generate.

"Good," said Timmy when they reached the coffee stage, "I want to talk with you on another matter. As a result of a phone-in organized by my Bristol radio station, we're aware that a number of old people in the Old Market area are being harassed into selling their properties by a company called Labgrove Estates. Someone acting for them uses strong-arm tactics and Helene happened to be at one of the houses when a man tried to force his way in and knocked the elderly tenant over. He was arrested and Helene will prefer charges if she's allowed to."

"That's terrible. One knows that such things go on but I never dreamed that it was taking place so close to home," said Mr Earnshaw.

"We've got agents in London who are investigating Labgrove Estates but the paper trail is complex and it occurred to me that you might be able to provide a short cut. Now at this point I have to assure you that you can trust us absolutely, anything that you say will never be attributed to you. I mentioned the phone-in that Helene and I conducted, and now we and my sister Liz, know that it was you who phoned-in and said that a senior member of the staff of your Department was accepting bribes from a contractor."

Mr Earnshaw gave Timmy a startled look and started to protest.

"Please don't get upset, no one will ever know but you'll appreciate that simple logic indicates that the only man this can mean is the Civil Engineer himself. What we want to know is the name of the company or person who is doing the bribing. It's them we're after, not your chief but, of course if they fall he might fall with them. I can see that it's not naked ambition that caused you to make your phone call but a sort of frustrated civic duty and I applaud you for having the courage to do it. Now, please tell us who it is."

"I'm surprised that you can think that I made such a call and even if I did, you promised anonymity," said Mr Earnshaw.

"There's no doubt at all that you made the call, Mr Earnshaw, voice prints are sometimes as good as fingerprints," said Helene, "and we're on your side, believe me."

"Well I don't know," said Mr Earnshaw "I don't want to be mixed up in a court case and that could happen."

"All that we want is to know who's behind these efforts to intimidate poor old people out of their homes, that's all and your name will never be mentioned."

"There are three companies who have shown an interest in developing two major sites in the Old Market area and clearly the one that owns the properties that must be acquired to free the sites for development would have an advantage. To have the active support of the City's Chief Civil Engineer would also be an advantage," said Mr Earnshaw.

"Which of the three has taken steps to ensure that it has the city Engineer's support?"

"A company that is new to this field called Gravlynch Consolidated."

"Thank you Mr Earnshaw, this conversation never took place."

"Isn't he the limit," said Liz "I make all sorts of promises to swap duties so that I can have lunch with these two and all they talk about is doing good deeds."

"Don't you believe it Mr Earnshaw," said Timmy. "This is the girl whose foresight undoubtedly saved a girl's life the other night and brought about the capture of a gang that was smuggling girls into Britain for prostitution."

"I heard about that on the news."

"That should give you all the reassurance you require," said Helene, "it was Timmy who had private detectives keep watch and film the goings-on at Portbury and he forced the police to take action but there was no mention of Hawkridge Media in the press, was there? So don't worry, all we wanted was that name."

"On your TV one day soon you may see the film we've made about the plight of the Arab girls which will include what went on at Portbury Dock. We're producing it but it may have a different name when you see it," said Timmy, "so please be reassured."

After lunch they went out to the radio station to discuss whether it was worth putting someone else in the Chuck Williams midnight to two a.m. slot.

Wednesday was an important day. Not only were Timmy and Helene in Bristol but the pair from Tolbrite were there as well that afternoon.

Will drove directly to Long Ashton and made the difficult turn into Providence without damaging the Tolbrite antique dealers Jaguar. He parked where he had parked before and he and Gloria walked down to the night-shift workers house.

Will rang the bell and the wife opened the door with a baby on her hip.

"Good afternoon. Remember us? We're from the radio station. We wonder if we could have a word with your husband."

She turned and shouted down the passage "Fred, there's those people from the radio want to talk to you," with which she turned on her heel and went into a room.

Her husband appeared, "What do you want now?"

"You remember last time I said that my boss might ask you to sign a copy of what you said, well, we've had it typed and here it is for you to sign, if you'd be so kind," said Will, getting breathless.

"Give it here," said Fred. He read the brief statement about seeing the dark Audi and signed it with a flourish.

They crossed the road to the house next door but one above the late Chuck Williams' house.

The husband opened the door. Before he could utter a word, Will said,

"We're not Jehovah's Witnesses, Mr Green, we're from the Radio, remember us?

A voice from the front room said, "Who's that George?"

"It's the people from the radio that came before."

"Well, bring them in here then, don't keep them standing out in the cold and put the kettle on for a nice cup of tea."

Will and Gloria greeted the old lady who was sitting exactly where she had been the last time they'd called.

"Hello Mrs Green, how are you today? You'll remember that I said that my boss might ask you to sign a statement saying what you told us the other day. Well, we've had it typed and here it is for you to sign, please."

"I remembered something else after you'd gone, didn't I George?" said the old lady.

Clearly George wasn't expected to answer and she went on,

"When the man who went up the Williams' steps turned his head, something shone or glittered for a moment on his left ear. I've thought about it and I'm sure it must have been a gold earring like some men wear."

"That's important," said Will "and if we'd known, it would have been part of your typed statement. Look, if we write it on the bottom you could sign it as well."

"I'll write it in my own hand," said the old lady and proceeded to do so in very legible script, signing both the typed portion and her manuscript addition.

Pleased at what he could see was an important item, Will joined Gloria and the old people at tea.

They made their excuses and climbed the hill to the antique dealer's car. Will phoned Tim to report the additional information. He then started the engine, stroked Gloria's knee, put the car in drive and made his way back to Tolbrite, stopping for an expense account meal en route, of course.

At the radio station, Timmy and Helene had found a very worried Joy.

"I'm sorry Timmy but these hate telephone calls are really getting to me. They're now mentioning my daughter's school and saying things like 'You wouldn't want anything to happen to her, so stop interfering in other peoples' business.' The calls have all been recorded when they come here but I'm now getting them at home."

"Have you told the police?" asked Helene.

"Yes, I mentioned it to the Inspector at the local police station and he asked me to let him listen to the tapes but, as he said, there's little that he can do until something happens and then it's too late. Hardly reassuring, with the school holidays coming up."

"Let me have the originals and we'll have the voices analysed to see if they appear on anything else we've recorded recently, it's a long shot but long shots sometimes score goals," said Timmy. "Meanwhile would you like some time off?"

"No, I'm better with something to do. I've arranged for a taxi to collect Petra from school and bring her here so that she doesn't go home to an empty house and in the school holidays we'll both be here all day and she'll have her dog with her to walk on the Down and I'll get one of the boys to go with her."

"How often do the threatening calls come?" Helene asked.

"Lately I've had one a day, sometimes in the morning, sometimes when I've gone to bed. I no longer want to answer the phone."

"Does the voice sound local and is there any pattern to the calls?"

"It sounds local. The morning calls come here and the evening calls are at home," said Joy." I've tried dialing 1471 but all I'm told is that the caller withheld their number."

"I'll have a word with Roger Hardwick, these calls must be something to do with the assistance this station has given them recently and they should return the compliment. Meanwhile we'll take the tapes and do two other things, one, employ Securifirm to put a man here and also keep an eye on your house and two, get Confidential Enquiries to snoop around a bit down here. Would you be happy to have a man? Stop grinning you two, this is serious."

"The answer is yes, thank you," said Joy. "Would he come inside or walk around the outside or sit in a car in the road?"

"I haven't a clue but it's probably a mixture of all of them," said Timmy.

"Well, it'll be a change to have a man about the house since Peter died," said Joy.

They had hardly finished when Helene's phone rang.

"Hello Helene, this is Will. I've been waiting for a chance to use your number. Much as I'd like to talk with you, I have to ask the dreaded question, here goes, Is Tim there?"

"Hello, Will, yes he's here, I'll put him on."

"Hello, Will, where are you?"

"Just leaving Providence, I've got some news for you that can't wait. When we went to the old lady who saw the murderer, she'd remembered something else, when the man turned his head something glinted on his left ear, she says like an earring."

"That's very interesting."

"I thought it might be important so I made her write it on the bottom of her statement and sign that too."

"Well done, I couldn't have done better myself." Timmy could have kicked himself the moment that he said it.

"We all know that Tim, that's why you need people like me to help you."

"Alright Will, tell me who's car are you road testing today?"

"The antique dealers Jag, goes like a bomb, will you be down at the week end?"

"Most probably, see you soon, goodbye."

To Helene and Joy "You heard all that, the old lady has remembered that the man had an earring in his left ear."

"So has Sally's husband," said Joy.

"Then on no account should we tell Sally, it could be fatal," said Helene.

"What do you intend to do with the statements that these people have signed," asked Joy.

"Give them to the police, I suppose. It's embarrassing because we keep doing or finding things they've missed. In the present instance, for example, we've got statements from people the police didn't interview because they were being considerate, the night –shift worker was asleep and the old woman was an invalid, so don't bother them."

"We might as well face up to it now and see if Roger can spare us a minute," said Helene. "I'm thinking more of Joy's threatening calls than the murder but the murder's the excuse for seeing him today."

"OK Angel, first I'll call Securifirm and then I'll call Roger."

## Chapter Fifteen

ROGER could spare them five minutes and they drove once more through the country roads to Portishead and on to the police headquarters.

"Good day Roger, I don't know if you'll like this but I had a friend of ours ask some questions of Chuck Williams neighbours."

Roger gave him a stony look that said meddling amateurs, and said,

"You realize that meddling in police enquiries could be a serious offence?"

"Our friend is not a private enquiry agent, just an ordinary citizen who went and spoke to some nice people," said Timmy.

"And he peppered Providence with copies of a letter from you," Roger said.

"Ah, so you weren't unaware of what we were up to?"

"No Tim. I was waiting for you to tell me if anything came out of it," smiled Roger.

"Our man used simple logic, the Williams house is close to the top of Providence, there's no space to park on Providence and few people come up to the top, so could the murderer have parked at the top and walked down?"

"And?"

"We also reasoned that your enquiries would be made by officers familiar with Long Ashton who would know that when people on Providence want to go anywhere they go down the hill and when they come back they come up the hill."

"And?"

"So we concentrated on the few houses above the Williams house."

"And?"

"Our man has got signed statements, very brief ones, from a man who saw a dark coloured Y registration Audi parked just round the corner at the top of Providence at eight-thirty that night and from an old lady who saw a six foot one inch tall man with an earring in his left ear walk down Providence at eight-thirty, up the Williams steps, down again and back up the hill."

"How long have you known this?" Roger asked.

"About the witnesses, for several days but what could be a vital piece of evidence, the earring, about an hour."

"Do you have any idea why these witnesses should suddenly come forward?"

"Look, Roger, you may not like this but they weren't interviewed by your officers. Your people were too considerate; the man who saw the Audi is a night-shift worker who was asleep when the police came. He was when my friend called, so my man went back in the afternoon. The old lady wasn't asked because her husband explained that she's an invalid. He didn't tell the police that she sits in a darkened bay window looking out most of the night. My friend asked the right questions."

"When can I have these statements?"

"Unfortunately they're on their way to Tolbrite. Would next week do or shall I have them sent to you tomorrow?"

"Tomorrow please."

"There's another thing. And here you can say that we've brought it on ourselves but it's still a matter for the police. Joy Philips my station manager at Bedminster Down is receiving threatening phone calls at the office and at home. We've always had abusive calls and some that threaten but these are different. They threaten her daughter as well. She has spoken to her local Inspector and all he could offer was sympathy and a promise that his officers would keep their eyes open. We understand his difficulties, so this afternoon I've arranged for Securifirm to place a 24-hour watch on the radio station and on Joy's house but I'd be grateful for police interest as well. I'm taking the tapes of these calls back with me to London to see what my experts can make of them."

"That's serious, I'd like to have copies of the tapes and I'll have a word with the local district officer and ask them to show themselves in the vicinity of her house and the child's school at coming-out time," said Roger. "You understand, I don't command anything bigger than this desk in my present job and I have to rely on other people's cooperation."

"We understand Roger and we're grateful for your help," said Helene. "We had lunch with Liz today, she was lucky to be able to get out they certainly get their pound of flesh out of the young doctors."

"I haven't seen her lately. I got the impression that she thinks I'm a bit dull, staid might be a better word, because I always seem to be deep in thought."

"I know they say that a copper's never off duty but you have to make the effort," said Timmy.

"The fact is that I have a personal problem that won't go away and even when I'm with someone as nice and, may I say, as beautiful, as Liz it keeps getting in the way. It's something that I alone can resolve and the time is coming when I can no longer duck the issue, it's the choice between my chosen career and the family business. There I've said it."

"Does it have to be as stark as that?"

"Yes. My elder brother had been running the company under my father's chairmanship and was due to take over completely next year but he was killed in a car accident some months ago and ever since my father has been on at me to quit the police and come back and take over the company. The MD of one of the subsidiaries is standing in and sees himself as the natural successor but my father's not too happy with the man and his pleas for me to take over are getting desperate."

"As I see it," said Timmy, "you have no choice. The police service will continue to run whether you're in it or not whereas your parents' company might not. In the long run would you get most satisfaction from being a Chief Constable, answerable in the final resort to a collection of petty politicians or the Chairman of a respected company answerable to whom? The shareholders? The family? Or yourself?"

"Since you started talking my brain has started to work," said Helene, "you're Hardwick Holdings, aren't you?"

"Yes, but I haven't exactly advertised it round here. The CC knows, of course."

"Well Roger, only you can decide and I see that we've taken up more than our allotted five minutes."

"Did Liz bring the Asian girl home?"

"Yes," answered Helene. "We left her there on Sunday with instructions to ring for translation services as required. So far I've had no phone calls but it's only three days."

"We really should go Roger, we've got to get back to London, Goodbye and thanks," said Timmy.

The driver of their hire-car consulted a timetable and took them to Parkway, Bristol's station on the main line from Wales where a train was due shortly and hence to Paddington. En route Helene and Timmy exchanged views on Hardwick Holdings, a large company with a finger in many pies, particularly in property, building supplies and construction.

Next day in the office Helene checked Hardwick Holdings and found that they owned ninety percent of Gravlynch Consolidated whose Managing Director was a Gerald White. She wondered if Gerald White was the stand-in that old Mr Hardwick didn't like. She phoned Mr Swift and told him. He said, "Isn't it curious, at the end of last week Mr Tim told me to look out for the name Hardwick, does he have a crystal ball?"

"I shouldn't say this about my husband, Mr Swift, but to be as successful as Timmy has been in building up an international business in such a few years, you need a dozen crystal balls."

"May I say unlike the Bouchier's, whose great wealth has been accumulated over many centuries," said Mr Swift.

"So you've been checking up on me. When I was a small girl living in my grandparents' chateau Bouchier, I heard an old Burgundian rhyme which roughly translated was 'Emperors may come and emperors may go but the Bouchier's go on for ever'. It will all be mine one day and I want Timmy and our children, when we have them, to love the place as much as I do."

"I'm sure they will but I'm trespassing on your kindness. I must get back to the paper chase."

"No, don't go, Timmy wants you to do a little snooping down in Bristol. Joy Philips the station manager has been getting threatening phone calls which have become much worse since we did that phone-in thing. We've got the tapes here for Bill Lawrence to analyse and we'll give you a copy of the latest in which her child is threatened. We've told the police and they promised to keep an eye on Joy's house and the school at coming-out time and Timmy's got Securifirm to put a 24 hour watch on her house and the radio station. But of course, that won't stop who's responsible. Timmy thinks a landlord or landlords are demanding extra money from poor tenants and using strong-arm methods to enforce it. They took exception to the phone-in and scared our reporter off when he visited the Council housing office. Timmy would like you to investigate."

"You know we don't do that sort of thing. Am I to take this as an instruction Mrs Hawkridge?"

"More a request I think. Please get the copy from Bill Lawrence and speak with Joy Philips and then we should meet to discuss what's to be done. For what it's worth, Bill will look for a voice match with anyone who's phoned the station in the past several months and we'll keep you informed. I'll tell Timmy and don't be surprised if he calls you but he's very busy."

She next called Lady Hawkridge

"Margaret, how are you getting on with Ah Ming, I haven't had any calls for translation, is she alright?"

"We are getting along famously. Mrs Holmes went through Liz's teenage clothes which are packed away in the storeroom, don't ask me why we kept them, and found some that fit her and she's been helping with the dusting and in the kitchen. We communicate in sign language. I've kept her away from Daddy because he tends to shout louder if people can't understand him. How are you both?"

"We're fine. We went to Bristol yesterday and had lunch with Liz. That wasn't why we went; Timmy had things to do, including seeing that policeman who, naturally, asked after Liz. I'll tell you all about it this weekend. Why I've phoned is to say that I would like your help in getting Christmas presents for the family, I'm just a newcomer and I need help. What we suggest is that you come back with us on Sunday and spend a few days helping me shop, if you would. At the same time we could talk about clothes for the wedding. I want Liz and Anne to be bridesmaids and David three a page. David two will be best man and he and the General will be in uniform, of course. I think it would be nice if my page could have a tiny uniform like his daddy's."

"Oh I'd love to come back with you and go round the shops it's so long since I've been up in town. I expect that it's all changed and all the places where I used to spend my dress allowance are now supermarkets or hamburger places."

"That's settled then. You decide how long you can leave the General and Timmy will see that you get back in time."

They met with Mr Swift the next day.

"The best lead that we've got to one of these landlords is centered in the Knowle West area in South Bristol," explained

Timmy. "This is an area which was once nearly all council owned houses. Many of the tenants took advantage of the measure that Margaret Thatcher introduced and bought their council houses and it's now a mixture of owner occupied and rented property. Many of the occupants of rented houses or flats can't afford the rents and the council makes up the difference, in many cases paying the whole rent. The law says that the money the council pays is to be paid to the tenant but many have been known to spend the money on other things and the landlord doesn't get his rent. So there is an arrangement under which the council pays the rent directly to the landlord. Unfortunately among the hundreds of good landlords there are a few rogues."

"What exactly do they do?" asked Mr Swift.

"They buy up property irrespective of its condition, do the minimum of decoration and repair, get the Rent Service to agree a fair rent and put tenants in. They   arrange for the council to pay the rent directly to them. They then ask the tenants for extra rent for services and if they don't pay, their windows are broken and wives and children are threatened. They then go to the owners of private property next door or nearby and undertake to provide protection from the rowdy newcomers at a price. If they don't pay, well you can imagine what happens."

"You want us to try and identify who these landlords are?"

"Yes, starting with the names that were mentioned in the phone-in and if possible, get evidence that could be used in court. The reason that I've chosen Knowle West is because our reporter was threatened almost as soon as he came out of the council housing office where he had been making enquiries. He was there ostensibly to record a programme on housing and asked who the big owners of rented property were and how many were paid directly, that sort of thing and bingo, when he came out there were two thugs waiting for him and threatened him."

"Did he tell the police?"

"Yes, it has been reported to the police," said Helene.

"What did you have in mind?" asked Mr Swift.

"The most direct way would be to have another phone-in to the Bristol station," said Timmy. "We would invite anyone who thinks that his landlord is charging more than the regulated or contract rent to phone in with no strings attached, and also anyone who has been threatened or paid money to avoid troublesome neighbours. The trouble with that is that it would render the station employees more liable to threats and physical attack."

"It's difficult to believe that we're talking of Britain in the twenty-first century," said Helene.

"The second line of enquiry would be to resume our probing at the council housing office but this time with a difference. Our man or woman asks questions and comes out. If nothing happens he or she asks questions at some rented houses. When the rough mobs arrive and start to threaten, the back-up team who have been photographing the encounter from a van move in and arrest the thugs. If I can arrange for a policeman to be in the back-up team, they get searched. Say that one of them has a mobile phone, we go back to the council office and make it ring the recall number and bingo we see at which desk it rings and we've got the inside man, that sort of thing."

"Do you have anyone in mind for this role?"

"Yes, Paula, and when the thugs move close she should scream and fall down as if punched, it'll make a better piece of evidence," said Timmy.

"Well, I'll say this, Mr Hawkridge you're never short of ideas, I'll have to think about it, it could be dangerous."

"Not half as dangerous as it might be for the staff of the radio station," said Helene.

Mr Swift phoned on the Friday morning.

"Good morning Mr Hawkridge, I've thought about what we discussed the other day and spoken with my people and we'd like to give it a go. I'll use three of the operatives who did the job at the dock, including Paula. When would you like them to start?"

"Good morning Mr Swift. I'd like your advice, I'm sure that you have more experience of the way that crooks think than I have. If you knew that the local radio station was asking your tenants to phone-in, would you be more likely or less likely to accost a troublesome reporter?"

"I don't know. A rational crook would realize that the game was nearly up when your station invited calls aimed at what he was doing and would start to draw his horns in but these people aren't rational and so I believe they would get even more dangerous and more likely to try to harm a radio reporter and radio station personnel."

"What does that boil down to, then, should I or should I not, have another phone-in?"

"If you want to bring matters to a head, go ahead with your broadcast."

"Fine," said Timmy, "it'll run for just one day with Helene and I taking the calls, she doesn't know that yet, and I suggest that our reporter and back-up go into action the next day asking the council housing officers if they heard the broadcast and whether they know if any tenant who they deal with called in, that sort of thing."

"When do you propose to do it Mr Hawkridge?"

"Helene must be in town with my mother the first three days of next week so I'll have Joy announce on Wednesday that the 0800 phone-in will take place between eight a.m. and eight p.m. the next day, Thursday, and your people can do their stuff on the Friday. Helene and I'll drive down on Wednesday evening and stay and see what happens on Friday before leaving for Tolbrite in the evening."

Timmy asked Penny to get Joy Philips; she buzzed him on line two.

"Hello Joy, I trust that all is well?"

"Yes Timmy, all is well with Hawkridge Radio Bristol, only the usual number of troublesome phone calls to report."

"That's what I want to talk with you about. We can't go on having you worried to death all the time and so I want to try to bring matters to a head by having a one-day phone-in aimed at people who think their landlord is breaking the law. I want the station to give it maximum publicity on the Wednesday, announcing that the phone-in will take place between eight a.m. and eight p.m. on the Thursday. Mr Swift and his people will be active the next day. Helene and I will man the phones all day on the Thursday and stick around on the Friday to see if we get results."

"That sounds alright when you live in London," said Joy, "but what if they attack us as we come to work and go home and what about our families? I've already been threatened."

"Would you like to take a week or two off, Joy?"

"No, I can't be away. Next Friday's the end of term and Petra's in the school Christmas play that evening. You've given us the Securifirm men and we'll be alright, don't worry."

"Good girl, I'll send you the announcement that I want you to make several times on Wednesday next among the local news items that you broadcast."

"Timmy, I nearly forgot. Sally's in a terrible state, the police have got new evidence and have taken her husband in, they said 'to assist them with their enquiries,' and won't let him come home. They suspect him of Chuck's murder. Did that young man who came here and went on to distribute your letter, did he have anything to do with it?"

"Yes Joy, it's all down to Will, he found the vital clues. It's a strange world, isn't it?"

They drove to Tolbrite that evening. En route Timmy told Helene what he had arranged with Mr Swift and Joy for the end of the following week.

They were greeted and hugged as usual and the Sergeant took their coats and bags to their room. They came down quickly for a drink with Timmy's parents.

"What have you been up to this week?" asked the General

"Nothing out of the ordinary, really, father," said Timmy

"Except that due to his machinations and with help from young Will, the police have now detained the man who killed the disc jockey Chuck Williams," said Helene.

"Young Will serviced the Volvo this week. The Sergeant says it's much livelier now. It'd be a pity to lose him," said the General.

"I don't think that the landlord's daughter would let that happen," said Margaret.

Helene turned to her and asked, "How is Ah Ming?"

"She's settling in very well. Mrs Holmes tends to mother her. Of course it's new to her but somewhere along the route she's travelled someone has taught her the rudiments of housekeeping and she's proving quite a help. I'd be grateful if you'd try to discover what she's making of us, when you see her tomorrow."

Saturday followed the usual pattern. Timmy worked at his papers and the ladies walked across the park. But before that Helene talked with Ah Ming.

Ah Ming was eternally grateful to be living in this lovely house with the English Lord and Lady and their boss servant Sergeant and his wife who were kind to her and had given her such wonderful clothes. She had never had clothes like these even when she was the favourite of an Arab man. She didn't want to be with men and would like to stay with the English Lord and Lady. She would like to do more things to show her gratitude; perhaps she could look after the lady's clothes. She didn't want to go outside, it was too cold and she would wait until the summer if the English Lord would let her. The English Lord had frightened her at first with his loud voice but the Sergeant had explained that he did this because he was a soldier.

Helene repeated this to her in-laws and to Liz when she arrived at teatime.

There was an early dinner on the Sunday before they departed for London with Margaret as a passenger amid fervent promises to phone every night, to take care and to return without fail not later than Wednesday in time for dinner. Liz left at the same time to return to Bristol. Helene had told her in the strictest confidence of the personal problem that Roger had; to choose between his career in the police and the family firm. Liz had no problem with that. Long live the family firm.

# Chapter Sixteen

AS Helene explained to Timmy afterwards, the three days that his mother spent with them were some of the happiest days yet. Margaret seemed to shed years as they revisited places she had known before her marriage and looked for things suitable for Christmas presents for the family. This would do for David three who was having a train set from his parents and that for little Anne who loved teddy bears. Who doesn't? Helene thought. Whisky would be fine for Daddy and David two. She rather thought that they had come to rely on getting it. This year they'll also get a case or two of Chateau Bouchier, planned Helene. For Sally-Ann let's get her something for herself, like a knitted suit, rather than something for the home or the children's room. What for Liz, she's more difficult, she's still got all those lovely clothes that Timmy bought her when she was at University College Hospital and lived at his house in Chelsea and acted as his hostess and party companion. Good old Liz kept the harpies away, thought Helene, but what can we get her for Christmas? Got it, we'll give her one of those satellite navigation things to put in her car.

Margaret said,

"We mustn't forget that the Maier's will be with us. I suggest that we give them something typically British that is small enough to go back with them as hand luggage."

"Fine, we'll look for something antique," said Helene, "and now the important question, What for Margaret? We also have to decide what the bridegroom's mother will wear at his wedding, undies, shoes, tights, dress and coat."

It took a moment for this to sink in,

"Oh, I thought that I'd wear my peach outfit, it doesn't clash with David's uniform."

"I'm going to ask my bridesmaids, Sally-Ann, Liz and little Anne to wear ivory dresses and I know that my mother will not wear dark colours, so Timmy and I want to give you two new dresses, one long and one for cocktails and coats and all the shoes and things that go with them. And it's no good saying No, Margaret, because we've made our minds up, all we have to do today is chose the style and light colour."

"Oh, I couldn't accept all that."

"Don't be silly, dear, it's your son and we're so very happy and want all those we love to share it. Come on now, we'll start in Beauchamp Place and I'm determined that you'll have at least one of your wedding frocks to wear on New Years Eve and I've got strict instructions to see that you get presents for the staff as usual and that includes Ah Ming," added Helene.

They decided that it would be nice to have a little party so that Margaret would have someone to chat with other than themselves so on the Tuesday evening they had the senior managers and wives to drinks and a buffet supper and Margaret was able to put faces to a few of the voices she had heard asking to speak to Timmy at Tolbrite, especially Penny who, Helene noticed, made sure that the other wives were included in any chatting group that formed. She really is a thoroughly nice girl.

Timmy came home to lunch next day and helped load a mountain of parcels and boxes into a hire car for his mother to take back to the Manor House with strict instructions that those wrapped in Christmas paper were not to be opened before the twenty-fifth. He said that they'd bring the heavy ones for his father and David and Mr Maier the weekend after next and Helene said that she would bring the clothes that had required slight alteration.

Margaret left for Tolbrite and they left for Bristol in mid-afternoon. They came within range of the Bristol transmitter just after they passed the junction for Bath. They heard the announcement about the phone-in, that the station would like to receive calls from any listener who felt that they were being forced to pay a landlord more money for rent than was proper and this included tenants who received some or all their rent as an allowance from the Council. The announcement was at pains to point out that callers didn't have to give their name or address, simply the facts about the money the landlord demanded and his name or his agent's name. The 0800 number, which would be open from eight o'clock in the morning until eight at night, was given and repeated at the end of the news.

Liz joined them at the Grand for dinner. She spoke of DCI Hardwick. She'd had dinner with him earlier in the week and mentioned that he seemed to have changed for the better; he actually flirted with her instead of sitting lost in thought. "Of course", she said, "he didn't know that she knew, but he seemed to be a man who had made up his mind about something."

The following morning they took a taxi to the station at Bedminster Down and at eight o'clock Helene was seated in the small room the undergraduates had used, tape recorder at the ready, awaiting calls, while Timmy discussed station matters with Joy.

The first call came at eight fifteen

*"Hello, is that those radio busybodies?"*

*"This is Hawkridge Radio Bristol,"* said Helene.

*"Well, keep your bloody nose out of things that are none of your business."* Click.

The next one came at eight thirty

*"Hello, is that the radio station?"*

*"This is Hawkridge Radio Bristol,"* said Helene.

*"Well, mind your own business if you know what's good for you."* Click.

Helene checked Bill Lawrence's phone number finder and both callers had withheld their number.

The next call was an hour later, a timid voice asked

*"Is that the radio that asked us to ring about our rent?"*

*"Yes,"* said Helene. *"Can we help you?"*

*"It's like this, see. I gets my rent paid by the council because I've got two kids and can't go out to work. My landlord, Mr Singh says that I've got to pay him another ten pounds a week for services like stopping people smashing the windows and things. I said I couldn't pay and next day someone smashed the windows and I've got them covered in plastic 'cos I ain't got money to mend them. They're passing the word around that anyone caught phoning you'll get done, you won't tell him I phoned, will you?"*

*"No, my dear, no one will know you phoned."*

She checked Bill's number finder and it said probably a public call box.

An hour later and one more person had called.

*"Hello, is this the phone-in about rents?"*

*"Yes, how can we help you?"*

*"I don't know if you can help but I'm being made to pay to live in the house I own."*

*"How is that?"* asked Helene.

*"We've lived here for nearly forty years. First it was a council house and then we bought it and became house owners and tarted it up a bit. Last year the old lady next door died and her son sold the house. The new owner rents it out and seems to put noisy and dirty people in it who cause a lot of bother to us neighbours. We complained to the people and that only made it worse. We complained to the landlord who said we could pay three hundred pounds to have them move to another place and we complained to the council and the police who said it was nothing to do with them. The landlord also said that if we will pay him twenty pounds a week he'd employ a man to keep the noisy people quiet."*

Half an hour later,

*"I rent one of the shops in Hartcliffe and have to pay a certain gentleman twenty pounds a week for protection against a gang of youths who mill around, block parking spaces and prevent people coming to my shop. One of my neighbours refused to pay and his shop window's been broken twice. Now nobody will insure him. I pay; it's that or go out of business. Now he's talking about putting it up to fifty pounds a week."*

*"Can you tell me who this man is?"* said Helene

*"We never see the big man, he sends his underlings but one of them did let slip that a Mr Singh would not be happy if we didn't pay."*

Timmy came in and gave her a cup of coffee

"How's it going Angel?"

"Calls aren't exactly pouring in but there have been two calls that have named a Mr Singh as a rent racketeer cum extortioner in the vicinity of Knowle West and somewhere called Hartcliffe."

"It's a start. Shall I take over for a while?"

Almost instantly the phone rang,

*"Hello, Hawkridge radio here, can I help you?"* said Timmy.

*"It's like this, the council pays part of my rent and I make up the rest. The council pays its part directly to the landlord who insists that I must pay fifteen pounds more than I should for services that he provides."*

*"That's illegal, what's your landlord's name and address."*

*"His name's Simpson and I don't know his address."*

*"That's also illegal. The law says that he must give you his address. What services does the landlord provide?"*

*"As far as I am aware, none, except occasionally someone sweeps the path."*

*"Thank you for calling. We'll look into it."*

The phone rang

*"You'll be sorry you poked your nose into things that don't concern you."*

*"Getting worried?"* said Timmy.

*"You see, you'll be sorry."*

Helene came back with a plate of sandwiches and two fresh mugs of coffee." It is half past twelve and I'm peckish, it must be the Bristol air."

The phone remained silent for nearly an hour.

*"Hello, is that the radio station?"*

*"Yes, can we help you?"*

*"I hope so,"* said a frail female voice, *"I spoke to you the last time and your lady came to see me. I want you to tell her that the man that knocked me down is back again, knocking on my door and banging things about at night. Tell her I don't mind so much now because I know you're after him."*

And thus it continued until eight p.m. when they summoned a cab and took the recording machine and tape back to the hotel for a late dinner and bed. Timmy smiled as she tucked her nightdress under the pillow 'in case the hotel catches fire.'

The next morning they were back at the radio station by nine o'clock and found the Confidential Enquiries team of Paula Simms, Fred Smart and Will Toms already there, awaiting the all clear to proceed with the council office ploy. Timmy gave them a summary of the twenty-seven calls that had been received. A number had been warnings to keep out, these might provide a clue when analysed, a number had been from people who felt that the rent they were paying was too high and a number had mentioned a Mr Singh and a Mr Simpson as bad landlords in the South Bristol area.

There seemed little possibility of getting the police to co-operate in what they planned to do. Ex-police sergeant Will Toms gave it as his opinion that police courts were rightly suspicious of this sort of sting operation and tended to give the accused a big benefit of the doubt, no matter how telling the evidence presented. Joy provided Paula with all the equipment of a radio reporter, a Hawkridge Media pass, a car with the station logo on the door and the names of the senior staff at the council housing office. Fred and Will would use their white van with video cameras mounted behind tinted windows. The plan was that when Paula came out of the council office, Will would be some distance ahead of her and the van would be parked between her car and the council office, wherever parking was possible with adequate camera angles. Fred would work the cameras. If the ungodly approached Paula, Will Toms would move towards them to be ready to help if required. Paula was reminded to keep her voice recorder switched on.

"There's one other place where they could expect to intercept me," said Paula "and that's back here at the station."

"True," said Fred "but there are probably more potential witnesses here than around the housing office."

"We could be wasting our time," said Timmy. "I'm as puzzled as you must be as to why someone felt it worthwhile to threaten Joy's young reporter when he made a routine enquiry at the council office. Anyone with a grain of sense who was in the extortion business must have realized that the game was as good as up the moment we asked people to phone-in and tell us about it."

"It's not uncommon for bullies to imagine that what works on small fry will work on bigger fry and come unstuck in the process," said Fred Smart.

"Perhaps that's the explanation. Judged by what happened to our radio reporter, the probability is that, if they do anything, the ungodly will do it between when Paula leaves the council office and when she drives off in her radio car," said Timmy. "Fred and Will's problem is where to have Paula park, to give them the maximum advantage for photography and the ability to come to her assistance if required. The closer she parks to the office, the more is the chance of having witnesses. Knowing you three, I'm not sure whether we want witnesses or not."

"I can answer that one," said Will Toms looking at his knuckles.

"We'll take the white van and have a look at possible parking places and suchlike and then come back and get Paula's car for the real thing," said Fred Smart.

"You had better wait until Joy has confirmed it with the housing manager," said Timmy.

Joy telephoned the housing manager in charge.

"Good morning Mr Humphries, this is Joy Philips of Hawkridge Radio Bristol. I phoned you a couple of days ago about one of my staff reporters visiting your office and you said OK, phone me when he wants to come. I'd like her; yes it's a girl, to come this morning. The reason for the urgency is that yesterday our station conducted another 0800 phone-in especially for people who feel that their landlords are making unreasonable charges. You probably heard about it."

"Yes, Mrs Philips I had heard what you were doing. The politest way I've heard it described this morning was muck raking."

"I hope that you corrected the less polite people, we are solely concerned that a son of Rachman doesn't exist in Bristol, a concern that I'm sure you share."

"Of course and we do our best to see that doesn't occur. Please remind me again what you're up to and how can I help?"

"We are making a series on the work of Bristol Council and some weeks ago one of our young reporters visited your office to get some background information on the work of the Housing Department. Because of our phone-in, housing has been given higher priority and I have to get more information in a hurry, so I want to send one of our young women to you this morning to put or get, whichever way you look at it, the woman's point of view. What time would is convenient for her to come?"

"Well, it's a bit sudden..."

"I did ring you two days ago, Mr Humphries."

"How about ten-thirty this morning but she'll have to be quick because Friday's a busy day?"

"Thank you so much, it's nice to deal with helpful people. Her names Paula Simms and she'll be with you at ten-thirty. Goodbye."

Timmy turned to the Confidential Enquiries team and said,

"You heard Joy go out on a limb for us. Mr Humphries is

expecting Paula Simms at half past ten and from then on it's all up to you. Good luck and remember that discretion is the better part of valour."

"Is that another of your crazy English proverbs? What does it mean?" asked Helene.

"I think it means if they're bigger than you are, run away," said Timmy "And, like most of our quotations it's probably a translation from the French."

"You needn't try to curry favour with us."

"Now that you raise the subject what's this about quote *your crazy English proverbs*, unquote, and us? Remember that not only was your father English, which makes you English but you're also married to an Englishman which also gives you English nationality, even if you do have a rather attractive French mother."

The usually calm Fred Smart had had enough of this small talk and was wound-up and ready to go "How long will it take us to get to this council office?"

"Ten minutes at the most," said Joy. "You go along the ring road, what I call the airport road, and after the second set of traffic lights take the next turning to the left. You can't miss the council office; it's a long, low, building on the right. You can park along the road. If it was me I'd go to the left where there's probably less passing traffic."

"That raises a question, I've assumed that what little parking there is at the office will be occupied," said Timmy. "If it's empty, does Paula drive in?"

"She must park in the road no matter how empty the office car park is," said Fred. He turned to the others. "Right then, we'll go off on our reconnaissance and aim to be back here by ten."

They returned at ten o'clock in high spirits. They had found the office with its car park full to overflowing and had selected suitable parking places, as Paula put it, just this side of the first speed hump.

Paula parked, locked the car and made her way to the council office. The white van was between her car and the office and facing away to allow photography from the back windows. She grinned at the invisible occupants as she passed.

She was taken to Mr Humphries and recorded a five minute interview on the work of the Housing Department which she found most interesting. Mr Humphries warmed to such an attractive and sympathetic reporter. "Is there any evidence of attempted fraud?" ventured Paula.

"Not possible," said Mr Humphries and explained the checks that his staff made.

"But the radio phone-in included several people who said that they were being ripped-of by unscrupulous landlords," said Paula.

"Unfortunately we might not know that was occurring unless the tenants came here and complained with evidence to support their claim."

"And you haven't had substantive evidence?" asked Paula.

"No, my staff is very keen on such things and would know if that was occurring."

Paula was given an escorted tour of the office and recorded everything that was said. She paid particular attention to the man concerned with rent allowances and repeated what she had said to his manager. He assured her that no tenant had brought substantive evidence to support an allegation of extortion. He explained that in many cases the council was not an interested party; it was simply a matter between a tenant and a private landlord. Paula pointed out that in all the complaints recorded in the phone-in, the council had been paying housing benefit.

After three quarters of an hour she thanked Mr Humphries for a most interesting visit and assured him that his comments would feature in the future programme. She left the office, crossed the road and walked up the short hill and turned left. Two men dressed in faded jeans, dark sweaters and donkey jackets with caps pulled well down on their heads were standing in conversation about ten feet from her car and Will was walking slowly along the opposite pavement. She walked on and as she came abreast the men, one of them grasped the shoulder strap of her recording machine and said, "You won't need that."

Paula reacted like any citizen, "What do you mean? Leave go or I'll call a policeman."

"Fat chance of seeing a copper round here, they know what's good for them," said the man with the brown cap. "You'll give me that radio thing and keep your nose out of it, if you know what's good for you."

"You're crazy," said Paula, "I've just been recording an interview on the work of that office, what business is that of yours. Who are you working for?"

"That's our business, give me that thing or else."

He lunged towards Paula who reeled back and fell to her knees screaming "Help! Help!"

Will came at the double, "What's going on?"

"You keep out of this Mate if you know what's good for you," said brown cap.

"Wadya mean," said Will, "you leave the girl alone." He half bent down, "You alright miss?"

"Help, he knocked me down and he's trying to steal my tape recorder."

"Police, Police," said Will at the top of his voice.

"Shut up you stupid git," said the one with the dark green cap and punched Will.

Will hit him in the stomach and the man collapsed groaning, his companion started to back away, only to be collared round the knees and brought down by Paula who seemed to be thrashing around wildly while on the ground.

Will made a sign to the white van that meant stop the cameras and went through the men's pockets. Sure enough there was a mobile phone, which disappeared quickly into his capacious pocket.

Paula regained her feet and helped Will restrain the men. Fred arrived with some cord, which he threw loosely around each man pinioning his arms to his side, saying, "I've called the police."

The distant noise of a siren heralded the arrival of the police. Will explained how he had come to the rescue of this young lady who had been knocked down by these two men who were trying to rob her. The men had then attacked him. Being an ex-sergeant in the Met, he knew how to handle people like that and he had used some cord that his friend had in his van to restrain them because they were violent.

A small crowd had gathered by this time. A woman in a blue apron with her hair in curlers volunteered,

"It was dreadful, I seen it all, this young lady was walking along when one of these men grabbed her satchel and punched her and she fell down. Then this gentleman ran up and they punched him as well but he gave as good as he got and hit the man and he fell down while the other man fell over the young lady, who was on the ground. Then this other gentleman came up and fetched a piece of rope because these two men were starting to fight again. Then you came ever so quickly, I must say." The constable took her name and address and walked across and checked that she would have been able to see what she claimed to have seen from her window.

Fred explained quietly to the constables that they were private investigators who had been hired by the radio station to keep an eye on the young lady because the station had received threats and the reporter who had come here before had been molested and threatened when he left. Hence the need to take precautions this time. He gave the address of Confidential Enquiries Limited and added that DCI Hardwick at police headquarters and other officers knew about the threats made to the radio station and its employees.

The policeman gave the three of them an old fashioned look, looked at Paula and said,

"Well, I like your bait. You'll all have to come down to the station and make formal statements."

"Is that the station we passed at the bottom of Kings Head Lane?" Will asked.

"Yes," said the policeman, "as soon as you can please, for I expect those two will be screaming for a lawyer the moment we get there."

They drove off and the small crowd dispersed with blue apron describing what she had seen for the umpteenth time.

Paula and Fred went back to the council office. Paula told Mr Humphries what had happened. He said,

"I wondered what all that noise was about."

She said, "Someone must have warned those two men that I was at this office. With your permission we want to make a small experiment, please come out into the general office."

None too graciously, Mr Humphries got up and led the way. Fred took out the mobile phone and after making sure that Humphries could see him do it, pressed the callback button. A second or so later a phone down the room rang. Fred put the phone in front of the manager's mouth and said "Speak."

"Hello," said Mr Humphries, "who's there?"

"Why, it's me, Peter Singh, Mr Humphries, what can I do for you, Sir?"

"Peter, please come to my room." He then turned to Fred and Paula and said,

"Before we go any further, I insist that you tell me what this is all about."

"When I was in here earlier," said Paula "I explained that Hawkridge Radio Bristol had received a number of calls from people who were being bullied into making extra payments for protection against strong arm merchants who made their life a misery if they couldn't pay. I asked if your staff had knowledge of this and was told by you and by the man you've just spoken to, that it couldn't happen. I completed my recording, which, by the way, is a genuine recording for the planned radio programme, and left. I was attacked almost as soon as I left. Unfortunately for the two men who attacked me, I had an escort and the men are now in police custody. The phone into which you spoke, fell from the pocket of one of the men and by use of the callback feature we know where the call that warned the thugs came from, it came from your man's number."

"I don't believe it. Mr Singh wouldn't do such a thing."

"No one has said that he did," said Fred. "All that we've established is that the call was made from Mr Singh's phone but I should tell you that several of the people who phoned-in mentioned the name Singh. I would have him in this room and one of us can ask him questions while you go out into the general office and ask if anyone else has used his phone in the past half hour. One of us will go with you in case someone says that you did, Mr Humphries. If they haven't then I would strongly recommend that for your own sake, you should send Mr Singh home without giving him the chance to use his computer terminal or access to his records."

"You've no authority to come in here making accusations against me and my staff. I'll do nothing until I've consulted my superiors."

"That's your choice, Mr Humphries," said Paula who realized that time was being wasted, "but you realize, of course, that if it is proved that an employee of the council housing office, your office, was associated with whatever racket is going on, then the council and it's lawyers may have something to say about it, especially if they have to pay damages to the folk who have been cheated." She went on,

"If you let it continue, for even five minutes after you have been warned, then the council will certainly be liable. As I said, it's your choice and you should note that everything that has taken place since we came in to your office has been recorded."

"What should I do?"

"Send Mr Singh home straight away and make certain that he touches nothing before he goes. Then get someone who is expert in the rent and benefits field to look at his work. I repeat, the name Singh was mentioned by several of the callers to the radio station phone-in," said Paula.

"I'll tell him that because some of the callers to your phone-in mentioned a Mr Singh, it would be wise for him to take the afternoon off." Mr Humphries suggested.

"As long as he is kept away from your records it doesn't matter what reason you give."

Humphries picked up his phone and asked his secretary to send Peter Singh in.

"Oh, but I can't," she said, "he's gone. He asked me to give you his apologies but he had an urgent phone call, it sounded as if it was from his father and he said he had to go. I saw him drive out of the entrance a few minutes ago."

Humphries hurried down the room and found a blank computer screen. "Never mind, our records are automatically dumped into secure memory each night so he can only have erased this mornings work."

"I wouldn't count on that," said Paula. "I think you'd better give us his address."

He buzzed his secretary,

"Give me Peter Singh's address, please, Sheila."

"He lives with his parents in Westbury Park, just off Durdham Down, here it is, The Larches, Royal Albert Road."

# Chapter Seventeen

THEY arrived back at Bedminster Down in high spirits having called at the police station and made their statements. Even the abrupt departure of Mr Singh might not be a bad thing if he disappeared forever from the present scene. Will handed the mobile phone to Timmy, suggesting that Bill Lawrence would be able to extract a number of telephone numbers from the phone's memory. Timmy could hardly believe that it had gone so well but Helene uttered a word of caution.

"A short while ago we were saying that we couldn't understand why a bad landlord would persist in using strong arm methods and threatening people after he had reason to suppose that enquiries by our radio station would virtually blow the top off his business. We thought that it would be more reasonable for such a landlord to quietly withdraw. This Peter Singh seems young to be a Rachman, could he be the son of Rachman, so to speak and could his disappearance this morning precipitate the departure of the father?"

"I can't believe that he would abandon what may be a large portfolio of property and simply vanish," said Timmy. "If he does it'll be an extraordinary change in behaviour, two hours ago what we assume to be his hirelings were molesting Paula. What I'd like to know is what did the father say to the young Singh that made him run? Was it the news of the arrest of the two thugs? Who told him? Did the police at Kings Head Road let the prisoners make phone calls?"

"If the father said leave at once, he must have something dramatic in mind," said Helene, "because if he intended to bluff the thing out, leaving his son in the council office would have been the smart thing to do, to make the authorities think twice about the questions that would be asked following a public prosecution."

"Yes, that's a good point, Angel. Let's not get carried away, perhaps the younger Singh's departure had nothing to do with rents and threats and was simply due to some small domestic crisis. Perhaps he's just having the afternoon off. In which case, why did he dump the computer data? The thing to do is to have someone go and talk with them."

"You can't be serious, Timmy, we can't do that."

"I am serious Angel, but I don't mean us. I think that the police will have good reason to talk with them after we give our evidence that Mr Singh has been responsible for threatening his tenants. I'll have a word with Roger. He must dread being told that we want to speak with him but, yes, I'll tell him the story, the least that the police should do is go to the house at Westbury Park and bring him in for questioning, if he's still there."

He telephoned the police headquarters on the number Roger had given him and was put through.

"I'm sorry to bother you, Roger, but there's something that I think you would wish to know. In our earlier phone-in and in the one we did yesterday, the name Singh came up as a landlord who threatened his tenants and demanded extra money for so called services. Some days ago we sent a radio reporter into the council office in South Bristol to make part of one of our programmes on local government. We're making a series. When he came out he was roughed-up by two men and told to stop asking questions. So this morning we sent another reporter but this time she was from Confidential Enquiries and had two male escorts nearby. When she came out she was attacked and pushed to the ground before being rescued by her colleagues who captured the two men and handed them over to your people at Kings Head Lane. One of her attackers dropped his mobile phone. Our agents wondered if the thugs had been alerted by someone in the housing office and if the phone could tell them who that someone was. So they went into the office and pressed the callback button and surprise, surprise it rang the phone of an employee called Peter Singh. While my people were talking to the manager, Mr Peter Singh took an outside call and made off in his car. The secretary said that she thought the call was from his father. He wiped out his computer memory before he went."

"You're going to ask me how the father knew that the hit-men had been arrested'? Hold on a moment." Timmy could hear a muttered conversation. Then Roger spoke again, "I can tell you that, they phoned a solicitor called Jones."

"I was also going to tell you that Peter Singh lives with his parents at The Larches, Royal Albert Road, Westbury Park," said Timmy, "and suggest that somebody should go and question him as soon as possible. The excuse would be twofold, the connection with the thugs this morning and the repeated mention of the name Singh as a threatening landlord."

"Both of those excuses are a bit shallow as far as prosecution is concerned but good enough to justify questioning, I think," said Roger "I'll ask the local station to bring him in for questioning."

"I'd bring in both father and son," muttered Helene.

"I heard that," said Roger. "Good morning. Helene and I think that's a good idea. There's nothing else that I should know, is there Tim, before I put my career on the line. Like you haven't already got your friend from the Tolbrite Garage asking questions at The Larches?"

"No I haven't, but the three operatives from Confidential Enquiries are here and if it would help, they could go and keep watch until your chaps get there."

"Thanks but no, I'll tell one of our patrol cars to bring them in now."

"Roger, Helene's making gestures, I'll put her on."

"Roger, what I want to say is that Timmy and I can't understand the Singh's behaviour. If they're intelligent they must have known that any extortion and protection racket would be blown the moment Timmy's radio station got on to it. In these circumstances a normal person would have drawn in his horns and hoped that the radio people would leave it at that. But no, they utter threats and send thugs to rough-up our people. The question is why do the Singh's think that they're fireproof or, put another way, what is so important that they have to hang on until the very last moment?"

"I get the point. Let us hope that we find some sort of an answer when we question them, Goodbye."

The police went to the large detached house in Westbury Park at lunchtime. Mr and Mrs Singh and their two grown up daughters were there but not the son, Peter. Mr Singh stated that Peter was away in his car and they didn't know when he would be back. He agreed to accompany the officers to the station after he had telephoned his lawyer, a Mr Jones, and arranged for him to be present.

At the police station the questioning went,

"There have been serious allegations that you or your agents have been demanding money for services from your tenants with real or implied threats that things will be made difficult for them if they don't pay. What have you got to say?"

"That is completely ridiculous .I don't have any tenants," said Mr Singh.

"You can't expect anyone to believe that you have no tenants in your properties?"

"I don't own any property other than the house my family lives in," said Mr Singh.

"You understand that we can check-up on this at the Land Registry, don't you?"

"You can check wherever you like, I have no tenants and I haven't threatened anybody."

"Who does own the flats and houses which the tenants know as 'Mr Singh's properties'?"

Mr Singh remained silent and when pressed, his solicitor intervened, to state that his client declined to answer the question; the disposition of the family estate was, he understood, not a matter of police enquiry.

"Does any member of your immediate family, and by this I mean your wife, son and two daughters, own any property occupied by tenants in the Bristol area?"

Mr Singh declined to answer.

"Your son Peter is employed by Bristol Council in its housing department. It would be a matter of great concern to the council and perhaps a matter that would come before the courts, if one of its housing department employees was found to be the owner of a number of properties whose tenants were in receipt of housing benefit, approved by that office, perhaps by that employee himself. Does your son own the properties?"

Mr Singh declined to answer.

"The facts now in our possession suggest that either you or your son engaged two men to threaten and molest agents of Hawkridge Radio Bristol who were making enquiries at the council housing office at which your son works. These two men, Russell Stanley Knowles and Frank George Howorth, are in custody and have made statements. No, Mr.Jones, we are not prepared to give you copies of those statements at the present time. What we require from your client is a statement of what he said to his son in the phone call that he made to him at about 11.45 this morning which caused his son to drop everything and run and where is his son Mr Peter Singh, at the present time?"

Mr Jones indicated that his client declined to answer.

"Very well, Mr Singh, there is no point in continuing this discussion. We will need to question you again when your son Peter is available and meanwhile you should not leave the neighbourhood."

Mr Singh, senior, and his lawyer departed.

Late that afternoon, DCI Roger Hardwick told Timmy and Helene the outcome.

"When they found that Peter Singh was not at The Larches, my officers had checked up on the registration numbers of the cars parked in the grounds. We checked these numbers with details of the four cars registered with the DVLA in the Singh name at that address and got the number of the missing car so that while we were being stone-walled by Singh senior, police forces were already looking for Singh, junior. They caught him at Heathrow, complete with his luggage, checking in for an Air India flight to Bombay. They're bringing him back at this moment. The customs officers and airport police nearly died when they found that one of his big suitcases was stuffed full of £20 and £50 notes and high value Euros. It'll take them all night to count it and it opens up the possibility of money laundering, but as you said at the outset, what did they think they were doing?"

Timmy thanked Roger for keeping them in the picture and said that he hoped that would be the end of the more vicious threats that the radio station and Joy Philips had been receiving. He told Roger that they were going down to Tolbrite for the week end and Roger said that he didn't know if Liz would be there, he was taking her to the theatre on Saturday evening.

They had earlier thanked Mr Swift's trio for their help and wished them God speed for their journey back to London. Now they said goodbye to Joy with the hope that there would be no more nasty phone threats and set off past the police station where they hoped that Knowles and Howorth were still being held, to join the A37

South into Somerset and Dorset, with Helene driving and Timmy distracting her in the nicest possible way.

Helene observed,

"Daddy had an Admiral friend who worked in the Ministry of Defence offices in Bath and moved to a village near Glastonbury some months before he was due to retire. He said that he had to learn to add half an hour sheep-time to his journeys in case someone was driving them from field to field along the road he was on. I hope that doesn't happen to us, well, I don't mind the delay it's just that I'm always sorry for the sheep, being prodded along and frightened. Would you still love me if I became a vegetarian, Timmy?"

"Angel, I'd still love you if you became a Confucian."

"Idiot, I mean not eating meat and things made from meat."

"Like what?"

"Well, I don't know; sausages?" ventured Helene.

"Your culinary education has serious gaps in it, Angel, if you think that there's any meat in a British sausage."

"Well, mincemeat, then, the stuff they make mince pies from," laughed Helene.

Somewhat later Helene raised the matter of the list of subjects raised in the original phone-in.

"Timmy, are you awake? You remember the list of possible offenders that we drew up following the month long phone-in, well, apart from the car thieves, most of the offenders have been dealt with, by that I mean that the police are dealing with them, all except the property developers who want to empty the houses around Old Market."

"True, my love, and in all cases we may modestly claim to have had a hand in it," said Timmy, mockingly.

"I'm being serious, there were the girl smugglers, I mean the smugglers of girls, the drug smugglers who are probably the same people, the Civil Engineer-who has still to be publicly unmasked, and the bad landlords. That only leaves the property developers and who's behind them, and we've got Mr Swift working on that."

"You missed out Chuck's murder where our man from Tolbrite provided the vital clues."

"True, I leave things out solely so that my lord and master can score his little points."

"Talking of little points, Angel, did I ever…"

"Stop it Timmy or we'll have a crash, there's a proper time and place for everything."

They arrived at the Manor House and were hugged by Margaret "I know that you've been in Bristol, in fact two people have told me so, your secretary Penny, such a delightful girl, and Liz."

"Another delightful girl," smiled Helene.

"Yes, she told me that you'd had dinner together on Wednesday and that she may not be down this weekend."

Helene and Timmy exchanged a private smile.

"Run along and change, it's lovely to actually have you here in time for dinner."

They changed and came down to say hello to the General. Helene kissed him and asked after his health and he, for his part, marveled that she had come into all their lives. They went into dinner shortly afterwards and to their surprise found Ah Ming helping the Sergeant serve. Over coffee Margaret told them of the remarkable progress the girl had made and her evident happiness to be of service. The Sergeant and his wife had taken her out in the car a few times and she no longer cringed at the sight of other people.

Before they went to sleep Timmy downloaded the e-mail that Penny had sent and had a brief look at the mail that she had forwarded by courier. Another pile would arrive in the morning.

"Timmy, darling," said Helene, nestling in his arms "do you think that Liz could be serious about Roger?"

"I don't know, Angel," said Timmy unconsciously stroking her naked body, "it's always difficult to tell with our Liz, I'm sure that she'd like to like him, if you see what I mean."

"No, I don't."

"You don't what?" said Timmy.

"See what you mean, oh, that's nice," said Helene.

"I could make it even nicer if you'd only stop talking about Liz and Roger."

"I was only wondering if she was serious."

"Doctors are always serious," said Timmy. "You've seen them on the TV looking grave and saying 'I'm sorry Mr Smith but your wobbly leg's serious.' The only time they smile is when a pretty nurse passes by."

"You're not being very helpful, are you?"

"I thought you liked me doing this."

"I'm not talking about what you're doing, I'm talking about, oh I give up, kiss me darling."

Saturday morning Timmy worked and Helene and Margaret, walked across the park to the village.

"You've no idea what a difference the Trust Fund's made," said Margaret "I realize now that inside me I   subconsciously dreaded coming into the village or going to the farms in case some unfortunate tenant drew my attention to their leaking roof or broken fences and I think that David felt the same.  Now we can at least look them in the eye and promise that something will be done."

"Yes, I've noticed that the General is out and about around the estate more these days."

"And he's adopted young Will, he takes him around at least once a week and asks his advice about repairs to farm machinery and buildings," said Margaret,   "I think   he's well on the way to accepting the suggestion you made some weeks ago that Will could be the Trust's Clerk of Works."

"We told you that we used him recently in Bristol and he unearthed the evidence that will probably convict a murderer, didn't we?" asked Helene.

"Yes, the more I hear about him the more impressed I am."

When they passed the Old Forge Garage young Will was engaged with a customer and they were spared the wolf whistle. Helene was just a little disappointed and she suspected so was Margaret. They stopped at the Cosy Tea Room and were fussed over by the misses Roberts. "Was Miss Elizabeth home this weekend, such a sweet girl and a doctor in a Bristol hospital, of course the sisters had seen that she was clever even when she was a tot and they had taught her in the village school…. Two teas, wasn't it?"

"No, Daisy, two black coffees."

In the chatter Margaret learned that "old Mrs Hardy had had a fall and was housebound and her daughter couldn't get there every day being in Salisbury and the neighbours were doing what they could."

They called at old Mrs Hardy's cottage on their way home and ascertained that she had food and milk.  Helene brought some firewood in from the pile down the garden and noticed the WC at the bottom of the garden. She knew that all the cottages were scheduled to get a bathroom in the next two years and made a mental note not to enquire about the old lady's temporary sanitary arrangements.

As they passed the garage there was a low whistle from beneath one of the cars. All was well in the world.

On their return Margaret had a quiet word with Timmy.

"Timmy dear, I'm embarrassed at that enormous pile of presents that I brought back from London, doubly embarrassed really because I was there and perhaps I should have hinted to Helene how much of your money she was spending on us."

"You're wrong on all counts mother, we want you to have all that you want and it wasn't my money that Helene was spending, it was her own."

"Well, I should have stopped her anyway."

"She'd have been very hurt if you had. Look Mother, I didn't know this until I married her but Helene's got more money than I have and has a whole lot more to come. Her mother's family own big estates and property in Burgundy. When her grandparents died they left Helene a quarter of their estate and the rest to her mother. Then there's great uncle Philipe, who owns a lot more of Burgundy and Helene's his heir too. So you see you shouldn't worry."

"Aren't we lucky Timmy, despite all that money, she's such a sweet person."

"You do appreciate the implications of Helene's family estates, don't you?"

"What implications?"

"I haven't discussed it with Helene but our children will be the heirs to the Bouchier lands and vineyards as well as Hawkridge Media and we'll have to bring them up to be totally at home in both countries, fluent in the languages, idioms, culture and customs of England and France, like their mother."

"With one son married to an American girl and the other married to a French girl, no one can say we're not doing our bit for international relations, can they?"

Helene knew with certainty that their afternoon walk in the Manor House Park would finish up at the Tolbrite Garage.

"Saw you this morning," said Will looking at Helene.

"I know, we heard you," said Helene.

"Well, you could've stopped to pass the time of day, seeing as your husband wasn't with you."

"Good day Will; this is me, over here, I'm Tim, her husband, remember?"

"Oh, hello Tim, how's things, did they arrest anyone for that murder?"

"Yes, they arrested the husband of Sally, Chuck's TV producer, because of the evidence you provided," said Timmy. "When they searched his garage they found the murder weapon hidden in a tool box."

"Makes you think, doesn't it? You know what I mean. Perhaps the murderer is a nice guy and the man he shot was a rotter, stealing his wife and wrecking his life. Did you hear that, I'm a poet as well as a detective?"

"You're a man of many parts, young Will," said Helene. "How's Gloria?"

"I'll let you into a secret but you mustn't tell, on pain of death like we used to swear when we were kids in the Long Wood, and that includes you, too, Helene. I used some of that money you gave me to buy an engagement ring for Gloria's Christmas present."

"Oh Will, we're so pleased for you both."

"Well it was those things I've done for you in France and Bristol where I took Gloria, like you take Helene that sort of made up my mind. She's nice to have around," said Will, grinning, "and she thinks I'm wonderful."

"Don't ever lose your modesty, will you young Will," said Timmy. "I'm told you've been helping my parents on the estate. Thanks."

"It's a pleasure to work for them. What I can't do myself I get reliable people for them and see that they're not being ripped off by some Bournemouth or Dorchester cowboy builder."

"Please keep it up and remember, if you need help ring us. We won't be here for Christmas we're going to spend it with Helene's mother in France but we'll be here to drink your and Gloria's health at the New Year. Remember, if you need help, ask."

# Chapter Eighteen

MARGARET took her nightly telephone call from Liz and came back to say that Liz would, after all, be down for lunch on the morrow and would like to bring Roger Hardwick.

When the family party returned from church the following morning Liz and Roger had already arrived. Liz introduced Roger to her parents and the Sergeant and explained that she had done a swap of duties and would have to be back in time to go on duty at 10 p.m. The General remarked that it was the same in the services when a man came home on leave, the first question anyone asked was always 'When are you going back?'

Liz took Roger for a walk in the park. From his favourite spot in his study over the main door the General could see them as they crossed the river towards the Long Wood. Some time later they came back and then made their way out of sight as she took him down the back drive. They reappeared some long time later coming up the main drive with red cheeks from the winter wind and the exertion of the walk. He wondered if Liz had been showing her policeman where the vicar's wife had found that fellows body.

They joined Timmy and Helene in the library.

"He's as bad as you are Timmy," said Liz "before I was allowed to pick him up this morning he had to check up on his crooks."

"They're Tim's crooks as much as mine," remarked Roger.

"Then tell us how they all are," said Helene who some time ago had pointed out to Timmy that you don't get anything unless you ask.

"It's difficult to know where to start."

"Your officers had questioned Mr Singh senior, arrested Mr Singh junior at Heathrow with a suitcase full of banknotes which your officers were counting and you had two men in custody for assault," said Timmy.

"I'll start with none of those, or rather I'll start with the Singh family's property. You remember that Mr Singh senior stated that he owned no rented property. Well, that's true. We managed to get the Land Registry to check late on Friday and it appears that the family own twenty-two housing units made up of eight houses divided into two flats and six houses. Each daughter owns four of the two-flat houses and the son owns the six separate houses. The parents own the house they all live in."

"We'll have to think about the reasons they choose to do it that way, could be death duties, marriage dowries or something much too subtle for the western mind," said Helene.

"Next. There's the money. The closely packed notes were £20 and £50, thousands of them, with a few 100 Euro bills, totalling roughly £360,000. We know what the Singh's were doing with this money; they were taking it to India. The question is, why? Was it to remove it because it's evidence of wrongdoing? If so, what wrong doing?"

"It's the money they extorted from those poor people in rents," ventured Liz.

"It can't all be that, kitten," said Timmy, "it's far too much. Think about it. Say that each property is let at £100 a week with the tenant responsible for all the outgoings, council tax, water, electricity, gas, repairs and so on, that's £2,200 a week gross income." He took out a pocket calculator. "That's £114,400 a year. But the landlord has to pay for insurance so the gross income becomes, say, £110,000. But they have to pay income tax and here the divided ownership shows to advantage since no share gets much into the 40 percent zone, if at all. Assuming that each Singh daughter and son pays the tax due, then the net income after tax can't be more than about £90,000 and remember this is with the landlord paying nothing towards the repair and upkeep and no repayment of any loan or mortgage on the properties, all highly unlikely. From this we have to deduct the family's living expenses, the house at Westbury Park, four cars, and so on, say about £600 a week, which means that the money in the suitcase would represent something like six years profit from renting and it's hardly likely that they would sit on a pile of cash that long."

"They probably fiddled their income tax," said Liz.

"Then it would be five years net income," said Helene.

"So the question that Mr Singh and his lawyer must answer," said Roger, "is 'where did this money come from?' This was put to Singh junior the moment we had him in for questioning but he refused to answer. We would have liked to keep him incommunicado for the whole weekend but he started screaming about his rights and racial discrimination so in the end we had to tell Mr Jones the lawyer that we had him. We're checking against the numbers of notes known to be stolen, of course."

"Where did the money come from?" said Liz. "Drugs spring to mind but if it is, you bet there are at least four people between the Singh's and the actual drug dealer."

"My guess is that it's from some sort of protection racket," said Helene.

"We haven't told the two muscle-men, Knowles and Howorth, that we've caught Singh junior," said Roger. "We told them, quite truthfully on the Friday afternoon, that he had run away. This led to an outburst by Howorth about not trusting our brethren from the sub-continent and a statement that they hadn't meant to harm the girl. By the way, your people were lucky. Knowles had a vicious knife in a leg sheath. They then admitted that Singh senior was the one who told them which tenants to rough-up to get the extra rent. We made them sign statements to that effect, so when he comes in to see his son tomorrow, we'll hold him on a charge of extortion and inciting threatening behavior."

"There are two things that puzzle me and if we can understand those, they might give us the answer," said Helene. "Why did he wipe out the computer memory and where did the 100 Euro notes come from, they're not forgeries, are they?"

"Oh God, not that again," said Timmy. "Anyone for Blandford?"

"Just because we unmasked a forger there in the autumn doesn't mean that they're all there my sweet," said Helene. "Ask Liz, she scoured the country for forger's ink last time and everybody had some."

"I don't think we can usefully take this much further, we must rely on Roger's chaps to look at all the things we've thought of and a lot more," said Timmy.

"Not so fast my pet, think about the two puzzle items that I mentioned, the computer and the Euro notes," said Helene. "Clearly there was something in the computer that they couldn't risk discovery. Say that they had created several phantom tenants for each flat and house. They complete the documents; remember there are five people in the Singh household with different handwriting, and Singh junior inputs the data into the computer with the rent payable to the landlord, one of the three Singh children. He doubtless found a way to input these data into the computers of whichever council housing office dealt with each house and those computers would input the Council finance department computers which would then pay the rent to the named landlord as a matter of routine until told otherwise."

"How would he get the signed documents into the files of the housing office dealing with houses outside the Bristol South area office without drawing attention to them?" asked Liz.

"I haven't the slightest idea. Perhaps there are a lot of files that pass between the various offices and he simply slipped them into one of the bundles or perhaps he didn't bother at all. I've got a nagging worry about how long they expected to be able to get away with it, because inevitably someone would have raised an innocent question and their house of cards would have come tumbling down," said Helene.

"Which, of course, your phone-in and subsequent enquiry at the housing office threatened to do," said Roger.

"How do you account for the Euros, Angel?" asked Timmy.

"Logic suggests that the Singhs wouldn't take Euros in payment for something unless they absolutely had to and it follows that the person making the payment only had Euros."

"Or the Singhs exchanged them for sterling at a profit," said Liz.

"Could be the same thing," said Helene, "perhaps the person with the Euros had no choice. Perhaps they were lodgers living in one of the flats or houses. Now who fits the bill, only got Euros, can't go out to change money and accommodated in a hovel? Why, illegal immigrants."

"We had a number of callers in the phone-in who complained about illegal immigrants, didn't we?" said Timmy. "We've probably got the phone numbers which may give a lead to the locality."

"I have to hand it to you two. It could well explain the large sum of money in the suitcase and where it came from," said Roger, "what would you suggest we should do next?"

"In the time available to him, Singh junior probably had insufficient time to wipe out his illegal entries in the other area housing office computers and the finance department machine," said

Timmy. "First thing tomorrow your officers should go to the finance office, tell them your suspicions and have them sort out all benefit payments in the name of Singh with a cross check on payments relating to the addresses of the sixteen flats and six houses and just for luck, all payments to The Larches, Westbury Park. On no account must you let Singh junior get near to a computer that's connected to a telephone line."

"Perhaps the daughters are computer whiz kids as well," said Helene.

"Let's hope that Indian culture doesn't encourage that," said Liz.

"What about all the call-centres in India?"

"What about the possibility that there are flats full of illegal immigrants," said Timmy, "who are all paying rent and perhaps hush money to the Singhs. What'll you do about that?"

"We've got a section that deals with illegals and I'll give them the addresses of the Singh properties. Ideally I'd like to keep them all under observation to establish which ones have illegals and then swoop on them all at the same time because you can bet that there's a Bristol Kurd network or an Afghan network or a Bosnian network or what have you," said Roger, "and an army of oddball lawyers ready to come out of the woodwork to defend their human rights."

"I don't know how long it will be before the residents of the Singh flats and houses learn that their landlords are under police examination and I don't know how fast your people work but would it be worth getting Mr Swift's agents to snoop around a bit before you signal the off?" asked Timmy.

"Having regard to the likely neighbourhoods I think that it would be wiser to leave things to the uniform branch who can call up the heavy squad if need be," said Roger. "Thanks all the same."

They were quiet for a few moments, each busy with his or her thoughts. Then Timmy said,

"Look Roger, there's something you should know and before I tell you, I ask you to trust us."

"Sounds ominous," said Roger.

"You'll remember our month-long phone-in. One item that came up was several old people in the Old Market area claimed that someone was trying to get them out of their houses and when Helene investigated she was pushed about by a thug."

"Yes, I remember," said Roger.

"We had a separate line of enquiry from the phone-in about a city official who was accepting bribes," said Timmy, "and we now know for a certainty that the official is the City Civil Engineer but we have no evidence at the present time other than the statement of someone who claims to know."

"Oh, yes, I remember, I was there when you had that nice man to lunch at the Grand and promised him that you wouldn't tell anyone," said Liz.

"True, but I haven't told Roger who our informant is, have I?"

"No, I suppose you haven't," grudgingly.

"The vital piece of data from that enquiry is that the firm doing the bribing is Gravlynch Consolidated in which Hardwick Holdings have a ninety percent share," said Timmy. "You can see how embarrassed we are about that."

"Not half as shocked and embarrassed as I am at this moment," said Roger.

"We're interested in two things, they may both lead to the same place or it could be that two different agents have a hand in what's going on. They are who is responsible for harassing the old tenants and who is handing out bribes to council officials? Shall I go on?"

"Of course," said Roger.

"Starting with the harassment. The firm sending letters to the tenants is Labgrove Estates with an accommodation address in Portman Square, manned, if that's the right word, by a girl who knows nothing about Labgrove Estates. But the building is owned and lived in by a Mr S.A.Awnsred who has told the young lady not to return any letters that arrive for a Mr S.A.Andrews but to give them to him to deal with."

"Not very original, but I suppose that they never think anyone will look," said Roger.

"We're using Confidential Enquiries on this," said Timmy. "So we searched for any company with a building connection with an S.A.Andrews on the Board and came up with Midshires Building Supplies of which we find Labgrove Estates is a wholly owned subsidiary. The majority shareholder in Midshires is Gravlynch Construction and a George Black is a member of each Board. Gravlynch Construction is a wholly owned subsidiary of Gravlynch

Consolidated. The Board of Gravlynch Construction has a Charles Smit and he is also a member of the Gravlynch Consolidated Board. Den Holdengraf MV holds the other ten percent of Consolidated. And, of course, the Managing Director of Consolidated, one Gerald White, is a member of the Hardwick Holdings Board."

"My God and stand-in Managing Director and would-be Chairman," said Roger.

"I'm sorry to spring this on you when you came out for a day with a pretty girl," said Timmy, "but we felt that you should know, especially since you told us of the career choice that faces you in the near future."

"I'm grateful to know," said Roger. "Off the top of my head I don't see what I can do at the moment other than to assist you in any way I can with an entrée to Hardwick Holdings but any probing there had better be done by me. I've told Liz of the decision that I must make and I think that what you've told me this afternoon makes it certain that I'll resign from the police service and take over the family firm. It'll certainly pay better."

"There's no proof at the moment that anyone other than one or more members of the Gravlynch Consolidated Board knows anything about the alleged bribe or that anyone other than S.A.Andrews knows anything about the harassment," said Timmy, "but it's unlikely that the MD of Consolidated, Gerald White, wouldn't know what was going on although, doubtless he took steps to keep well away from the actual bribing."

"I was so sorry for the people living in those houses that I wondered if we should buy the properties ourselves, with guarantees of full life occupancy for present occupiers," said Helene, "but there are too many pitfalls and we'd be foolish to get mixed up in it. All we can do is to get the property developers off the people's backs. The problem that both Timmy and I have is that we have some sympathy with any prospective developer, it really is a splendid site, there are two of them actually, both crying out for development and held up by three or four run down properties."

Margaret slipped quietly into the room and said "I've come to join you for tea. David will be in, in a moment."

"Margaret, we're so rude to hide ourselves away and talk shop," said Helene, "please forgive us."

"Silly, you must talk about the things that occupy your minds. I hope it doesn't mean that you'll go rushing off to Qatar or somewhere." She looked around the library, "I do so love this room. I used to sit in here when David was away fighting in Borneo and the Falklands. Timmy and Liz will remember how we'd gather round the fire on winters afternoons and make toast on a long handled fork."

"Oh, yes Mummy, I've always liked toast made that way," said Liz, "I can see our faces now, all aglow with the fire light as you read to us and we nibbled toast and you told us not to get buttery fingers on the pages. And Christmas was always just round the corner."

The General followed a laden Sergeant in and sat down cozily next to his wife.

"You know there's nothing better than muffins for tea on a winter's afternoon. As a boy I used to watch the shadows gather across the park and judge when to come in for tea. My stomach was always half an hour ahead of Greenwich but cook always had something to keep me going until it was proper teatime."

Ah Ming appeared and silently refilled their cups. Liz gave Roger a warning glance and he grinned lopsidedly at her. When she had gone Liz remarked,

"That dress looks better on her than it ever did on me."

"I can't believe that," said gallant Roger.

"Don't eat too much, David, I've asked Mrs Holmes to serve an early dinner so that Elizabeth can get back to Bristol in time to go on duty."

Roger turned to the General "If you'd excuse me Sir, Timmy has just told me of a problem that he and Helene and Liz, may I say, have uncovered concerning my family firm, Hardwick Holdings, and I'd like to pursue it a little more if I may."

"Carry on, my boy, I'm bound to hear all about it in due course," said the General.

"My question, Tim, is what is our next move going to be? We don't want to scare these rotters off before we've got the evidence to charge them, do we?"

"First, let's deal with the harassment. If you could let us know all that you know officially about the man who barged past Helene and knocked the old lady down, I'll put Confidential Enquiries on to him

191

to try to find out who his paymaster is. That might start us up the company ladder."

"I can see no reason why I shouldn't tell you all that the man's solicitor knows," said Roger. "I'd better not write to you or phone it, I'll give it to Liz."

"Next, the bribe," said Timmy, "Here I am mindful that we gave our word that we wouldn't drag our informant into the public eye and I want to honour that undertaking. That might mean that the matter never comes to court and that might suit all parties, mightn't it?"

"It'd be the best solution as far as protecting my father is concerned," said Roger.

"I think that Helene and I should talk to the guilty Civil Engineer and invite him to confess and retire early from his job," said Timmy. "A condition would be that he would have to tell us who bribed him. Then we'll interview that person and so on up the company tree until we get to Gravlynch Consolidated. We've no evidence that it went higher than that. We'd be gambling that at each level the offender will assume that the person at the next level down has spilled the beans and that his co-operation and silence will avoid court proceedings. If she's free, we'd love to have Liz join us because I've noticed that she has the same effect on men as does Helene."

"Flatterer, "said Liz "but it's true, isn't it? You should see me on ward rounds. I can make the lame walk."

"You should have learnt by now, young Tim, that she has an answer for everything," said her father.

"Ignore that family banter Roger, what do you think?" asked Timmy.

"I think it's worth a try and it might be the best way to deal with it. If we go in officially, they rush to get lawyers, everything is on the record and people simply clam up."

"Good, that's settled then. Now he can get on with running a few radio stations and record companies," said Helene.

"It's probably best that we see him in his office without warning him of the subject," said Timmy as if Helene hadn't spoken "If we approach him at home he's bound to ask why and somehow he might alert his paymaster and the last thing we want is for them to contrive a collective defence. What we'll do is get into his secretary's office and barge in when he has no-one with him, muttering Gravlynch Consolidated before he can have us thrown out."

"That's what I said, isn't it Liz?" said Helene. "After he's been to Bristol next week he'll be able to get on with running a few radio stations and recording companies."

"Angel, I heard you the first time and you missed out your outfit that makes TV programmes."

"When can we expect you in Bristol? I can get away for lunch if you give me a day or two's notice," said Liz.

"Let's plan on Wednesday. It all depends on whether our target man is in office that day but for lunchtime planning take it as fixed," said Helene. "Can you make it that day, Roger?"

"I'll try. The problem with being at headquarters is the time it takes to get back to civilization and finding a parking place when one has."

"Surely you can park at Bridewell" said Liz.

"There speaks a girl who's never seen Bridewell," said Timmy. "Would it help if we all met at that place Liz took us to last time?"

"Good idea, then that's agreed, let's say one o'clock and Timmy books the table, he's got staff to do those things, haven't you brother dear?"

## Chapter Nineteen

THE next morning Penny greeted Timmy as if he had returned from safari in darkest Africa and made a small moue at the pile of paper and dictation tapes that he placed on her desk. She asked if he had caught any terrorists or murderers during his absence in Bristol. Shortly afterwards she buzzed him to say that his sister, Elizabeth, was on line one.

"Hello kitten, did you have a good journey back and is all well with you?"

"Yes thanks, Roger just went by in one of his blue and yellow's and he left a note at reception. The bit that I think you want most is George Arthur Simmonds, 6A Gage Street. I say Timmy, he's already on police bail for assault, be careful, he seems to be a nasty type, judged by what it says here."

"Don't worry baby, I'll delegate him to Mr Swift's chaps."

He asked Penny to arrange for Mr Swift to see him sometime that day.

After his management meeting and individual meetings, Penny put her head in to say that Mr Swift was waiting and she had sort of asked Helene if she was coming and Helene was outside talking to Mr Swift. "Why don't you come in as well, Penny?" said Timmy grinning. "I'm sure that Sid would like to know what's going on."

"I'll keep half an ear on you through the phone while I get on with all that work you brought back," she said cheerfully and stood to one side as Helene and Mr Swift came in.

"Morning Mr Swift, I hope that Helene has given you an idea of what's been going on since your trio arrested those two thugs on Friday last?"

"Yes, it sounds as if you've discovered another nest of crooks. Perhaps you'd fill me in, in more detail and what further help my people might give."

Timmy explained the weekend's events.

"We think it's time to short circuit the enquiries you've been making about Labgrove Estates by leaning on the man Paula arrested and make him tell us who's instructing him to make life unbearable for the tenants of the houses."

"How do you propose to do that, Mr Hawkridge?"

"Well I thought that you might have a number of large friends who we could dress up in white shirts and blue suits and uniform caps like Security guards or policemen and pick up Mr George Arthur Simmonds and put him in your white van and ask him the question. I'm sure that he'd tell them rather than face a charge of assault or something."

"That sort of action could make big headlines and I can't risk my people doing something like you suggest, I'm sorry Mr Hawkridge." He paused for a moment and added, "but since we were in on the ground floor, so to speak, I'll talk to my people and see what they might suggest. When would you like the information?"

"Splendid chap," said Timmy, "the sooner the better. Sometime this week would be marvelous, Helene and I plan to be in Bristol on Wednesday to tackle the top end of the same puzzle by visiting the City Chief Civil Engineer who we think has been bribed."

"I wouldn't want to do anything that could end up in court."

"Please don't worry, Mr Swift," said Helene, "there are good reasons why we wouldn't want this thing to come to court. What Timmy is up to is to nip the thing in the bud without stirring up a lot of mud that would harm innocent people as well as the one or two guilty ones."

"I see, another one of your reverse blackmail efforts, Mr Hawkridge," said Mr Swift. "But you're just talking to people whereas you were asking me to sail close to breaking the law."

"I suppose you could put it that way. Look, please forget that this conversation ever took place, Helene and I will deal with George Simmonds. Good day Mr Swift thanks for coming over."

"I could supply someone like Will Toms or Paula to watch your backs."

"That's a good idea," said Helene quickly "I'll keep in touch with you and tell you when we'll be in Bristol. We'll probably base ourselves at the radio station; at least we can all park there."

"Yes, let's do that," said Timmy, recovering his good humour, "we'll be glad to have them around."

When Mr Swift had gone Helene said,

"Darling he's a nice man who has to protect his business the same as you do and your idea of picking this George Simmonds up on the street was a bit James Bond, wasn't it?"

"Angel, I could see it all in my minds eye, actually I had to amend my scenario as I spoke. I had those four chaps dressed in white shirts and blue trousers, not blue suits and then I remembered that it's winter."

"You are an idiot. How do you plan we should tackle him?"

"I suppose that we'll just be ourselves and give him two alternatives, he either tells us what we want to know and gets a few pounds or we press the earlier assault charge and he goes to jail," said Timmy.

"The difficulty is getting him somewhere so that we can pop the question and afterwards how do we know that he's told the truth?"

"We'll ask Mr Swift's people to watch for an opportunity and act on their advice," said Timmy. "As for honesty, we'll tell him that if he tricks us he can still go to jail. He has to trust us, not the other way round, my love."

"How do you intend to handle the Civil Engineer?"

"I'll get Joy to telephone him, following up the recordings that we made of his organization. The programme is ready for transmission and she could suggest that we're doing the well mannered thing and telling him in advance."

"You're never at a loss for ideas, are you, darling Timmy?"

"No and I've got a good one now."

"Go away Timmy, this sofa's not for that sort of thing and you've probably smudged my make-up and I love you," all in one breath.

Joy phoned back in the afternoon to say that Mr Hopkinson, the Chief Civil Engineer could spare them ten minutes at eleven o'clock on Wednesday.

Helene arranged that Paula would be in Bristol on Tuesday and Wednesday to discover the pattern of Mr Simmond's movements and accompany them if and when they tackled him. She phoned Liz and arranged to meet for lunch at the hotel on the northern ring road. She mentioned that Paula might be with them and asked if Joy should book a table for four or five. "Five please," said Liz.

They went by rail to Bristol and were at the radio station by ten-thirty. Paula had left a message that the omens were good and she would be outside the civil engineering office when they came out.

They arrived at the office and were ushered in to meet Mr Hopkinson. After the introductions Timmy said,

"The radio programme about your department is quite interesting and will be transmitted soon. That's not what we want to speak about. We want to ask you about Gravlynch Consolidated."

"I don't understand, why should I want to discuss Gravlynch Consolidated with you?"

"We have it on good authority that Gravlynch Consolidated have made certain payments to you, payments that you wouldn't show on your income tax return."

"Rubbish, I'll have you thrown out."

"Very well, then my radio stations will broadcast what we know in their national news bulletins and you can sue me for deformation and face the consequences."

"What exactly do you think you know?"

"Well, we know about the whole chain of companies, Midshires, Gravlynch Construction and Gravlynch Consolidated with Hardwick Holdings on the top. Oh and we mustn't forget little Labgrove Estates trying to force the old people to sell their houses to your friends," said Timmy. "Look, Mr Hopkinson, we have no wish to send you to prison, we simply want to know who within the management of those companies originated this crime and see that they leave the company."

Helene said "I'm sure that you must have already regretted the impulse that made you take their money and then found that there was no way out. We're offering you a way out."

"If you only knew how I've regretted it," said Mr Hopkinson, "it was forced on me."

That's what they all say, thought Timmy.

"How was that?" asked Helene, a keen believer in the keep 'em talking school.

"I met this man at the Institution of Civil Engineers dinner, we were having a drink afterwards and he mentioned that he was interested in developing the Old Market sites. He asked me to see that his proposals got a fair hearing and I said that I would. I'd had a few drinks. The next month when my bank statement arrived, I found that ten thousand pounds had been deposited in it. I told the bank that it was a mistake and they checked and said it was correct. I then had a letter from a man called George Black of Gravlynch Construction, saying that he was a friend of the man I had met at the dinner and saying how pleased they were at my acceptance of their small gift towards my wife's operation."

"And have you had any further contact with anyone in these firms," asked Timmy, "and have you still got the letter?"

"No."

"Tell me, Mr Hopkinson, when did this take place, how long have you had the money, you haven't spent it, have you?"

"Well yes, you see I must have told this chap at the dinner that my wife was ill and had to have private treatment and the ten thousand helped towards that."

"Oh dear, never mind, I hope she's better?" said Helene.

"She died three months later."

"Oh, I'm sorry," said Helene.

"I miss her terribly and I wake in the night realizing that it was all in vain, I lost my professional honour as well as my wife."

"Do you have any idea who the man you met at dinner was?" asked Timmy.

"Yes, I saw a picture of him in one of the civil engineering journals. His name is Gerald White and he's the Managing Director of Gravlynch Consolidated. I think he's on several other boards, including Hardwick's."

"Thank you for telling us your story Mr Hopkinson," said Timmy. "I'm sure that I speak for both of us when I say that we recognize the dreadful dilemma that you faced when ten thousand pounds came from out of the blue to pay for your wife's treatment and the remorse you now feel. Believe me as far as we are concerned your secret is safe."

"It's my intention to retire in the spring and I hope that will mark the end of this painful business."

As Helene remarked later, it seemed that the old people who wouldn't sell their houses to Labgrove Estates were the people who had saved the day.

When they emerged from the civil engineering department Paula was waiting. Helene hugged her and Timmy shook her hand.

"Gosh it's good to see you two again, it's always a pleasure and we always manage to have a laugh amid all the unpleasantness. I bring you good news. I thought that it would be a shame to have you bother with George Arthur Simmonds so this morning I had a little chat with him. The name you want is S.A. Andrews. He was particular about the S.A. because it reminded him of the Sally Army where, I gather he has been fed and housed in the past."

"That's wonderful, the last time I saw you together you had him down on the ground in an arm lock. How did you do it, or shouldn't we ask?" said Helene.

"He took a little convincing but I expect that his leg will be better in a day or two. It made him maudlin so I had to listen to the story of his life and when I left I gave him fifty pounds, was that alright?"

"Bless you, I'd have given him a hundred for that name," said Timmy. "Here's a hundred, you can buy yourself a present with the change. We're meeting Liz for lunch and have reserved a seat for you but since we've finished early you might prefer to have us drop you at the station and make a quick getaway for London."

"That's what I'll do if you don't mind then I'll get back before the rush hour."

Thus it was that there were only four of them for lunch.

Timmy and Helene reported on the morning's events. They now had three names. S.A.Andrews was behind the intimidation of the old householders and it looked as if Gerald White and George Black were both behind the bribing of a city official.

Timmy asked, "How do you think we should play it, Roger?"

"I don't know. Gerald White will be a tougher nut to crack than the city engineer seems to have been and we don't want it to develop into an action for slander. The man in the middle, George Black, is a new one to me. Clearly he knows all about the bribe and must be considered a Gerald White man and any approach to him will immediately be known by White."

"Is there any means of checking the two firm's accounts to find a record of the payment?" asked Liz.

"I doubt it, there'll be thousands of transactions during a year," said Helene.

"But not for precisely ten thousand pounds in some non-material, non-labour account, surely?" said Liz.

"You may have a point, Liz," said Timmy, "and we might have to ask Roger's father to have a special audit if all else fails. Another approach would be for his father to sack both men stating that he has no confidence in them. That could be costly in redundancy payments."

"On an earlier occasion I said that it would solve a lot of problems if so and so died and the next day he was found dead. It caused no end of bother so I won't say it or at the very least I'll cross my fingers," said Helene.

"Thank you for that helpful suggestion, Angel. How about if we interview them simultaneously, Helene and I do George Black and you two do Gerald White, or should we split it Liz and I and Helene and you, Roger? Because you're a policeman your role would be to get Helene into his room and then keep quiet."

"Not possible, I'm afraid. If I learn that a felony has been attempted I must take official action."

"The problem is we have no evidence. They can admit that money may have been paid by someone in their company if we and Mr Hopkinson say so but claim total ignorance and personal innocence themselves," said Helene.

"There's a nasty trick they could play. They could say that your brother authorized the payment," said Liz.

"Perhaps the best course is as follows," said Timmy. "Roger tells his father all that we've discussed around this table. We'll come and assist if you want. He tells him that he will resign from the police force and take over the family firm. That clips Gerald White's wings for a start. We shouldn't underestimate Roger's father, why doesn't he trust Gerald White? He might already have sufficient evidence for this new scandal to tip the balance and enable him to fire the man."

"I'm absolutely certain that my father will stand no nonsense. He'll kick him off the Holding company Board and make his life hell thereafter. I think he'd rather enjoy it," said Roger.

"And as his father's deputy and successor," said Helene, "Roger takes a personal interest in Gravlynch Consolidated and in Gravlynch Construction and Messers White and Black in particular, hinting at some knowledge that he gained in the police in Bristol."

"So we're agreed that as far as the top-down approach is concerned, Helene and I do nothing for the present and you'll speak with your father, Roger," said Timmy. "We'll have a go at Mr S.A.Andrews of Labgrove Estates about intimidating old people in Old Market."

"I'm glad that's finished," smiled Liz, "now perhaps we can talk about something nice and really interesting, like the number of people suffering from the common cold this winter or something equally absorbing to the non-medical world."

"Changing the subject, how are you getting on with the Singh's?"

"You really are the limit, Timmy," said Liz "but I'd like to know as well. Come on Roger, spill the beans, have you put them on the rack yet?"

"The expression is that 'they are helping the police with their enquiries'. Actually they are refusing to say a word other than, *the police are racist pigs*. That's a direct quote from Mrs Singh. It'll probably be on the news tonight. In the early hours of this morning police and immigration service officers raided all the Singh properties and found no less than fifty-seven illegal immigrants in six of them. They are of several nationalities and the questioning has been slow but as far as it had got when I left to come here, some of them claimed to have paid the Singh's thousands to get them into Britain and hide them until it was safe to move on. It's going to be a big case."

"Will the Singh's be able to use the contents of that suitcase to pay their legal expenses?" asked the ever- practical Liz.

"No, that's now evidence but they might be able to raise a loan on the strength of their claim that they are innocent and the money is rightfully theirs," said Roger.

"I suppose that their defence will be that they let the properties to one man and his family and unknown to them, he had sublet to all these other people. I expect the younger Singh will produce rent books in the name of individual occupiers and tenancy agreements prohibiting sub-letting," said Helene.

"To think that all this started with your extended phone-in," said Liz, "perhaps you should do the same at all your stations, Timmy."

"God forbid," laughed Roger, "I don't think the British police forces have the resources to deal with what would emerge."

Before they parted it was agreed that Timmy and Helene would try to see Mr S.A.Andrews on the Friday and that Roger would journey to Marlow to brief his father over the weekend. If she could get away, Liz would go with him.

On Friday Timmy had Penny telephone the office in Portman Square, and say that she wished to use them as an accommodation address and would like to come round that afternoon to meet the owner and sign the papers. She was told that Mr Awnsred would be available at two-thirty.

Timmy and Helene took a cab and announced themselves to the young lady in the basement office. After a minute or so they were ushered into Mr Awnsred's office on the ground floor.

"I understand that you wish to use my address service, Ms, I don't think I caught your name."

"The name's Hawkridge of Hawkridge Media and we haven't come to discuss accommodation addresses but the activity of Labgrove Estates in Bristol," said Timmy.

"I don't know what you're talking about, I know nothing about Labgrove Estates other than they're one of my customers downstairs. I must ask you to leave or I'll call the police"

"Please call the police and I'll tell them that your name isn't Awnsred but Andrews and that you're the man who runs Labgrove Estates and that you hired a man called George Arthur Simmonds to harass the owners of certain properties in the Old Market area of Bristol into selling their properties to Labgrove Estates. Do you still want to call the police?"

"You've got no proof of any of this nonsense," said Andrews.

"Oh yes we have," said Helene. "We've got two things, the first is that Mr Simmonds is on police bail for knocking an old lady down when attempting to enter one of the properties and secondly we've got his signed statement that you instructed him to do it."

"You'll never make that stick. I didn't tell him to knock the old fools down," said Andrews.

"The fact is that in law he was your agent acting on your instructions," said Timmy. "Juries still remember Rachman, Mr Andrews, what do you think they will do about you?"

"I told them that we should get compulsory purchase orders but they wanted to do it on the cheap."

"Who are they, Mr Andrews?" asked Helene. "We're not the police and it's the people at the top we want, the people that use people like you to do their dirty work and then walk away with fat bonus's, leaving you to take the blame."

"I can't see that we've done wrong. I can't be blamed if someone goes a bit over the top. They're good sites and they're ripe for development. It's George Black's idea. He said he'd get me a seat on the Gravlynch Construction Board if I could get the Old Market site cleared."

"Did you have anything to do with anyone else, Mr Andrews?" asked Helene.

"He said that Gerald White would be pleased."

"That's all we wanted to know," said Timmy. "We suggest that you keep quiet about our visit. You wouldn't want George Black to know that you named him would you?"

"It's only your word against mine," said Andrews

"But you see it's not. We've got George Simmonds statement and both Helene and I have recorded every word that has been spoken in this room this afternoon. You wouldn't want us to visit this George Black and play the tapes, would you? So sit tight and keep your own counsel. Good day Mr Andrews, we'll tell the young lady downstairs that we've decided not to use this address."

When they got back to Canary Wharf Timmy phoned Roger.

"Roger, its Tim here. Is it OK to talk, I mean you're not in a meeting?"

"No, go ahead Tim, did you go and see the Labgrove Estate man?"

"Yes with satisfactory results. Both Helene and I recorded everything that was said and I could send it down the wire for your people to record. He named George Black and mentioned Gerald White."

"That's splendid. Could you ask your people to use the same phone number that they used to send us the girls at Portbury tapes?"

"Fine, we'll do it right away. Have you arranged to see your father?"

"Yes, we're going to Marlow on Saturday afternoon. Liz is coming with me I'd like her to meet my parents."

"Well done old chap, see you soon. Goodbye"

As he said to Helene as they drove down to Tolbrite that evening, it looks as if his baby sister likes Roger more than she has admitted.

# Chapter Twenty

THEY were hugged on arrival by Margaret and enjoined to hurry down. The Sergeant confirmed that the cases of whisky and Chateau Bouchier had arrived and were in the cellar. As he remarked to Timmy, "You couldn't have got that lot in the car."

They joined Margaret and the General.

"Liz told me that you all had lunch together in Bristol on Wednesday and you insisted on talking cops and robbers through the whole meal."

"We got the impression that she rather enjoyed it," said Helene.

"Yes, that's the impression that I got down the phone. As she said, it's Roger's business."

"It won't be Roger's business for much longer," said Helene, "Timmy spoke with him this afternoon and he's going up to Marlow to see his father on Saturday to confirm that he's going to leave the police and take over the family firm. Liz is going with him."

"Well, he seems a nice chap and the discipline of the police service will help him in business, you'll see," said the General.

"You realize that this is the last weekend before Christmas," said Margaret, "the Maier's are arriving next Thursday and David, Sally-Ann and the children the next day. When are you two going to France?"

"Christmas is a busy time for Timmy's stations and so we're not going until sometime on the 23rd and coming back on the 28th. I hope that Mama won't think that our visit is too short because she and Matilde are coming back to London with us for a few days before we all come down here for the New Year, so we'll be together for nearly ten days. I want to be there much longer in the summer, we're going to stay on for two weeks at least after our wedding, aren't we my love?"

"Of course, I want to see more of the countryside as well as you."

"You know, Margaret, sometimes he uses English in a very peculiar way."

"I learnt a long time ago that with children you have to learn to use the meaning that suits you best."

"In this case I should be blushing then," grinned Helene.

They left after tea on Sunday promising to ring the moment they were in France and that they would all be down, Mama and Matilde as well, before lunch on the day before New Years Eve.

They landed at Dijon at teatime on the 23$^{rd}$ December. Helene's mother and Matilde were there to meet them, muffled in furs against the east wind with the elderly chauffeur, Jules, hovering ready to take their cases.

"Oh little one, it's so lovely to see you and thank you Timmy for bringing her home for Christmas. My, but you both look so happy, marriage must agree with you."

"Mama, everything is wonderful, we're so lucky. I now understand how you felt about daddy. When I was growing up I sometimes thought that you were soppy but now I understand."

"You'll understand even more when you have little ones of your own."

They spent a relaxing evening with so much to talk about. For the first time Helene told her mother what had really happened on the way to visit her in the autumn and all about the body in the Manor House Park. She went on to explain the phone-in on Timmy's Bristol radio station and what that had led to, capturing a murderer, stopping girls and drugs being smuggled in, catching a family who were smuggling in illegal immigrants and stopping old people being harassed out of their homes, not to mention stopping a few other crooks.

"We could do with something like that in most of our cities," said Claire-Marie, "why don't you build some radio stations in France, you've got them in England, America and Canada why not take a giant leap and set up a station here?"

"Oh Timmy, why not do that? I could manage them for you and Mama would see that we got a lot of advertising from her friends," said Helene.

"I rather thought that I would manage them for you," said Claire-Marie. "I'm bored to tears sometimes and I could do with a challenge or two."

"Now that's more like it," said Timmy. "I'm not backing a scheme that puts you in France, Angel, and me in London. We'll call it Radio Bouchier. What I like about the idea is that we could present each nation to the other in the best light, starting with small beginnings and building on it. You know what I mean, attractive French artists on the English stations and vice versa."

"It would be an uphill struggle Timmy," said Claire-Marie. "A stubborn Frenchman makes a mule look the spirit of cooperativeness. Come to think of it, the English are the same. But it would be a bit of a lark. Helene's papa used to say that flying under bridges was a bit of a lark. He got into trouble once for doing it but luckily his C.O. had flown under the same bridge the week before, so he got off."

"How do we go about it?" asked Helene.

"First we study the French government regulations concerning the allocation of frequencies, the rules controlling broadcasting and advertising on the air, the profitability of the existing stations, and the extent to which the populous areas are already covered," said Timmy, "there's no point in getting into a business that's already over-subscribed."

"Leave that to me," said Claire-Marie.

"You really mean it, Mama, don't you?" said Helene.

"Yes, what I want is Timmy's knowledge and experience, I'll provide the money, it is about time I did something other than produce wine."

"That's agreed then," said Timmy, "you collect copies of the statutory regulations, balance sheets and areas at present covered by one, two and three stations, the important parts of which Helene will have to explain to me and I'll get my chaps to prepare specifications for typical stations and the sort of programmes my stations in England and Canada put out. Above all, it's vital that as few people as possible know what you're planning. There are some nasty people about."

"We could start with a station in Dijon, oh, alright little one, I'll keep quiet."

Christmas Eve was one of the nicest days Timmy could remember. They toured the villages of the Bouchier estates and admired the decorations, listened to carols, ate small pies, drank toasts and arrived home feeling that they couldn't eat another thing, ever. He delighted in his bride, she glowed with happiness, she met old school friends and kissed their babies, always with an eye for him. He was introduced to them all and kissed by some. They had a late dinner and at eleven thirty dressed once more in warm clothes were driven by Jules to the local church for the watch-night service. Claire-Marie said that it was expected of her and she enjoyed it. Timmy knew that back in Tolbrite his family was doing the identical thing, because it was expected of them and they enjoyed it.

Christmas Day passed peacefully. There were presents to unwrap and toasts to be drunk with the servants and they went to morning Mass. Timmy had realized some time ago that although he had always gone to church and made the required responses, Helene's religion was more profound and personal than his. Kneeling beside her he thought that perhaps this explained why such a beautiful creature had remained unwed until she had met him. Her hand crept into his. "I always say a special prayer for us, Timmy."

Boxing Day morning he was taken to visit more of Helene's friends. Uncle Philipe came to lunch and they dined with him that evening.

A good deal of the day after Boxing Day seemed to be taken up with preparations for the next day's departure and observing the mountain of cases in the hall the following morning he thanked God that they had a private aircraft and wouldn't have to wrestle that lot through Heathrow. The following morning they were off to Dijon airport and the baggage seemed to be no problem at all.

By lunchtime they were back in Cheyne Walk and Helene had taken charge. While he was at work she would see that her mother and Matilde were entertained. This included a visit to the Hawkridge Media headquarters at Canary Wharf where Claire-Marie brought the place to a halt. The staff had got used to the beautiful Helene but now there were two of them, Helene and this beautiful, elegant, long legged sister; it just couldn't be her mother, she didn't look old enough. And behind them, beaming was Timmy.

As Penny said to Sid that night "When he's with Helene our Timmy looks like a dog with two tails. Today he looked like a dog with four. You can see where our Helene gets her looks from."

They dined in all their favourite restaurants, went to that peculiarly British institution the pantomime, did a couple of museums and went to the sales. They gave a small party for their neighbours and were entertained in turn.

On the afternoon of the 30th they packed what luggage they could get in, in the back of the Bentley and the rest into one of the firm's vans and drove to Tolbrite. Timmy sat in the back with Matilde who chatted happily of the place names she thought that she recognized from the various airfields Helene's father had served at when in the RAF.

Helene drove slowly past the Old Forge Garage and gave young Will a small toot on the horn. Will responded with an elaborate salute and a cheerful wave. As they drove towards the main drive, Helene told Matilde about the bond between Will and the Hawkridge children and family.

Thomas the gamekeeper was at his post in the Lodge and raised his hat. Timmy realized that Claire-Marie was about to get the full treatment and as Helene drew up, Margaret and the General came to greet them. The Sergeant opened the car doors and Claire-Marie got out with a flash of long legs as Helene came round the bonnet. There was a moment of silence and then two small figures and two little dogs erupted from the house, "Mummy, Mummy, Uncle Timmy and Helene are here."

Everyone was introduced to everyone, including the dogs and the party moved indoors to meet Sally-Ann and her parents who said that they hoped that her husband, also a David, would be able to be there on the morrow. Margaret explained that her daughter, Elizabeth had been home for Christmas but would see in the New Year at her friend Roger Hardwick's home in Marlow, if she could get away from the hospital. Helene and Timmy took care to see that Matilde met everyone. Little David explained that they all had the same name, he was David three, Daddy was David two and Granddad General was David one. And I'm Anne with an e and Mummy's Ann without an e, explained his sister, and the dogs are Maxi and Oliver.

Claire-Marie confessed that it would take her a moment or two to remember all this but Helene could see that she was pleased.

Matilde had the room next to Claire-Marie and shared her bathroom.

The children were allowed to stay up for dinner with the grown ups and contributed to the happiness of the occasion. Claire-Marie explained to the Maiers that she knew all about the radio stations that they had let Timmy put in their hotels and that she was busy collecting information so that Timmy could build some for her, starting in a small way in Dijon – with a defiant little smile at Helene. If necessary she would buy an hotel to put it in. Mr Maier thought that would be a splendid idea, Timmy's people brought custom to the hotels and their restaurants and he'd noticed that the hotels with a radio station always seemed to be livelier than those that didn't have them. He suggested that she should 'come on over and see for herself'. Claire-Marie said that she'd suggest some possible dates, it would have to be early in the year, adding that it was about time she visited the US importers who handled her wines.

The following day the General took them around the estate and they met the vicar and Mrs Ford. When they got back at lunchtime they found the children and Sally-Ann excited because the elder son, David had arrived. There were more introductions and explanations about being on duty yesterday, which prompted memories of when daddy had drawn the short straw and she had been smuggled in to lighten his duty hours. Timmy could see both the General and the Major thinking that sort of thing wouldn't happen in the Army or perhaps the converse, that sort of thing could only happen in the Air Force. This, of course prompted Mr Maier's recollections of his time in the US Army. The children sat each side of Matilde and loved every minute of it. Margaret thought the lunch a success, no one was left out of the conversation and they all cleared their plates.

In the early afternoon Helene and Timmy took Claire-Marie and Matilde for a general tour of the district including Bournemouth and Dorchester. She remarked that "this had been more of an army area than an air force area in their time but daddy had been at Tangmere for a while. There were some good pubs round there."

Helene was driving and she stopped opposite the garage and walked round and opened the passenger door for her mother to get out. Timmy knew exactly what she was up to. Claire-Marie swung round and got out with a remarkable display of her legs before Will's startled gaze. "Strewth," he said, "there's two of 'em."

Helene walked over and said, "Will, I want you to meet my mother. Mama, this is Will, one of Timmy and my best friends."

After a while Timmy ventured, "This is me over here Will, you remember me?"

As Will said to Gloria, later "You could hardly tell them apart, fancy having a mother who looks like a blooming film star."

After dinner Timmy said that the whole party should go to the Tolbrite Arms so that the squire could see in the New Year with his people. Matilde said that she would see to the children and they all walked across the park. Their arrival doubled the population of the bar and after a rather hushed moment and the General-cum-squire introducing Madam Bouchier-Taylor and the Maier's to the assembled company, everyone entered into the spirit of the thing.

Helene nudged Timmy and looked down at her fingers. He looked at Gloria's left hand and the sparkling ring she now wore and asked her where Will was. "He won't be a minute, he's down the cellar."

When Will appeared, Timmy called for silence and proposed a toast of congratulations to our good friends, young Will and Gloria.

Helene pressed close to Timmy and said, "You've no idea how much Mama has come to life again since we've been together, look at her now, perched on a bar stool, legs crossed and perhaps showing a little more thigh than she should, and loving every minute of it. And look at Margaret in her high fashion frock, she looks ten years younger and is herself a center of attention. Isn't it lovely and aren't we lucky?"

Claire-Marie caught her daughter's eye as the General paused beside her.

"Bless you little one, you might not believe it but I spent some of the happiest times of my life perched on a bar stool and showing my legs in village pubs adopted by the RAF squadron, listening to those splendid young men talking flying shop. They believed that what they were doing was worth risking their lives for. They were fine men and your daddy was one of them."

The General moved close to Margaret and as the church clock chimed midnight, raised his glass and called in his best parade ground voice, "A Happy New Year to you all."

Printed in the United Kingdom
by Lightning Source UK Ltd.
111659UKS00001B/211-213